Passport for a Pilgrim

James Leasor
'Of all the operators in the overcrowded fiction thriller field, the one character who looks like having a long life is Dr Jason Love. He was invented by James Leasor in *Passport to Oblivion**, and carried on bravely in *Passport to Peril** and *Passport in Suspense** and now makes his fourth appearance.

Dr Love is the quiet type, a mild-mannered doctor practising in Somerset, who collects the emblems of famous cars and owns an incredible Cord front-wheel drive. Unlike the usual agent who picks his teeth with a gunsight and wears a dirty raincoat, Dr Love is polite and gets involved in dreadful adventures with great reluctance . . .

Such a nice man, but when he is angry and in danger Love is more like a leopard than a red, red rose. In one mad, desperate moment he even uses a shovel as a weapon, in another a fire extinguisher. Love's many admirers will not be disappointed with *Passport for a Pilgrim.'*   *Sunday Mirror*

'Most ingenious and exciting'   *Birmingham Post*

'Plenty of thrills'   *The Sunday Times*

'Fiendish espionage . . . red-blooded climax.'
                                        Eastern Daily Press

'The invention, suspense and excitement is non-stop.'   *Current Literature*

*All Dr Love's previous adventures are obtainable in PAN Books.

JAMES LEASOR

Passport for a Pilgrim

UNABRIDGED

PAN BOOKS LTD · LONDON

First published 1968 by William Heinemann Ltd.
This edition published 1970 by Pan Books Ltd,
33 Tothill Street, London, S.W.1

330 02487 6

Printed in Great Britain by
Cox & Wyman Ltd,
London, Reading and Fakenham

For Jeremy,
Andrew and Stuart

Prologue

*Tirana, Albania, June 12th; Cairo, Egypt, June 14th;
Damascus, Syria, June 27th*

It was that hour of evening when the whole valley trembled
on the hinge of darkness. The dusk blew flights of birds
across the grey, exhausted desert, and lights in the scattered
houses beyond Tirana glittered like glass eyes.

Krasna stood on the small concrete balcony of his flat
overlooking the Place Skanderbeg. It was a view of which he
never tired; somehow he felt that it symbolized all he had
achieved, rising from an orphan child to become one of the
three most renowned surgeons in Albania, entitled to such
rare privileges as his own apartment, his own Skoda Octavia
car. Of course, the flat was drab, and the car was three years
old, but still, everything was relative; and compared with the
poverty from which he had sprung and which still engulfed
so many of his countrymen, he had succeeded beyond all
expectation.

Every town had still a statue or a square named after
Skanderbeg, the Albanian who, four hundred years earlier,
had rid his country of Turkish domination to give it an inde-
pendence that had only lasted as long as his own life. Yet
such was his fame that many of the older men still wore
black coats in mourning for his death.

Krasna wondered, not for the first time, what Skanderbeg
would have thought of his country's present plight, where
few people earned more than £10 a month; where children
were taught to inform on their families; where, although
closer to London in terms of distance than Athens, and only
a little farther away than Rome, no Western tourists ever
came, and no direct flights or railway lines joined Tirana to
other European capitals.

What would it be like to live in Western Europe or in the
United States? He often found himself thinking this almost
treasonable thought. Once, at a medical convention in

Beirut, he had seen American magazines which were not imported into Albania; one contained an article, with coloured photographs, on a day in a New York surgeon's life. This man owned a fine house of white horizontal wood planks in the country, two cars, a motor-boat, a deep freeze, and all kinds of apparatus in his kitchen – a mixer, electric can-opener, waste disposer, and so on. Of course, Albanian housewives did not need such intricate mechanical devices – or was it simply because they had never had the chance of using them?

Krasna pushed that thought from his mind because he felt it was somehow disloyal. After all, surely even in America he could not have prospered better than he had prospered here? Perhaps he was tired or disillusioned; or maybe it was the time of life through which all men passed, when doctrine and dogma were clouded by doubt, when truth itself seemed illusory, as hard to distinguish as a waning moon on a foggy night; when, in a kind of masculine menopause, you finally admitted to yourself, if to no one else, that there were heights you would never reach, that you were lucky to have done as well as you had.

He leaned over the balcony rail so that he could see couples sitting beneath the shabby canvas awnings of the cafés, drinking glasses of raki, the colourless spirit made from plums and grapes, and small tumblers of ouzo, the local absinth. Up and down the street, past the concrete blocks of workers' flats that towered symbolically in the gardens of the great houses once owned by the old families who had flourished under alien rule, hawkers touted brass flagons of lemon juice, metal cups jangling at their leather belts. He poured himself a glass of raki, regarded the street lights through the lens of the liquid, then sipped it, savouring the fire that ran in his veins.

Tonight his son, Issan – at thirty-two one of the most outstanding anaesthetists with whom he had ever worked – was leaving with him for four days in Cairo, as members of the Albanian Delegation of Solidarity with Pan-Arab Scientists. He wanted Issan to have opportunities he had never known, and in other countries, with higher rewards than Albania could offer. Surely that was one of the reasons you had children? Was it disloyal to think like this?

Krasna had only prospered himself through the Italian occupation of Albania before the second world war.

He had been drafted into the Italian Army, detailed as a medical orderly, and then had so impressed his regimental medical officers that they put forward his name for promotion.

Now it so happened that the Italians needed some examples of Fascist generosity that they could praise; Krasna and several other surprised conscripts therefore found themselves relieved of their military duties to enrol as medical students at Tirana University.

This was his first chance. His second came later in the desert, at Bizerta and Benghazi, when he was able to operate on severely wounded soldiers. Gradually, he began to specialize in new techniques for brain operations. He had a vast supply of patients for his experiments, and as a growing number were successful, his reputation spread to base hospitals in Italy. After the war, he had returned to Tirana and then found it impossible to leave. His wife had died, he had a small son to bring up, and the Communist government refused to allow him to take the boy out of the country. If he went, he would have to leave Issan behind. So he stayed.

Krasna stepped back into the room, feeling the carpet rough beneath his feet, and caught sight of his own face, lined and hard and brown, wrinkled around the eyes from the intensity of concentration in so many complex operations. He was still fit, with hardly any fat, despite his age. He ran a hand through his thinning, black hair; he had worn well.

The sun had almost disappeared behind the mountains, so that for a moment they seemed to crouch like the dark spine of some enormous, brooding beast. He thought of the empty country beyond the city, stretching into ever-deepening darkness, where wild beasts prowled, the most dangerous not always those that walked on four legs. There were too many ugly rumours of purges and arrests, of torturings in houses high in the hills, to discount them entirely. He had seen fear in the faces of many of his friends, and once or twice someone had been on the edge of speaking to him – it had almost seemed of warning him – and then they had thought better of it, and he had not seen them again.

But why should he feel uneasy, when he was so successful, so friendly with so many influential people? What had he ever done against his country, wretched and ruined though it was through the blind, bigoted folly of its rulers, and their incomprehensible dependence on China? The Albanian dictator, Enver Hoxha, would not sign the simplest decree without the approval of the Chinese ambassador. Was it now a crime even to think of other, freer ways of life?

He knew the answer before he phrased the question, and he turned back into the room to pull the curtains across the open balcony, before he switched on the light, because, even at twelve stories high, he still kept some of the old bourgeois dislike of being overlooked by neighbours.

The outside door of the apartment clicked gently; he had left it on the latch for Issan. Soon, he would see, like a disembodied ghost between the two curtains, the pale handsome face of his son. It was the moment of each day to which he looked forward with the most pleasure.

'Issan,' he called.

There was a faint movement behind the curtains. Then they moved more roughly, so that the old-fashioned runners screamed on their brass rail.

Then all the lights went on.

A man was standing between the curtains, but he was not Issan. This was a short man in a grey suit so tightly buttoned that the creases ran like horizontal grooves across his belly. He wore a black felt hat, greasy around the band with sweat and hair oil. In his right hand he held an automatic.

This must be a robber, thought Krasna, one of those people he had read about in the evening papers, who terrorized outlying collective farms with weapons stolen from some military armoury, sometimes holding up country buses, robbing the occupants of their watches, even gold rings.

'Who are you?' Krasna asked him roughly. 'Do you want money?'

If it was only money, he would give him what little he had to humour him, and when he had gone he would simply pick up the internal telephone and speak to the caretaker in the basement; the man would be seized as he stepped from the lift.

'Stand over by the far corner,' ordered the man. 'I don't want money. Put both your hands on your head. If you move, I'll shoot.'

He crossed the room, pulled a knife from a sheath beneath his right shoulder, snipped the leads of the telephone; the bell gave a tiny ring as he cut the wires.

'I am from the Policíja,' he explained. 'You are coming back to headquarters for questioning.'

'For questioning? What about?'

General Ackermann, the head of the Policíja, the Secret Police, was an old friend. This ridiculous business, whatever it was, could be sorted out in minutes, man to man. But why cut the telephone wire? Could it be to prevent him telephoning the General? Or perhaps Ackermann himself had been deposed? Perhaps he was going to be questioned simply because he had been friendly with him? The nuances of loyalty and distrust, of envy and betrayal, were as delicate as they could be dangerous.

'I'm expecting someone,' added Krasna carefully.

'You're expecting your son,' corrected the man. 'We want him, too. It is a political matter.'

'A political matter?'

How could it be, when all his adult life he had so carefully avoided all involvement in politics?

Something about the man's face, the flesh grey and cold like mortuary marble; something about his eyes, without feeling, without warmth, bright as the eyes of a serpent, stilled Krasna's voice in his throat. He swallowed, and could feel his heart begin to drum an alarum under his shirt. Fear poured adrenalin through his veins. He leaned back against the wall; his sweat was damp between his shoulders.

The door clicked again. The automatic came an inch nearer to his stomach. He heard Issan's voice behind the other side of the curtain.

'Why the bright lights?'

Krasna wanted to cry out a warning, to tell him to shout down the lift-well for help, to ring the lift bell, anything; but his voice remained locked in his throat.

Issan came through the gap in the curtains. His smile faded when he saw the gunman.

'Who? . . .' he began.

'Shut up,' said the man. 'You're also coming with me.'

'Where to?' asked Issan. He was taller than the man with the gun, and stronger. Surely they could both overpower this man, even if he were armed? But then what?

'I know what you're thinking,' said the man, 'but don't try it. There are others in a car outside. If I'm not down within a certain time, they'll come up, and there's only one way out of here. By the lift. I only came alone to be more discreet. As a compliment to your father.'

He smiled, but it was only a muscular contraction of his lips; his eyes stayed dark as the muzzle of his gun.

'Go into the bedroom and pack as many clothes as you can get into a briefcase,' he said. 'You will need an overcoat. It is cold in the hills – where we're going.'

He turned slightly towards the door, jerking his automatic at Krasna to make him move. For an instant the muzzle pointed towards the wall. In that fraction of a second, Issan hit him.

The edge of his right hand came down on the gunman's arm, hard as a rod. The bone snapped as the trigger finger tightened. The noise of the explosion in the tiny concrete room seemed as loud as a cannon. Issan's knee came up into the man's groin. He folded forward in his tight suit, his face a blind mask of agony. Krasna hit him as he fell. He lay on the carpet, a little bile at his mouth, his fists clenched against the pain.

'Who is he?' asked Issan, dusting his hands, as though to rid them of any contact with him.

'Policija.'

Reaction had dried Krasna's mouth; his tongue had turned to cotton wool. He sat down shakily.

'But why? What have you done? We're loyal Party members.'

While Issan dredged his mind for reasons, Krasna sat, head in his hands, looking at the man on the floor. Was he dead or just stunned? He leaned over and held his wrist; there was no pulse beat. He felt no regret, no nothing; it was as though he had been unconsciously preparing himself for some catastrophe; his life had been too good to stay that way.

'They don't need reasons,' he said at last, flatly. 'Someone says something about you. Or someone else writes an anonymous letter. You know that as well as I do. If there's nothing, they make something. The question is, what are we going to do now? That man's dead.'

'Why don't you ring General Ackermann?' Issan asked. 'You know him.'

Krasna glanced at the telephone wires.

'He cut the wires,' he explained. 'And if we go to headquarters at this hour, he probably won't be there. And what do we say to him, anyway? That we've killed the man he sent to escort us?'

He did not like to add to his own fear – that Ackermann might be in trouble himself.

'You operated on his sister when she had a brain tumour,' Issan persisted. 'You saved her life.'

'So I did. And Dr Grussman saved the General's life when he removed one of his kidneys last year. But that didn't save old Grussman, did it, when someone said he was an enemy of the state? No, we've got to leave quickly – get out of the country.'

'But won't that show we're guilty of whatever they're accusing us of doing or being?'

'We are already guilty, just because we've been accused. Also, we've killed a man. If we flee, at least we will still be alive. We can start again.'

'But where?'

'The United Arab Republic. Egypt. Syria. We'll go to Cairo as we intended – on the flight tonight. Then we'll see.'

He glanced at his watch; it was already nine o'clock.

'Won't the police have warned the airport?'

'Why? They wouldn't imagine we'd try to get away. Anyway, it's a risk we'll have to take. Unless you've a better suggestion?'

Issan shook his head.

'Then let's get out of here. We've only minutes before someone else comes up.'

They pulled two fibre cases from the store cupboard in the little hall and then stood, minds blocked with urgency, wondering what they should take, what they would need. It was one thing packing for a short stay; another, packing for ever. A seventeenth-century print of a boar-hunt, some small pieces of early Albanian armour, little things like these marked the progress of Krasna's life like milestones, but what use were they when you were running away?

They shut the flat door carefully behind them and took the lift down to the first floor. From the landing, a window overlooked the road. Krasna saw a Skoda taxi parked outside the front of the building, with a small van behind it. Fronds of smoke plumed their exhausts; the engines were running for a quick departure. They could not possibly leave by the front door.

They tiptoed down the back stairs, through the spring-loaded doors to the back yard, where Krasna kept his car. He unlocked it, started the engine, drove behind the boiler house, out through the almost empty streets towards the airport. By his side, Issan kept glancing through their rear window; no one was following them.

In the airport entrance hall, a few globular lights lit up the curiously dated architecture of Communist countries. It was as though, aesthetically, time had stopped for them in the mid-nineteen-thirties when Communism still seemed to offer a road to a better world, not just a tomb for personal initiative.

Krasna parked the car, locked the door from force of habit, wondering sadly who would unlock it and when, then together they walked up the steps.

Half a dozen middle-aged men in the peculiarly-cut brown suits and light plastic raincoats, which were as much a uniform as anything the soldiers wore, stood in the hall, surrounded by brown fibre suitcases and wicker baskets. One or two greeted them with arms raised in extravagant welcome, as though they had not seen them for years instead of only two hours before. Krasna wondered whether any of them had been responsible for their caller. He waved back as casually as he could, walked over to the ticket counter, then pushed his two tickets under the metal grille to the clerk.

The man checked them against a typed list of names, ticked off two, tore out one page from each of the ticket folders, handed them two boarding cards, went back to adding up rows of figures on a hand adding-machine. So far, so safe. As Krasna had thought, the Policíja had not thought it necessary to warn the airport.

He and Issan exchanged brief glances of relief. Issan set his watch against the huge clock that hung from a roof girder. They would be called in ten minutes. They drifted over to the little group, and forced platitudes out of their mouths as the big hands jerked slowly round the white clock-face above their heads.

When the loudspeakers first began to crackle, Krasna thought his heart would freeze, but the announcement was simply that their plane was ready. They walked with the others towards the departures door. A plainclothes policeman stood with the airline official; Krasna looked up at him, but he was looking over Krasna's shoulder, at someone who stood behind him. He nodded briefly. Krasna felt a hand clamp on his upper left arm. His heart beat in his head like a drum; sweat poured off his body.

He turned slowly, like an automaton, a puppet with his neck pulled by string; he could feel the muscles around his mouth harden like ridges of bone. He could not have spoken to save his life, for his throat had constricted so that he could barely breathe. Above him, the lights in the airport roof danced like a constellation of stars gone mad.

A man in a grey uniform with red facings on his jacket was smiling, holding out his right arm, over which hung a plastic raincoat. His raincoat. The man was speaking, but although Krasna watched his lips move, saw his Adam's apple go up and down with the movement of speech, he was under such strain that he could not understand what he said. He might have been talking through a thick glass screen; it was like watching a silent film. Then Krasna swallowed and breathed, and the lights stopped dancing, and he heard the words. Of course, he had left his own raincoat on the ticket counter. He bowed stiffly and found his voice.

'Thank you,' he said.

'It is my pleasure, Comrade surgeon,' said the man.

They were all bowing and smiling to him. He was a man of consequence, of esteem, of position; he was a success. He followed Issan up the aluminium steps into the aircraft and the door shut behind them. He sat down, looking straight ahead. Then the machine trembled and the lights dimmed, and they were away.

In Cairo, the delegates stayed in the hotel always chosen

for such outings; a small seedy place with peeling stucco on the front walls and ancient shutters powdered and cracked by the suns of too many summers.

Aspidistras in the gloomy entrance hall gathered dust on dark-green leaves; the lamp shade hanging from the centre of the ceiling wore a pink cotton cover, four corners weighed down by snail-shells.

Krasna and Issan were on separate floors, which neither had expected. They slept uneasily through that first night, and the next day seemed clogged with meetings, fraternal resolutions and receptions. Neither had any experience in defection. If they walked into a police station, would not their embassy be consulted – and reply that they were already wanted for murder? What chance would they have then? They decided to wait, to see whether some sign or portent might appear as a guide. So when they went to bed, on the second night, fear and indecision had eroded resolution.

Krasna was asleep when the knocking awakened him. He swung himself out of bed and sat listening. Who could it be calling at this hour? His mouth felt sour with interrupted sleep, and the tiled floor was cold to his bare feet. He switched on his bedside light.

'Who is it?' he called thickly.

'Me,' Issan replied. 'For God's sake, let me in.'

Krasna unlocked the door and bolted it behind his son.

'What's wrong?' he asked.

In the light of the street lamp through the window Issan's face glistened with fear.

'They're after us,' he said.

'Who?' asked Krasna, his mind still fuddled.

'Ackermann. He's here. In Cairo. I've seen him. I couldn't sleep and I went out for a stroll. I don't know if he saw me.'

'What was he doing?'

'Coming out of a house.'

'You're sure?'

'Certain.'

'How long ago was this?'

'Just now. I went back to my room. I didn't put on the light, but I looked out of the window. A man was outside.'

'He might be trying to pick up a girl,' Krasna suggested.

'Not there,' retorted Issan. 'Not that man.'

'So?'

'So I came out through the back door, down the service stairs, round here.'

'I don't believe a word of it,' said Krasna, reassuring himself as much as Issan. 'You're tired. You must have seen someone who looked like Ackermann.'

'I saw Ackermann,' Issan insisted doggedly.

'I'll come back to your room with you,' said Krasna. He unlocked the door. The corridor was empty under its old-fashioned lights; outside some doors, pairs of shoes waited patiently to be cleaned.

They were halfway across the hall when the night bell rang; they could see the outline of a man's body against the frosted glass. They stopped, looked at each other. A larger-than-life photograph of President Nasser watched them toothily from the wall. The night porter slept in a straight-backed wooden chair under it, his feet on top of his scuffed shoes, his mouth open. A fly marked time on his lower lip.

The man outside the door rang for a second time. The porter swam back to wakefulness, rubbed his eyes, flexed his toes, walked slowly to the door, opened it. The man who came in wore a belted raincoat and a soft black felt hat. Dressed like that, Krasna thought he was either a policeman or a ponce.

Some of Issan's panic began to infect him. They hurried through the back regions of the hotel to Issan's room, locked the door and did not switch on the light. As Krasna opened his mouth to speak, the telephone rang. Issan picked it up, with the automatic reflex of a man whose life has been ruled by the telephone; the night porter was on the line speaking in French.

'Monsieur Issan?'

Krasna put his hand over the mouthpiece and shook his head. Issan took away the hand.

'Who wants him?' he asked.

'There is a police officer to see him.'

'You've got the wrong room. Now don't wake me up again.' He slammed down the receiver, not out of anger, but because his hand was shaking.

17

'We've got to go,' said Krasna urgently. 'Now.'

He opened the bedside cupboard, pulled out a bottle of Japanese whisky, filled two tooth glasses. They drank in silence; the cheap spirit shot fire around their frightened bodies and, with the sudden rough warmth, came a small return of courage.

'Where can we go?' asked Issan wretchedly. The hotel receptionist still had their passports. And if the police were already seeking them, it was obviously absurd to go to a police station and ask for asylum.

'There's only one possible way out,' said Krasna. 'Go to Damascus. We won't need passports. They'll not think of looking for us there.'

'Why shouldn't they? It's Communist, too, isn't it?'

'That's what I mean. If you're looking for a prisoner who's escaped, you don't start looking for him in another jail.'

The telephone rang for a second time. They stood in silence, looking at the amber liquid in their glasses. In a corner of the room, a brass tap dripped into a cracked basin; lights of passing cars drew patterns on the far wall. Mosquitoes whined in the far corners. The telephone went on ringing.

Krasna reached out and touched his son's hand. 'We'll leave our luggage,' he said. 'That may give us a small start.' Issan nodded; he could not trust himself to speak.

They went out down the fire escape, past sewage smells from old waste pipes tacked to the crumbling walls.

Each delegate had been given a small folding map of Cairo and its museums, its railway stations and embassies. They also had thirty Egyptian pounds each, for local spending money; this would have to get them north. They took the night train to Natrub on the coast, and then sold Issan's watch to buy tickets on a cargo boat that carried occasional passengers.

In Damascus they rented two small rooms, about half a mile apart, near the main bazaar. Krasna knew they could make enough to keep themselves in food by concocting syrups for quacks in the souk who sold rubbishy medicines for such diverse diseases as cancer and syphilis.

They only needed a living, until it was safe to return to Cairo or until, perhaps, they might do some sufficiently powerful politician a favour, and he would give them passports in Syrian names, and then they could travel anywhere, to new lives, perhaps even to the New World.

They had been in Damascus for nearly two weeks when Issan came to see Krasna, his face as grey with terror as it had been in Cairo.

Krasna locked the door automatically behind him.

'What's wrong?' he asked resignedly.

'Ackermann's here.'

'He can't be.'

'He is. I saw him in the souk tonight. In a silver shop.'

'He saw you?'

'I don't know. As soon as I recognized him I ducked down that alleyway by that shop that sells tin kettles and hurricane lamps. I stayed there, watching him until he went out.'

'Maybe he didn't see you?' Krasna suggested hopefully.

'If he didn't, he will next time. He must guess we're here, for we can't get out of the Republic. So if we're not in Egypt, we've got to be.'

'When some animals in the jungle are hunted,' said Krasna slowly, 'they turn the tables and become the hunters. That's what we're going to do. Now.'

'How?'

'I've bought a gun,' explained Krasna simply.

He crossed to the bureau of unpainted plain wood, opened the right-hand drawer, pulled out a Lüger.

'Where did you get it?'

'In the souk. With a dozen rounds.'

'You can't shoot him in the street.'

'I may have to,' said Krasna. 'It's his life or ours.'

The colour was coming back into Issan's face. He wiped his brow with his handkerchief.

'It's murder,' he said doubtfully.

Krasna shrugged.

'Have you a better solution?'

Issan shook his head.

'Do you think he's on his own?'

'I don't know,' said Krasna. 'But he'll be on his own when I get him. I'm not running away any more. Then I'm going to the American Embassy. Or the British. We've got something to offer in exchange for asylum. They'll listen to us.'

'Why not go now?'

'It's too late. They'd be closed. And they're probably watched.'

Krasna let the gun slip down into the side pocket of his jacket. He could feel it, heavy, uncomfortable, and yet comforting against his body.

'Anyhow,' he said, 'maybe he's not after us at all. Maybe he's after someone else.'

He didn't sound very convincing, even to himself.

'Now,' he said more harshly. 'Back to your room, get some sleep. Come here at eight in the morning and we'll go to the Embassy. Together.'

Krasna held open the door for his son and watched him walk down the empty street, past the shuttered shops and the beggars who slept in their rags; past the dustbins where cats lurked and stray dogs fought and copulated according to age and inclination. Then he shut the door, locked it in his careful fashion, poured himself a whisky, stood looking at himself in the mirror above the dresser. His face looked back at him, like the face of a stranger; sallow skin, grey smudges under his eyes, calipers of strain on either side of his mouth. What a difference a few days could make!

He sipped the whisky, looking into his mirrored eyes, his thoughts turning like a gramophone record. Instead of running away like this, instead of shooting one man, and risk having not only the Albanian police after him, but the Syrians as well, it would be better to go to the American Embassy, even at this hour. They were mad to postpone it any longer. What if it was watched? Some duty officer or guard would let them in.

He walked up and down the threadbare carpet, clotted with dirt, poured himself a second drink, his thoughts jagged as a mind of broken fingernails.

Then he reached his decision. He turned out the light and looked through the mesh curtain at the road.

It seemed empty. He unbolted the door, opened it half an inch. The night air was chill and damp, heavy with the smell of oil which saturated the whole city, that seemed to soak up from the sand beneath, from measureless black walls that one day would be tapped, to make fortunes for other people, in other countries. He closed the door behind him, leaned back against it to make sure the catch was holding, and then set off for Issan's room.

He lived three flights up in a block off The Street Called Straight. The building was new, of rough precast concrete, near the Kaysam Gate where St Paul was said to have been lowered over the wall in a basket to escape the anger of the Jews. As Krasna walked up the gritty staircase, he hoped that the omen of successful escape was propitious. Naked light bulbs burned on the landing; outside a shabby door stood two prams and a bicycle with a torn mudguard. He knocked on the door in the tattoo he and Issan had between them. There was no answer. He put his hand in his pocket, took out the key, turned it in the lock.

As soon as he was inside the door, he knew something was wrong. There was a smell of cigar smoke, and Issan didn't smoke cigars. He felt fear catch in his throat, and flicked on the light.

The curtains were drawn and a copper vase had been placed on the sill to hold them together, to prevent anyone outside from seeing what had happened inside.

All Issan's books had been thrown from the bookcase; a chair was broken, a table lay on its side. Issan's flowers withered in a pool of water on the brown-tiled floor.

Krasna prowled around the edges of the room. There was blood on the front page of a newspaper, on the imprint of a foot, blood on the tiles. That there had been a fight was obvious, and whoever had been waiting for Issan had captured him. Surely it could only be Ackermann?

Krasna felt fear grow like an enormous physical lump in his chest, which threatened to choke him. If they had discovered where Issan lived, then it was almost certain they would soon beat Krasna's address out of him.

A car went past outside, tyres squealing as it made a sharp turn on the greasy road. Krasna stopped breathing as though the driver could hear him, from that far away. The car went on, and then came the call of prayer from the mosque, loud and metallic, and somehow menacing in a tongue he could not understand.

He crossed to the basin in the corner of the room and ran the tap, cupping his right hand under it, drinking eagerly, sprinkling some water on his face, trying to clear his mind. It was surely only a matter of time before he was discovered; already he could feel the boot in his kidneys, the knee in his groin, the hard edge of a hand splintering the bridge of his nose. He knew their methods. He had signed too many death certificates in the past not to know how their victims had died; and invariably they took a long time to die.

The fear of physical pain, the anguish of not knowing what had happened to his son, threatened to overwhelm him; it was as though he was already on the rack. But where could he go? He felt like an animal running blindly in a circle.

To stay where he was for an instant longer was to invite discovery. He would go back to his own room – just in case Issan had managed to break away and flee there. Then he would go to the American Embassy. Surely he would not be turned away? Not when he told them what he had to tell, what price he could offer in return for security? But what if he would not be accepted?

Wild ideas of starting a fire in his room, of finding a body to dress in his clothes, fumed through his brain and evaporated. He flicked off the light, opened the door a few inches, stood behind it, listening until he was certain no one was waiting outside.

He walked down the stairs, half crouching as though under fire, one hand balled into a fist, the other holding the automatic in his pocket, but the street was as empty as the staircase.

The night air dried the sweat on his forehead. He began to walk quickly, but not to run, because a running man always attracted attention. He went through back alleys, where houses leaned out towards each other, almost touching across the narrow curving road, as though eager for company, anxious to whisper to each other the terrible secrets of the centuries.

Outside his own room, he waited for a full minute listening, but there was no sound from within, no chink of light beneath the door. He pushed the key in the lock, turned it, kicked open the door with the toe of his foot. He could see the familiar outline of the curtain, the old armchair with the frills round its legs, the marble table, the tattered edge of a rug. He shut the door behind him, and leaned against it to regain his breath. His heart was still thumping inside him like the wings of a captured bird. He waited until it slowed, then he put on the light.

Across the room, in the cane chair which he used for breakfast, a man was sitting.

Krasna had never seen him before, and yet he could have seen him a hundred times, because there was nothing remarkable about him. He was broad-shouldered in a dark suit,

'My dear Dr Krasna,' he said in French. His voice boomed like a mellow bell around the shabby room; the voice was of power, of infinite authority.

'My dear Dr Krasna, it was very kind of you to come back and save me a long wait, or, even worse, a journey through unfamiliar streets. I have searched for you for a long time, but I thought you would return here before you contemplated any other – ah – journey.'

'Are you from Ackermann?'

Now that the worst had happened, all fear had drained from Krasna's body. He stood, exhausted by inertia and reaction, a shell of a man. He remembered the gun in his pocket, but what use was it there – what use was anything now when there was nowhere to run to, and no chance to run?

The man smiled; white china teeth glittered like stones in his mouth. He gave an almost imperceptible nod. Another man, who had been waiting behind the curtain with the ether mask, rammed it over Krasna's face.

The rest was brief pain and long darkness, a hiss of gas and the slow, silent fall past centuries of stars.

Chapter One

The grey carpet dipped slightly and safety-belt signs flashed with silent impatience. The stewardess braced her legs against the growing angle of the floor, as the Air France Caravelle began its long slide down the sky to Damascus.

To Dr Jason Love, who remembered when a journey as long as the flight from England to Syria could take weeks, the idea of accomplishing it in a few hours in an armchair (meanwhile enjoying escalope de mer saronis, côte de veau en casserole, salad, champagne, and even his favourite Gitanes, doubly pleasant since they were free) seemed altogether remarkable.

In time, possibly in very little time, all this elegance in the air which the French understood so well, just as the British understood sumptuousness at sea, would seem as dated as the old Atlantic queens – and he meant the ships, not any of their passengers. But until travellers could be fired by capsule into space, propelled by rocket or maybe even dehydrated in one country to be rehydrated in another, Air France certainly seemed a most comfortable and civilized way of travel.

He dutifully buckled on his belt, stubbed out his cigarette and watched the violet clouds of evening pour past the window. He felt relaxed and at ease, looking forward to Damascus. On the flight he had been reading the classic guide, Murray's *'Book for Travellers in Syria and Palestine,* including an account in the geography, history, antiquities and inhabitants of these countries'. Although published in 1858, it still provided an interesting companion for a first visit. Love opened it up again as the plane came in to land.

'Passports,' he read, 'are not generally required, but it is so easy for the traveller to provide himself with one that the precaution should never be omitted.'

Well, no one would argue overmuch on that.

'Travellers should also bear in mind that there is scarcely a district in Syria in which amateur bandits may not be met with, ready to take advantage of the unarmed solitary wayfarer ... I would therefore advise everyone in travelling always to have a revolver within reach, and an attendant not far off – this may save some disagreeable encounters, and can do no harm.'

He would not dispute this, either, but he had neither revolver nor attendant, and as a doctor on his way to a convention of general practitioners at the New Omayad Hotel in Damascus, with another few days to be spent sight-seeing throughout Syria, then crossing to the Lebanon for Baalbek and finally going down to Jordan and Jerusalem, he did not visualize the need for either.

He glanced without interest at the other passengers, his mind free-wheeling. What did they all do for a living? Were firms paying their fares – or had they bought their own tickets?

That man across the aisle, sleeping, mouth open, shoes and tie loosened, seat tipped back – was he a director or one of the directed? The couple behind him, the middle-aged man in the dark-blue, unpressed suit, small bright eyes darting from side to side like snakes' tongues, holding hands with the mean woman in the fur coat, with the cupid's bow of mauve lipstick flattering her thin, hard, bloodless mouth – were they married or single? And what, if anything, did they think about him?

His mind turned back easily to his home in Bishop's Combe in Somerset. He hoped the locum had settled in well; that Mrs Hunter, his housekeeper, was coping with the builders who were due to decorate his hall; that the builders were honest men. He should have removed his collection of forty car nameplates from the rafters before he came away, for some, such as Schneider and Voisin, were so rare he could never hope to replace them. And although he had collected these epitaphs of dreamers and brave individualists over the years purely for the pleasure they gave him with their quaint heraldry, they had, like his Cord car, acquired a scarcity value out of all proportion to their original cost.

Usually, on his foreign trips, he found one or two new

badges – that of a Crossley-Burney in Amsterdam; an Imperia in Lisbon; a Star in San Sebastian. He was generally luckier in hot countries than cold, because a dry climate discouraged damp and death-watch beetle in wooden frames. Why, in the South of France, in that large breakers' yard on the coast road between Nice and Antibes, he had even seen a Bugatti Royale, one of those mechanical leviathans that Le Patron would only sell to kings – including with each a guarantee, not for the life of the car, but for the life of its owner.

This was Love's first visit to Syria: he wondered what the old car situation would be like there. You never knew your luck. Also, he relished the prospect of anything and anyone new and undiscovered, any fresh experience, for the older and more selective one grew, the fewer people, places and experiences fell into this ever-dwindling category. Eventually, there would only be one experience left to sample: the last. Death.

The word reminded him of a rather distasteful chore he intended to do as soon as possible, otherwise it would hang over him, like mental indigestion. One of his patients, Colonel Head, who lived in a converted millhouse at the far end of the village, had called on Love after surgery on the previous evening.

Head was a retired soldier, who had spent twenty-two years with the First Fifth Mahrattas in India, and now, as a widower, eked out his pension by keeping bees and selling honey to tourist shops in Minehead and Ilfracombe.

'I'd like to ask you a favour, Doctor,' he had begun in his brusque, direct way, as though he were addressing a new intake of subalterns on the traditions of the regiment. 'We've known each other long enough for you to realize that I don't ask many, so I hope you won't think I'm on the scrounge, eh?'

He paused for a denial. Love made it, poured a treble whisky for the Colonel, a double Bacardi for himself.

'Right. Then here it comes. You're off to Damascus, and Clarissa was killed somewhere out in Syria last week.'

He paused, cleared his throat, uncertain how to continue. Love nodded sympathetically. He had watched the Colonel's only daughter grow from a cheerful schoolgirl with a gold band around her teeth, winning prizes with her pony, Andy, at gymkhanas as far afield as Bath and Bridgwater, to an equally cheerful nurse, who had left a year ago to work as a voluntary helper in India.

She had been born in Bombay and some relations still lived there. When her year was up, she decided not to come home by boat, but to drive back overland, in her Austin Healey Sprite. About twenty miles out of Damascus, so the Colonel told him, Clarissa had skidded on a curve – banked the wrong way, as the fifth secretary in the British Embassy there explained in a letter, and damp because of an early morning mist. She had crashed into another car, and died on the way to hospital.

Her passport, some travellers' cheques, a few letters and two suitcases found in her car boot, had been flown back to her father by the British Embassy in Damascus, along with a certificate of death, and a returnable receipt for these belongings.

'You've heard nothing more?' asked Love. But what more could the Colonel hear? The dead were notably bad at communicating with the living, whatever the mediums might claim.

'Nothing. The fifth secretary fellow out there was very helpful, but he couldn't add anything to what he'd said in his first cable. Which brings me to the reason for coming here.

'I can't get out to Syria, Doctor. For one thing, you won't let me fly because of my angina, and apart from that, I just can't afford it – the air fare alone is over two hundred quid. So I was wondering whether, since you'll be in Damascus for a few days in any case, you could take a few photographs of Clarissa's grave?

'She's buried in the Christian cemetery, wherever that is. And perhaps you could ask at the Embassy if some arrangement could be made for looking after her grave? You know, putting flowers on it each Christmas Day and on her birthday, and so on. Well, that's the favour, Doctor. Is it asking too much?'

'It's asking nothing,' Love replied at once. 'I'll make it my business to photograph the grave. Then I'll check with the British Embassy. And if there's anything I can find out about the accident I'll bring you back a full report.'

'Thank you,' said the Colonel gratefully. 'I thought you'd say that . . .'

The Caravelle wheels bumped once, twice on the tarmac. The pilot reversed his engines, and the plane sighed to a stop outside the little airport building. In the customs hall, a few old men in shoddy dark suits sat stoically on wooden benches, looking out at the plane through long windows set in metal frames that had been fashionable thirty years ago.

A trough of sand under the window was littered with cigarette butts; the plants in it had died because bored spectators had pinched their fleshy leaves. These old men would never do that; they were too poor even to be bored.

A group of Bulgarians on some mission of socialist solidarity were filing out on to the tarmac as Love picked up his bag from the customs counter. They wore the curiously outmoded clothes he had seen on middle-European emigrants in Canada – plastic shoes, very wide trousers, belted raincoats.

They all had large heads, with strong oily features, like living wood carvings; their mouths glittered with gold-tipped teeth. They left behind them a smell of garlic and sweat and cheap hair oil; Love thought it would have been more pleasant to leave nothing behind. He hailed a taxi, a blue and yellow De Soto, and told the driver, the New Omayad.

The road into Damascus was almost empty except for a few Tatra Army trucks growling along in low gear. A little rain began to fall unexpectedly, and flags of orange, amber, purple, covered with Syrian writing he couldn't decipher, fluttered damply in the trees. Policemen on point duty wore brown leather jackets, white gauntlets and leggings; they could have been cavalry colonels or old-fashioned country butchers. All had moustaches, like actors from a film of the thirties; Don Ameche, Cesar Romero.

Here and there, men jogged along importantly on donkeys piled with tin suitcases. On a street corner, a hawker sold oranges from a three-wheeled cart. Opposite him, a beggar lay on the ground, fat and defeated, bloated with flies, clutching a handful of lottery tickets no one bothered to buy.

So this was the city the Arabs called The Bride of the Desert, the gateway of God.

Love's hotel took its name from the Omayad, a dynasty that had ruled the country 1,300 years earlier.

They had lived hard – one Omayad was said to have killed 120,000 of his people before the rest submitted and accepted his rule – but they carried out irrigation projects and other schemes to benefit their subjects. Under the Omayad rule, poets had flourished – and so had Syria; its empire stretched from Spain in the west to China in the east, and north into Russia.

They wouldn't be at home in the hotel now, thought Love, looking at the indifferent architecture, the grey concrete walls. But they might have approved of the high school students across the road, who were rehearsing some military parade. The air reverberated with beaten drums and the baying of bugles.

Love paid off his taxi, went up the steps through the swing doors, signed for his room, 247, collected a card giving details of the convention meetings. The first was what the card described as 'an informal get together' at ten o'clock on the following morning in the main lounge.

They would have their meals at tables of five or six, and the organizer, one Dr Erasmus Plugge of Goole, whom Love had met briefly at a conference on malaria in Teheran a couple of years previously, added his hope that they would 'all move around'.

Like musical chairs, thought Love, remembering Plugge, without notable enthusiasm or warmth, as a man who smoked herbal tobacco and wore suits of unbelievable tweediness; the cloth almost had built-in burrs. The Plugges of this world invariably organized meetings, protests, campaigns, conventions, for only in crowds could they submerge their own inadequacies. Ah, well, sufficient unto the night was the evil thereof.

He took the lift to the second floor, let himself into his room. It was no worse than he had expected; perhaps a little better. The door opened into a tiny tiled hall, with the bathroom on the right, his bedroom straight ahead. A mosquito screen covered the window.

Love threw open the shutters: the window overlooked a rubbish tip towards a spine of hills. A few parked cars glistened at the side of the road, the rain returned the gloss on their paint that the sun had removed. A strong smell of oil seeped up from the soaking earth. On the rubbish tip, an old man was carefully shredding a handcart of posters in Syrian script. He made a damp white heap, and then slowly pushed the cart away and left the sodden pyramid behind him, a paper memorial. Was this really the site of the Garden of Eden? Love closed the window, unpacked, had a bath, went to bed.

His sleep was punctuated by a bellow from a mosque he had not seen, somewhere behind the hotel. The muezzin was calling the faithful to prayer, but not as the priests had for centuries called on them to worship Allah, the one true god. This summons was electrically taped, transistorized and then amplified tenfold. It went out automatically, without benefit of clergy.

'God is most great.
'I bear witness that there is no god but God.
'I bear witness that Muhammad is the apostle of God.
'Come to prayer. Prayer is better than sleep.'

Not always, Love thought. It depends on who is praying and who is sleeping. Also, to whom and with whom. Then the hands of the time clock in the mosque passed on, linked switches clicked off the recording mechanism, and, like the priests, like their congregation, like Love, the machine slept.

The Convention's 'get together' next morning was all Love had hoped it wouldn't be. Country doctors in tweeds smoked curved briars. Ascetic town doctors stood about in awkward groups, with pale faces, folded copies of the *New Scientist* in their jacket pockets. All the delegates had tags on their lapels with their names and areas. Wives, in hats bright with lacquered berries, hung mental prices on each other's clothes, and everyone threw well-honed clichés at each other and caught them skilfully.

The lunch promised to be even worse; you could never be sure who would be put at your table. He looked at his watch; five minutes past eleven. Instead of making talk so small that it was practically microscopic, he might as well use the next two hours to photograph Clarissa Head's grave, and see the Embassy secretary, Mr Jackson. The first lecture in the afternoon came after a reception at three in the Musée de L'Armée, wherever that was. He had plenty of time.

He went up to his room, loaded his Ikonta, skimmed through the papers that Colonel Head had given him: Clarissa's death certificate with the name of Dr Suleiman, who had signed it, and his address; a photograph taken of her some years ago with her pony; the letter from the fifth secretary in the Embassy with the address of the Christian cemetery.

A taxi driver wearing a grey linen suit and open-toed sandals saluted Love as he came out through the swing doors of the hotel.

'Taxi, sir?' he asked hopefully. 'I speak English.'

'That makes two of us,' said Love. 'I want to go to the Christian cemetery.' But not, he thought to himself, in a horizontal position.

'Please?' asked the driver, less hopefully.

'Cemetery,' said Love. 'Tombs. The dead.'

'One moment.' The driver spoke to a colleague who asked Love in French what he meant.

Love explained; the sentence was translated.

The first driver nodded approvingly.

'You see, as I said, I speak English.'

It didn't seem worth arguing about, and each was entitled to his own opinion. Love climbed into the taxi. A white plastic crucifix dangled under the rear-view mirror. The driver took off as though starting for the 24 hours' Le Mans race, whipped dangerously in front of a lorry and a bus, and, having earned the anger of both drivers, sat back thankfully in his seat. The crucifix jangled against the windscreen; maybe the driver was pushing his luck.

'Which part do you want?' he asked.

'The gates,' said Love. The Christian cemetery wouldn't be very big in a Moslem country. He could find a newly dug grave easily enough.

They slid through the town, past dusty, trampled gardens, and open-fronted shops where dead fish rested pinkish scales on slabs of melting ice and animal carcasses provided raw landing grounds for flies. The air still felt heavy with the smell of oil he had noticed on the previous evening. Everywhere, an impressive past reached out to a mediocre present:

great archways and pillars crumbled to dust under centuries of sun. Workmen scraped that dust to make cement for new blocks of flats as architecturally inspiring as a telephone exchange in Gospel Oak.

The driver turned off the Boulevard Baghdad, past concrete houses wearing pale-green shutters, primly closed like spinsters' eyes, lest they saw any of the surrounding poverty. Some houses were half finished, and some would never be finished. The air of futility lay as heavy as the smell of oil. Only a few yards behind imposing houses stood rows of crumbling shacks, with mud roofs and walls, where chickens and children ignored each other in the sunshine. In Syria, it seemed, there was no middle class; you were either rich or poor.

'Here we are, sir,' said the taxi driver.

He stopped by two metal gates, padlocked together with a rusting chain. The green paint on the vertical metal spikes of a fence set in a stone wall, a legacy from French colonial days, had long since blistered and grown dull.

Love climbed out of the car. As he had thought, the cemetery was not very large. He pulled hopefully at the gates; the chain clanked uninvitingly. This was a hazard he had not expected. What was there to steal in a cemetery, apart from bodies? And what value could they have? Were there no Christian relatives here who ever came to visit a grave? He began to understand Colonel Head's wish to have someone arrange for flowers.

He climbed up on the wall, hauled himself over the spikes, jumped down inside. The nearest newly-made grave had no name, not even a number. He walked along rows of strange, forgotten headstones, some sunk wearily on their sides, others quaintly carved like stone chests of drawers, filing cabinets of the dead.

The second new grave had a French inscription: 'Jean Pascard 1908–1968. Priez pour lui.' This was not for him. He remembered the words of the seventeenth-century author and physician, Sir Thomas Browne, about epitaphs: 'Gentile Inscriptions precisely delivered the extent of men's lives, seldom the manner of their deaths, which history itself so often leaves obscure.'

At the head of the third grave stood a raw wooden stake

with a strip of zinc tacked to it. Love bent down, read the letters that had been punched into the metal: 'Clarissa Eve Head, British subject. Grave No 73402.' A wreath marked, 'From the British Embassy', had withered in the sun. The flowers looked smaller in death than life. Like people, Love thought: like all of us.

He stood back, pushed his camera control over to automatic, photographed the grave from both sides, then from the top and bottom. He had expected something a little better than this small mound of dry earth. Photographs of this impersonal resting place for such a cheerful girl as Clarissa would carry no comfort for the Colonel.

He glanced at his watch; it was still only half past eleven. He climbed back over the wall.

'Where to now?' the driver asked him, as he sank back on the blue plastic seat.

Where to indeed? Why not the British Embassy to see this fifth secretary who had written to Colonel Head?

'Do you know the British Embassy?' he asked.

'Please?'

Oh, no, thought Love, not this again. He took out the letter from the Embassy in Maliki Road and showed the address to the driver. He mouthed the words once or twice, then let in his clutch.

The British Embassy looked like an apartment building; all fawn stucco with white edges, and green roll-down shutters to protect the windows in case of riots. Air coolers stood out like little hat boxes on the lower verandahs. Next door was a grocery shop, then a red, white, and black sentry box with a glass front, to protect the sentry from the wind and baking sun. A Union Jack hung limply from a mast like a barber's pole.

He walked through the door under the Royal Arms, waited beneath Annigoni's portrait of the Queen, and looked at announcements for such activities as Morris dancing and madrigal singing which the English quaintly think will interest foreigners. A pleasant-faced girl in a linen dress came out from an inner room.

'Can I help you?' she asked.

'I would like to see the fifth secretary, Mr Jackson.'

'And your name?'

'Dr Jason Love. I'm over here on a medical convention for this week.'

'Oh, yes. I'll see if he's free.'

Doors shut softly on vacuum stops. She returned with a young man in an alpaca jacket, thin and small, with a dark moustache which he stroked with the side of his left index finger.

'You wish to see me?' he said dubiously in a voice that provincial bank managers reserve for clients with small accounts who seek large overdrafts.

'If you are Mr Jackson, yes,' said Love, holding out his hand. 'One of my patients back in Somerset – Colonel Head – asked if I would see you about the death of his daughter.'

'His daughter? Ah, yes. Miss Head. A very sad business. Please come in.'

He opened a side door into a side room papered with trade charts and advertisements for Lancashire cotton and die-casting machinery from Sheffield. He sat down behind a small plain table. A coloured picture of the Queen and Prince Philip looked down on them. On the desk was a bad photograph of a girl with fuzzy hair and rimless spectacles; possibly his wife.

'Now, how can I help you?' Jackson asked, offering him a cigarette.

Love sat down in a cane chair that creaked under him. It was government issue, and not very well made.

'Anything about the accident.'

'Right. I've my Day Book here with all occurrences – people losing their passports, hikers getting stuck without any money – that sort of thing.'

He put on a pair of reading glasses, thumbed back over the closely written pages, neat and small, like himself.

'Ah, yes, here we are. At four o'clock on that afternoon I was duty dog. A telephone message came in from the People's Clinic that a female British subject had been killed in a car crash. She had been moved to the Clinic but was DOA – dead on arrival. Would I go down and collect her stuff? This was Miss Head, of course.'

'Of course,' said Love. 'Who else?'

'Well,' Jackson went on, rather relishing his role, 'I went

down in my car, said who I was, and was shown' - he consulted the book again – 'two suitcases, a duffle bag, a handbag, a briefcase, all with luggage tags marked Miss Clarissa E. Head.

'I opened the handbag and found her passport, travellers' cheques to the value of £98 and some Syrian pounds, and fifty Indian rupees, in a money clip. Total value, at the prevailing rates, approximately £114 15s od. Her car had been towed away.'

'Where to?'

'Let me see. Yes, here it is. The Atlas Service Garage, Hassan Boulevard.

'I examined her passport, No X.5371482, issued in London on the seventeenth of May two years ago. The hospital intern asked if I wished to see the doctor who signed the death certificate. Naturally, I said I did – this was Dr Suleiman. He is not known to me personally, but our own Embassy doctor was away in Aleppo – he still is – and our deputy had just had his appendix out that very morning.

'Dr Suleiman's very well qualified. I checked on him, of course. He is an Armenian. Took his MD at Heidelberg in 1935, and then practised in France. Came out here just before the war. Anyway, that day he'd been seeing some other patient in the Clinic, and he asked if I wanted to examine the body.

'Well, I didn't want to, really. My business is the living, not the dead, if you follow me. But I thought I ought to see it, at least.'

How sad that inevitably he and she both became it with death, thought Love.

'Where was it?'

'In the morgue. A small building, air-conditioned – you need that out here, you know. Well, I went in with Dr Suleiman. There was a sort of table with a sheet over it. He drew back the sheet and I could see Miss Head's face on the slab. I compared her with her passport photograph. They were obviously the same person.'

Love showed him the photograph Colonel Head had given him.

'That's the girl.'

'And then what did you do?' asked Love.

'I went out, loaded her bags in my car, came back here and made my report. The other car involved had disappeared – that's not unusual here, you know, if there aren't any witnesses.'

'Was Clarissa driving into Damascus or out of it?'

'On her way here. Dr Suleiman told me. I informed her father.'

'What about the burial? How was that arranged?'

'Suleiman said that in this weather it would be a good thing to have that done as soon as possible. I quite agreed, of course.'

'Was she buried that evening?'

'As soon as a grave could be dug. The Anglican padre here carried out the burial service. If we don't know what they are, we always say C of E. Would you like to see him?'

'No. I don't think that's necessary. But her father did ask me if you could arrange for flowers to be put on her grave at Christmas and on her birthday, and her grave looked after. Could that be done?'

'Certainly,' said Jackson brightly, glad to be able to say something positive. 'But not, of course, until we are in receipt of funds.'

'Would it cost a great deal?' asked Love.

'About £25 a year.'

Jackson shut the book, took off his glasses, wiped them carefully, slipped them back in their case, put the case back in his pocket.

'Thank you,' said Love, getting the message. 'I'm sure her father will be glad that you looked after everything in such a businesslike way.'

Jackson bowed. He thought he had done pretty well himself, actually.

Love walked out into the sunshine. The hills behind the city trembled in the heat as though noon might be too much for them to bear. How many conquests had they already seen in this ancient land, how many wars were left to come? The taxi driver stood picking his teeth with a sharpened goose quill, and watching two girls in Syrian army uniform, wondering just what they wore underneath.

'Where to now?' he asked.

A good question. Love glanced at his watch. He had still

more than an hour before lunch. He'd use it to see Dr Suleiman, and then he had surely done all that Colonel Head could expect him to do. He climbed into the car, pointed to Suleiman's address on the death certificate.

'Ah,' said the driver comprehendingly. 'El Koubry Street. I got good friend in the souk. Give you special price.'

Love shook his head. He had already accepted too many bargains at special prices from other people's good friends. They littered his study in Bishop's Combe, and were the cause of frequent edged remarks from his housekeeper, Mrs Hunter.

The driver accelerated away towards the city, past gardens where, according to their inclination and their hormones, some men knelt at prayer on mats and rugs facing Mecca, and others strolled hand-in-hand over the dusty trodden spears of grass.

The streets grew narrower and more crowded, with the buildings all stone, their small windows prudently slatted by shutters and screens, outside walls strung with wires and naked electric bulbs. The open fronts of shops were stacked with trays of sweetmeats, cheap suits, yellow plastic toys and tin kettles. The road shrank until the car could hardly pass between the walls and the jostling crowds. Stalls on either side leaned outwards, outbidding each other with plastic brassières, coat hangers, bales of cloth. Torn, peeling advertisements in unknown script, showing Syrian soldiers with bayonets bravely facing unseen enemies, hung from concrete electricity pylons.

The souk was a network of alleys, all roofed, like St Pancras Station, with glass and latticed girders resting on stone pillars; only these pillars had been there in the days of the Apostles, which was more than even the Victorian Society could claim for St Pancras.

A man filled a plastic amphora from a tap. Others, keffiehs around their mouths as though to stifle any cries, sat behind stalls of sickly sweetmeats, khaki woollen gloves, rolls of damask, tin pots, funnels, hurricane lamps.

The air crackled with the braying of donkeys, the harsh cries of sellers, the weary impatience of car horns. Men ran alongside Love's car, tapping frantically on the glass.

'I know you friend of mine. Special price. Only to look, not to buy.' The car stopped: Love climbed out into the crowd.

'Which way to El Koubry Street?' he asked the nearest shopkeeper, a man in a bright blue suit with a bristly moustache like a black toothbrush stuck on his upper lip.

'Before you go there, sir, just you see my special goldwork. All done here on the premises. Nothing done outside whatever.'

He pulled Love into an open doorway. Under glass counters, gold and silver bracelets glittered like tiny curled snakes. In the background, unseen hammers tapped as craftsmen beat out new designs in a hidden room. Against the far wall lay stone heads from Palmyra, rotted by centuries in the sun; then a .45 Colt, half rusted and minus a firing pin, its wooden stock eaten away by worms. Who had used it, and when and where? And, more important, had they hit their target?

Love turned away.

'Not today,' he said. 'I only want to see Dr Suleiman.'

'We were at high school together,' the man in blue replied instantly. 'He's a very good friend of mine.'

'Then please be a very good friend of mine, and lead me to him.'

'Perhaps you will buy something in my shop on your way back? Yes?'

Anything could happen, but some things were more possible than probable; this, Love thought, was one of those.

They walked through the back of the shop, past two men weaving a carpet on an upright loom, and out behind an ancient courtway with wooden doors, where water dripped like a damp metronome, and ageless men waited behind trays of grain for Allah to send them buyers. But what if Allah did not know his part of the deal?

The cries of the market faded. The alley was now too narrow for any car; houses opened small front doors directly on to paving stones. The sun was nearly overhead, and children skipped in and out of the thin wedge of light down the centre of the alley. A dog growled at them and then began to scratch for fleas. The man in the blue suit said, 'We are just now here.'

He paused outside a pair of wooden doors, pulled a brass bell handle. A servant appeared in a military jacket with brass buttons. What they sell in the King's Road today was used in Damascus yesterday; I was Lord Kitchener's valet.

'He will take you,' said the man in blue. 'Then perhaps you come back to my shop?'

'Perhaps.'

Love followed the servant across a courtyard where water trickled into a pool; a lemon tree bowed low with fruit. They crossed a verandah of blue tiles into a room where carpets hung from the walls. By the side of leather easy chairs, octagonal small tables, inlaid with mosaic and mother of pearl, waited for someone to place a glass on them. A bird with bright red plumage whistled to itself in a bamboo cage, stopped to look at Love, put its head on one side, and whistled at him.

'Please to be seated,' said the servant in English.

Love sat down in a chair overlooking the pond. The flat oily leaves of the giant water lilies trembled as fish swam beneath them. There was no other sign of life.

'You wish to see me?' asked a voice behind him.

Love turned.

'If you are Dr Suleiman, yes.'

'I am Dr Suleiman.'

He was dark and tall and fiftyish, wearing a dacron suit and white shoes. His skin was yellowish and oily. He could have been Syrian or Armenian, or just a sunburned used-car salesman from Warren Street after a package holiday on the Costa Brava.

'I'm a doctor,' explained Love and gave his name. 'Over here from England. I understand you signed the death certificate for the daughter of a patient of mine – Clarissa Head – who was killed in a car crash about two weeks ago?'

'Ah, yes,' said Suleiman, frowning as though the effort of memory caused him physical pain. 'A young, dark girl in one of those English sports cars? Yes?'

'That would describe her.'

He handed Suleiman the photograph; Clarissa smiled out at them, her head against the pony's neck.

'And you have come all the way from England just for this?'

'Not exactly. Primarily, I'm here for the medical convention at the New Omayad.'

'Of course, the convention. Would you like some coffee?'

Love wouldn't, but he knew enough about Arabian hospitality not to say so. Suleiman clapped his hands. The servant appeared, holding a beaten brass tray with two white cups and saucers, a silver coffee pot. He must have been waiting outside the door with it. Or maybe they kept coffee on the boil all the time in Arab households?

Suleiman poured, handed him a cup.

'No sugar, you see.'

'I see.'

'But possibly not the reason, Dr Love. That is really an Arabic compliment. It means we consider you sweet enough as a friend, so you do not need the artificial sweetness of sugar.'

Love bowed his thanks. Someone should have written a good line of dialogue here for him to say. He wished he could have done so himself. They sipped the gritty, bitter liquid seriously and in silence, as though they had no other way of getting rid of it.

'Now,' said Suleiman, putting down his empty cup, wiping his thin lips with a silk handkerchief. 'This girl. I cannot really tell you much. As you may know, she was dead when I saw her.'

'Who treated her?' asked Love, trying to keep distaste out of his face as he swallowed the sugarless grinds.

'The casualty officer, Dr Hanania. I am not acquainted with him personally. He's very young, you know.'

He smiled deprecatingly, as though one did not become acquainted personally with the very young.

'I saw his report on the cause of death. A sudden blow to the forehead causing injury to the brain, which proved fatal. Her injuries were consistent with that.'

'Anyone else injured?'

'I don't think so. Not that I heard, anyhow.'

'Is there anyone at the hospital who could help me?'

'In what way?'

Dr Suleiman's face registered pained surprise: had he not helped the Englishman enough?

'Any more details. Just for the girl's father.'

'I'm not on particularly friendly terms with the superintendent, otherwise I would be happy to introduce you to him. As a matter of fact, I am on rather bad terms with him. My wife was once his wife. You understand?'

'Perfectly,' said Love.

'You say you are at this convention? Then I may see something of you. I am addressing the convention this afternoon in the Archaeology Museum on trachoma, and how we have almost stamped it out.'

'I'll look forward to that,' said Love, and tried to mean it.

He stood up.

'If I went to the clinic myself,' he asked, 'could I see this fellow Hanania?'

'I don't see why not. And if I can help you in any other way . . .' Suleiman's voice trailed off vaguely. The bird in the cage began to whistle. It had heard too many interviews end in that room not to recognize the signs as quickly as Love.

Suleiman led Love across the courtyard to a wooden door, about four inches thick, strong as a railway sleeper, and studded with iron nails. When he opened it, the roar of the bazaar rushed in; the courtyard had been so cool, so quiet, that Love had forgotten the hubbub just beyond the door.

'We are quite peaceful here,' said Suleiman, guessing his thoughts. 'But only a few feet away there is all the stress of the market-place, the fierce struggle to survive.'

'You look as though you've won that struggle.'

'Only temporarily, Doctor. Nothing in this world is permanent. Only death. And then, may I say with Saladin, who fought against your Richard the Lionheart, "Oh, God, receive this soul, and open to him the doors of paradise, that last conquest for which he hoped." '

Suleiman held out his hand, cold as a bird's claw, and then closed the door. Oiled bolts flicked obediently into place. Love's taxi driver came up to him, grinning as though they had been separated for weeks, and his meter had been ticking all that time.

'Now, where will you go, sir?'

'The People's Clinic,' said Love. He still had half an hour before he should be back at the hotel. This would be positively his last call.

They sped past shops selling carved wooden camels for suburban dining rooms, past old air-raid shelters and new showrooms for Czechoslovakian machinery, out towards the desert. Men chopped huge chunks of rocks beside the edge of the road; a sheep walked in a polished leather collar behind a shepherd.

The driver stopped outside a concrete block of a building, impersonal as a barracks, and ringed with a barbed-wire fence.

'The Clinic, sir,' he announced.

A few soldiers lounged about in dusty khaki uniforms and scuffed shoes, smoking hand-rolled cigarettes. The Syrian flag drooped dispiritedly from a pole; a poster with Nasser's portrait peeled from a tree trunk. Above the flat porch over the front door was a sign in Arabic and English: 'People's Clinic'.

Love walked through the front door into an entrance hall, cool with brown and white tiles. At the back stood a larger-than-life statue of a Syrian soldier, grenade in one hand, rifle in the other, braver in bronze than reality, a strange welcome to a hospital. A porter approached Love.

'Dr Hanania?' asked Love, hopefully.

The porter shrugged his shoulders; he spoke no English. Also, he did not like the English. He didn't trust them any more than the Americans; they were all in league with the Israelis. He walked out of the door and spat into the dust to show what he thought of them. Then he spat again in case Love had missed the message.

Love waited for a few moments, hoping the man would return with someone who could speak English, but he just stood there, looking at nothing. Love took a few paces down the corridor. Nameplates, some in script, others in French and English, were screwed on each door. If he walked far enough, perhaps he would see Dr Hanania's name, or an inquiry office, or even just someone who spoke English?

On the ground floor he found nothing and no one. He walked up the stairs and along the corridor looking at the names on some doors, the numbers on others. The corridor ended in a small round landing with a window overlooking the courtyard; through it he saw the porter talking to his driver. The man spat for a third time; maybe he didn't like drivers either.

Two white doors opened side by side from this landing. Outside them stood a Syrian soldier with fixed bayonet, the

43

blade as dirty as his boots. Perhaps Hanania was behind this door? Or maybe the superintendent warranted a guard? This seemed more feasible. He would knock on the door and see what happened.

'Dr Hanania?' he asked hopefully. 'The superintendent?'

The sentry shrugged his shoulders, and glanced to left and right, hoping someone else would appear.

'Do you speak French?'

The soldier took a tighter grip on his rifle.

Love nodded towards the door, and made a step forward. The soldier sprang to attention. It was better to be on the safe side; there were so many foreigners in the city: Russians, Czechs, Poles, and Love was clearly a foreigner and must be on some official business, otherwise how could he have come upstairs without being challenged?

Love knocked on the door and waited. No one answered. He knocked again, louder this time. Then he turned the handle, opened the door a few inches to see whether anyone was inside.

The room was small, white and impersonal; a green shade over the far window filtered the sunshine. The result was vaguely aquatic, like a scene beneath the sea.

In the centre of the brown vinyl floor was a white hospital bed, raised high on its rubber castors. Beyond this bed, on a white table, stood a flask of water with a strip of white muslin, edged by glass beads, over the top.

As Love stood, with the door open a few inches, a sudden draught made the curtain flap at the window. The person in the bed turned around slowly and looked at him. Love stared back in disbelief and amazement.

He was looking at Clarissa Head, whose death certificate he carried in his pocket, whose grave in the cemetery he had just photographed.

Chapter Two

Damascus, Syria, June 28th

Love took a step inside the door and reached out with professional reaction to feel Clarissa's pulse. It beat slowly but steadily; she was probably under sedation.

'Clarissa,' he said softly. 'Clarissa. Do you recognize me? Dr Love. From Bishop's Combe, in Somerset. Remember?'

Clarissa shook her head under its white bandage. Her face was bruised and cut.

'No,' she said dully. 'I have never been there.'

She watched him without recognition or comprehension. Yet she was the same girl he had known since childhood, whose career as a nurse he had followed through her parents' letters.

By what incredible mistake, by what unbelievable bureaucratic idiocy, could she have been described as dead? After all, Jackson was certain she was dead; he had seen the body. So had Dr Suleiman, who had actually signed the certificate for her death.

'Clarissa.'

He spoke more sharply now. She had the symptoms of concussion.

'Who are you?' she asked drowsily. 'Go away. I want to sleep.'

Her voice sounded huskier than he remembered it. 'What do you want? Why are you here?'

'Your father,' Love replied. 'He is worried about you.'

'My father?' she repeated mystified. 'Why should he be worried?'

'He thought you were dead.'

'Dead?'

Her face puckered.

'How could he think that? I've had a car crash, that's all. Nothing serious. But I feel giddy when I stand up. I'll be all

45

right in a day or two. Maybe even in a few hours. I know. The doctor told me.'

'What doctor? Suleiman? Hanania?'

She shrugged.

'I don't know his name. Why all the questions?'

Love's grip tightened on her wrist.

'You must remember me,' he said slowly, enunciating each word as though he were speaking to a foreigner; and, in a sense, he was. 'Think. Dr Love. Bishop's Combe. Somerset.'

Clarissa shook her head wearily.

'What do you want here?'

They were back where they had begun; indeed, they had never left home base. He must find the superintendent of the hospital, or Dr Hanania. There was bound to be some simple explanation, and when Clarissa was well enough – and when he discovered what was wrong with her – she could be flown home. He had nothing to gain by trying to make her talk now, before he knew more about her case.

He turned back towards the door, and as he did so two hands behind him seized his arms just above the elbows.

He flexed his muscles; the fingers tightened their grip. If he moved quickly he would break his arms; Love didn't move quickly. He looked over his shoulder instead. A man in white rubber surgical boots and a white coat was holding him. A gauze operating mask hung on its tape beneath his chin; he had pushed his white, chef-like surgeon's hat to the back of his head.

'What are you doing here?' the man demanded roughly in English. He turned to the sentry who was peering round the door post.

The sentry mumbled something.

'I'm a doctor,' explained Love. 'Dr Love. This girl is the daughter of one of my patients in England. I am trying to find out what's wrong with her.'

'She's very seriously ill,' said the man. 'That's what's wrong with her. And in England do you usually go butting into wards, interfering with other doctors' cases – even if their parents may be your patients?'

'I was trying to find Dr Hanania, but no one seemed to know anything about him. So I came up the stairs to see if he was here.'

'He isn't. He has gone to Beirut. What do you want to see him about?'

'I understand he treated this girl. Dr Suleiman gave me his name.'

The grip on Love's arms relaxed slightly.

'Ah, yes, Dr Suleiman. But we cannot have strangers coming into wards unannounced like this. Where are you staying, Doctor, in case the superintendent wishes to contact you?'

'The New Omayad.'

They moved out of the room, along the corridor, down the stairs. Once, as a boy, Love had been marched out of his local cinema by the manager because someone in the audience claimed he had aimed a pea-shooter at him. The same incongruous absurdity he had felt then, being propelled down the shabby red staircase between the glossy stares of Myrna Loy and Deanna Durbin and W. C. Fields from framed photos on the walls, he felt again. This was ridiculous. Worse, it was happening.

'You have a car here?'

Love nodded. He still felt too bewildered to think clearly, let alone speak his thoughts. He took a pace out into the bright sunshine; the grip on his arms relaxed. As his taxi drew up, he glanced back at the other man. He was still standing in the doorway, watching him. He watched Love's taxi out of sight, then went upstairs silently on the rubber-soled boots, and along the corridor, into Clarissa's room. She lay quiet, head turned away, as though asleep.

The man stood in silence, looking down at her, wondering about her, then he went into the room next door. It was the same size, but a telephone stood on the bedside table. He shut the door carefully behind him, turned the key, tried the handle to make sure that the lock was holding. You could never be certain with anything made in Egypt.

He picked up the telephone, dialled a number, waited for it to ring four times, replaced the receiver, picked it up again, dialled the number a second time. There was a click as the receiver at the other end was picked up, and then breathing in his ear.

'I am at the Clinic,' he said quickly. 'There's been a visitor. An Englishman. I found him with the girl.'

47

'How did he get in with a sentry on duty? And where were you?' asked the man at the other end of the line.

'The sentry says he thought he was an official. He claims to be a doctor. A Dr Love. I was only away a minute.'

'Your orders are to be in that room all the time, except when you are reporting,' said the man sharply. 'Who is this English doctor?'

'He says he was her parents' doctor in England. He's over here for the medical convention. At the Omayad.'

'Now go back into the room. And don't come out on any pretext until you are relieved. Understand?'

'I understand.'

He replaced the receiver, stood looking at it for a moment, running one finger around its dial as though he wished he had someone else to call. The sentry saluted him as he went out and into Clarissa's room.

Five miles to the west, where the three minarets of the great Omayad mosque pointed sharp stone fingers to the sky, a visible reminder of the trinity of god, the man he had telephoned was also looking at the instrument as though it could somehow provide an answer to a problem. Across the alleyway, in an upper room of the Madinet-el-Arus, the Minaret of the Bride, a needle dipped, a grooved disc began to turn. From linked loudspeakers in the three minarets the braying call to prayer went out.

Across the city, the faithful kicked off their shoes, and knelt on mats, placing first their hands, palms down, on the dusty ground, then their faces, cheeks against the warmth of the paving slabs, remembering Allah, the one true God, and Muhammed, his one true prophet, the man closest to god.

To the man in the upper room above the silversmith's shop, behind the souk, this call was simply another interruption. He had forced himself to think against the constant background of noise from the bazaar, and the incessant chipping of masons' hammers as they relaid the vast courtyard of the mosque, the endless annoyance of dust and grit blown in by the warm wind, but these electronic calls to prayer irritated and confused him. And yet he should be used to them, because he had once been a Muslim.

That's the reason, he thought. I've been too many people once, but never for long enough, so that I've become a sort of human chameleon, willing to merge into almost any background, but never entirely successfully. That's why I am who I am and where I am; I'm like an actor who never knows the whole script, only one tiny scene in a play without beginning or end, often without meaning.

And when this play ends, will there be another? He was growing too old for insecurity; it nagged him like an aching tooth, and yet, with his abilities, surely he could do better for himself somehow, somewhere. But, where and how?

He shut the window, pulled the curtains across it irritably in an attempt to dim the noise. He was a square, compact man with broad shoulders, wearing a black silk shirt, a black pullover and a pair of dacron trousers. Every so often he would clench his teeth and draw his lips back so that the muscles and arteries on his neck stood out like smooth ropes. It was a habit that acted as a warning signal to others. When they saw this they knew he was worried or angry or both. Now, he was only worried.

He paced up and down the room, his feet making no noise on the thick carpet. The eyes of the other two men in the room followed him as though he were in a cage. He knew they would guess who had telephoned him, but that was no concern of theirs. He bent back his mind to his present problems.

'You know the time well enough,' he said, trying to channel his thoughts into their proper course. 'If we'd been going according to schedule, we'd all be out by now. Are you *sure* you know what you're about?'

The older of the two men nodded. He had a big round head, too large for his body, and large goitrous eyes like huge pale marbles.

'It wasn't our fault this happened,' he said defensively. 'It was an accident.'

'I'm not saying it's anyone's fault,' retorted Khalif, 'but we're going to be blamed if we don't keep the second rendezvous, which is in exactly twenty-four hours from six this evening.'

The prayer call ended, and he looked out over the crammed street. Men beneath him were rolling up prayer mats. He wished, not for the first time, that he had something he could believe in; if not a religion, then something else that could fill a void in his soul; something to bring a deeper dimension into his life.

The older he grew, the more he longed for stability. He thought suddenly, for no real reason at all, of his boyhood in Cyprus in Kyrenia; the smell of the thyme and salt; gourds drying in the sun; wine, dark as evening. He had been happy there; but would he be happy if he went back now? He turned from the window.

'All right,' he said. 'I needn't tell you what this will mean if there's any other hold-up.'

He peered at them in the hot room as though he were trying to memorize their faces, trying to will them into an acceptance of the risks involved, the price of failure.

'There won't be,' the man with the puffed-out eyes assured him.

His chair made no sound on the thick Persian carpet as he pushed it back. They walked down the side stairs. The first man went out directly into the souk; the second, through a maze of alleyways to come out near the Bab Al-Faradisse, the Gate of Mercury, about five hundred yards away.

Khalif stayed where he was, thinking. He picked up a spent match from the ashtray, split it, began to pick his teeth with the shaped end. He had a broken molar in his lower jaw, and yet he would rather endure its sharp stabs of pain than visit the dentist; he hated the sight of blood and the appurtenances of surgery. Which was odd, when one considered his job.

This Dr Love person. It seemed an innocent enough mistake on the part of some visiting doctor, who probably couldn't speak the language. But when you were playing for stakes as high as his, you could not afford the slightest risk of failure. He would have a sentry posted on the door who could speak English and French. No, he would never find such a soldier; it was useless having some idiot peasant conditioned by years of colonial rule, first Turkish, then French, so that he sprang to attention at the approach of any European. He would withdraw the sentry altogether and put extra guards into the grounds around the Clinic. No one would question this, but if they did he could always claim he wanted to make spot checks to stop pilfering or some such plausible reason.

The hammers of the workmen came up faintly through the glass. He stood watching them, the match still at his mouth, unconsciously admiring their economical mechanical movements. Their work looked so easy, but it was so exhausting that you were old, burned-out and arthritic by forty-five. Yet what about him? If he failed, he would never reach that age. Even so, he was glad he no longer needed to work with his hands. That was the whole object of having a brain, he thought.

Khalif picked up the telephone and dialled a number. If he had a brain, he might as well use it; that's what his old father used to say. He could find no flaw in the advice.

Chapter Three

Covent Garden, London, June 28th

Sir Robert L— the head of MI6, the overseas section of the British Intelligence Service, stood behind the green leather-topped desk in his office overlooking Whitehall, his back to the white Adam fireplace, and swung his monocle from the end of its silk cord, allowing himself the luxury of exercising his natural irritability.

Colonel Douglas MacGillivray, his deputy, a dour, red-haired Scot, who had seen this performance too many times for it to impress him, even if it had ever done so, sat back in the saddleback chair Sir Robert had bought when the old Conservative Club had been demolished years before, and puffed at his cheroot. From time to time he dusted a speck of ash from a trouser leg.

Both, in their own way, tried to give entirely different impressions to the outside world. And both, in their own way, succeeded. Sir Robert, white-haired, consciously resembling the original Man of Distinction in the American advertisements, with a careful puff of silk handkerchief at his sleeve, farmed a small estate in Wiltshire, where his

51

neighbours thought he had a part-time job in London with a Service charity.

Sometimes one or two of them, in London with an hour to spare, would call unannounced at the Charity's address in Victoria Street, but always he was out. They would joke about this when they met over drinks on the following Sunday morning at one or other of their houses, but always Sir Robert had some vague excuse – and the promise that next time he'd be delighted to see them.

Like all members of the Service he controlled, he was known by a letter or a number. In his case, it was 'C', because during the first world war the man in charge of the British Secret Service had been Captain – later Sir – Mansfield Cumming. In those days, in an attempt to preserve his anonymity, he had signed his reports with the initial 'C' only and the habit had become a custom.

Sir Mansfield, a more colourful character than Sir Robert, had shared Sir Robert's enthusiasm for fast cars – he drove a Napier, while Sir Robert had one of the last S.3 Bentley Continentals. Once, after a motor accident on a lonely road, Cumming had been pinned beneath his car, and it was said he had been forced to cut off his own leg with a penknife to drag himself free.

Years later, interviewing strangers in his office, Cumming derived a certain dry amusement by casually picking up a paper knife from his desk and then suddenly driving it with all his force into his false leg. Sir Robert envied him this ploy, but not the loss of his leg.

MacGillivray, for his part, sought escape from the hard and often bitter reality of his job by living a dream life through the illustrated pages of auctioneers' catalogues and *Country Life* advertisements. As the knights of King Arthur's Court had sought the Holy Grail, so, with equal assiduity, he sought the perfect country house, far from crowds, ringed in by rolling hills purpled with Scottish heather, with rivers where salmon always leapt obediently and log fires burned without soot in the hall.

Instead, still with the rank of colonel to which he had risen in the Gunners, he lived in an old-fashioned flat off the Brompton Road, nursed a £1,800 overdraft (the ceiling the bank manager would allow him was £2,000) and endeavoured to keep one step or sometimes only half a pace ahead of present potential enemies of the Government of Her Britannic Majesty Queen Elizabeth.

His wife imagined that he was a director of Sensoby and Ransom, a fruit importing agency in Covent Garden. She could never quite understand the odd hours he had to keep, but then she knew no other fruit importers, and he reassured her with explanations that he had to take telephone calls from all sorts of countries with big time differences, that although the hour might be late in London it was early in Florida which shipped so many oranges to his firm.

Fortunately, she was an unsuspicious woman, otherwise she might have queried this explanation, or the reasons he gave for switching from running a travel agency, to managing a timber import-export business, to being managing director of the fruit business. All were of course convenient covers for his real career. They provided a believable background against which people could come and go at all hours without any comment, although the neighbouring offices would have been highly surprised at the identities and assignments of these ordinary-looking business men.

Years of experience in human nature, of knowing facts that outran the most outrageous fiction, of calculating the price of treachery in lust, in money or occasionally in titles or public honour, had left MacGillivray with profound reservations about the human animal.

He believed, however, that the mind of everyone who reached first rank in their career had what he called 'a special little wheel'. This special mental wheel might be geared to making a million over a property venture, to perfecting a scientific process, or to turning a hostile political meeting into a gathering of admirers. In his own case, he prided himself on having such a wheel, geared to world events, to coincidences that should never coincide, to apparently chance happenings that owed nothing whatever to chance.

It was about one of these that he now argued with Sir Robert – and whatever special wheel Sir Robert might have in his mind, it certainly was not geared to this.

'I still can't see the connection,' he said stubbornly, for the third time.

MacGillivray's fingers did the drum work for the first verse of 'God Save the Queen' on Sir Robert's desk before he replied.

'I agree it's a long shot, sir,' he said patiently, 'but our whole business is full of long shots.'

'Don't start telling me what our business is full of,' retorted Sir Robert testily. 'It's full of rockets for me for not finding that apparently half our men are really spying against us. It's full of soft and unsatisfactory reasons for not kicking diplomats out of the country who are no more diplomats than my backside. It's full of frustration everywhere, and on every level.

'Now, to recap. From what you tell me, a BOAC VC10, flying from Bombay to London, comes down at Cairo to refuel. The passengers have an hour at the airport, and when the plane takes off, this British neurologist, Dr Ronald, can't be found. Right?'

'Right.'

'This is odd as Ronald is supremely successful, on the staff of two London teaching hospitals. He's got a flat in Wimpole Street, a house in Sussex, a pleasant wife, two grown-up sons, no money problems. Even so, he's just gone over the hill.

'All right, that's event one. Now you also tell me that some Albanian surgeon Krasna – another brain expert – has disappeared with his son, who's his anaesthetist. The only possible link between these two events is that they both disappeared in Cairo. So far, so bad. What's known about this Albanian?'

'Very little, and nothing political. Apparently, the head of their Secret Police, General Ackermann, was ordered to investigate Krasna's disappearance himself. After all, Krasna's operated on members of the President's family. He's one of their very best surgeons – even allowed his own flat and car.

'Anyway, Ackermann took off for Cairo and apparently just missed them. The only other country Krasna and son could have gone to without a passport was Syria. I understand Ackermann flew up to Damascus, but had no luck there, either. So back he went to Albania, very down in the mouth.'

'Ah,' said Sir Robert thoughtfully. It was not unpleasant

to hear that his rivals in other countries also had their difficulties.

'Was this fellow – what's his name – Krasna – working on the same thing as Ronald?'

'Not exactly. But it was also connected with the brain.'

'What?'

'Aspects of memory.'

'Oh, my God,' said Sir Robert, 'This is ridiculous. What the hell has that to do with us?'

'I've got two people in the waiting room who can tell you more about their work than I can, and how it concerns us, sir,' interrupted MacGillivray. 'One is Professor Cartwright of the Neurological Research Institute at Cambridge. The other is Sir John Dean, the brain surgeon.'

'I used to know Dean slightly,' said Sir Robert. 'Pleasant fellow. Had a boat near mine on the Hamble.'

'He's worked with Ronald.'

Sir Robert nodded, pressed the intercom button on his desk, asked his orderly to send up two men who were waiting downstairs to see him, and then glanced surreptitiously at his watch. It was Friday, and he was anxious to be away to Wiltshire. If he could finish with them in ten minutes, he might still beat most of the traffic.

Cartwright was thin and cadaverous, his skin pale, as though he lived on leaves and roots and rarely saw the sun. His bald head had a monkish fringe of hair around it, like a grey, fuzzy halo. He wore an old-fashioned, double-breasted suit with a silver chain through his buttonhole to an American silver watch in his breast pocket. A fine layer of dandruff dusted his stooping shoulders. Sir Robert, who disliked slovenliness, concealed his feelings behind a mechanical smile.

Sir John Dean was much more to his liking; he approved of his dark-blue mohair suit, his elastic-sided, highly polished shoes, the flash of hand-made Harvie and Hudson shirt cuff at his wrist. Also, he owned a polychromatic blue Bentley Continental, the same model as Sir Robert's which was parked outside, in Little Scotland Place.

Sir Robert and Sir John chatted briefly about the relative merits of steam turbines and diesel engines, and the predatory, iniquitous way in which harbourmasters of Riviera

55

ports seemed to imagine that simply because you owned an ocean-going yacht, you could also afford to pay their inflated harbour dues.

'Right, gentlemen,' said Sir Robert at last, 'I understand you can help me with some details of the work of Dr Ronald and the Albanian surgeon, who have both apparently chosen to disappear in Cairo?'

Cartwright glanced at his colleague and then nodded.

'Sir John here knows Dr Ronald, so I'll deal with the Albanian. In brief, he is way ahead of us in the extent and scope of his experiments into the nature of memory, and the possibility of controlled telepathic communication.

'I don't want to get technical, Sir Robert, but almost every layman has had some experience – or heard of someone who has had some experience – involving ESP – extra-sensory perception.

'Two different people in different towns may think of the same thing at the same time. You are just going to make some remark at a dinner party when someone else says exactly the words you were going to use, and so on. There are even mediums, usually highly strung, sensitive people, who can pick up other people's thoughts. But Krasna has gone very much further than this sort of Christmas party trick.

'He is able – I assume he is still alive, so I use the present tense – to conduct an operation that can turn anyone into what is virtually a human transmitting station – and, given help – without their knowledge.

'Say this were to be done for purposes of espionage, Sir Robert. Some minor official in a foreign embassy in London that you wished to know more about, would be involved in an arranged accident, or given a delayed action injection jab in a packed train or bus.

'He could then be removed, ostensibly by an ordinary ambulance, to a safe room in some hospital. Here, with Krasna's technique, a minute transistor, attached to an electrode as fine as a hair, would be inserted into the base of his brain. It would be tuned to the thoughts of his colleagues in the Embassy.

'The patient would then be released from hospital and return to work, without any knowledge whatever of what had *really* happened to him.

'After a few days, he could be re-admitted to hospital again, for observation, or some such excuse, and kept there for, say, twenty-four hours.

'The electrode would be connected to an electronic device linked to a memory bank computer. All the thoughts of the people to whom he had been tuned would be transferred to tape. The electrode and transistor could then be removed, and he would leave the hospital, again knowing nothing whatever of the part he had played, never imagining how he had been used.'

Cartwright paused. The room overflowed with silence.

'How do you know this, Professor?' asked Sir Robert, all thought gone of missing the traffic. 'After all, this doctor is working behind the Curtain.'

'We've done some work on this problem ourselves. Starting with epileptic patients, using electrical stimulation of the brain, ESB, we have embedded a fine metallic electrode, a millionth of an inch across, in the brain and linked up electrically to stimulate the cells.

'We have then had patients recall conversations, meetings, experiences, word by word – that took place twenty or thirty years ago.

'We have actually been able to tune into people's memories, things they've forgotten about and would sincerely deny had ever happened.

'We can even tap a particular year, going through the layers of memory, peeling them like an onion skin, or as you can tell the age of a tree by the rings on its trunk. But Krasna's way ahead of all this.

'He first became interested in brain surgery during the war. We heard about him at one of those overseas medical conventions that provide us with an excuse for a working holiday at some place we couldn't otherwise afford. Two of my colleagues went to a convention in Beirut last year. Krasna wasn't there, but two representatives from his hospital were. They let drop enough for our people to know how far ahead of us he was.'

Sir Robert stood up, and looked out at the street. A tired wind from the grey wastes of suburbia drove specks of rain against the outer windows. He felt tired himself. It would be good to be back in his farm in Wiltshire, away if only for a weekend from the ever-increasing complications of his job. Soon it would be unsafe even to think against a government's policy, let alone to speak against it.

This discovery would inevitably change the whole technique of his work, for usually the most difficult part of the agent's job was not to discover some fact which another country wanted to keep secret, but to transmit the news without being discovered himself.

Soon there would be no more need to use speeded-up radio signals, or microdots; no need to transmit messages along an infra-red ray or a laser beam. You would only need a man – who wouldn't even know he was working for you – and who could be expendable and also unpaid. Well, the Treasury would like that part of it.

'Do you think someone – maybe the Russians – wanted Krasna for this?' he asked.

Cartwright shrugged.

'I don't think anything,' he said. 'But it's obvious that this secret is one of the ultimates of research – and it has so many applications. We're working towards the same end here, and I've no doubt that, within a year or two, either the Americans or ourselves will come through with something like an answer.

'But this character in Albania has that answer *now*. You get him and you also gain a lead that's so valuable it is simply impossible to put a price on it. Not only in espionage, but commercially. What would one giant combine pay to learn their rivals' secrets? See what I mean?'

They all saw. In the silence, they could hear the muted traffic murmur through the double glass of the windows. MacGillivray glanced up from examining the pattern of the carpet and Sir John looked at his Rolex. He didn't like hearing other people talk so much; he preferred the sound of his own voice to anyone else's. Also, he had an appointment with a patient in Charles Street in seven minutes, a property tycoon so rich and so careful that he kept his Canalettos bolted to the wall.

'I must leave soon,' he said. 'So could I interrupt with what I know about Ronald's work?'

'Please,' said Sir Robert.

'He has been conducting some very advanced experiments

involving the transmission of behaviour patterns – the memory of a secret code in your business, Bob – or plans or processes in the commercial world – from one person to another.

'This has been studied for the last four or five years, largely in the States, starting with experiments on planaria, which are primitive worms that live in mud.

'The break-through experiment involved putting some of these worms in a Y-shaped tube, and then passing an electric shock intermittently across one arm of the tube. After a time, the worms learned to avoid this arm and concentrated on the other, safe arm.

'They were then chopped up like liver and fed to other planaria, who hadn't had the benefit of a Y-type education, and so knew nothing about the electric arm.

'After this cannibal meal, however, the uneducated worms immediately got the message and avoided the electrocuted arm of the tube. A case of digesting a skill, if you like.'

He smiled at the others; hoping they would approve of his pun. They didn't return his smile; he went on rather more quickly.

'In the experiments with higher creatures, they have injected fish with the antibiotic puromycin, and human beings with RNA, which is ribonucleic acid. I—'

'What does this mean in terms of everyday experience?' interrupted MacGillivray. He did not wish to be led along some endless scientific labyrinth unless the journey had a positive application to his own problems.

'It can mean so many things,' replied Sir John. 'But from your point of view, it means transferring entire behaviour patterns from one person to another, simply by injecting RNA acid, plus some other substance that Ronald evolved. You could make a pacifist war-like, a coward, a hero – and vice versa.'

'Would you have to inject them individually?'

'Not necessarily. The acid can be taken by mouth, and the permutations of behaviour are limitless, as you can imagine.'

'I rather wish I didn't,' said Sir Robert with feeling.

'Well, is there anything else, gentlemen?' asked Sir John, standing up, hoping there wasn't.

'Not now, gentlemen,' Sir Robert replied. 'But we have your private numbers in case we do need your advice urgently. The Colonel and I are most grateful for your kindness in coming along at short notice. A most illuminating talk. Most illuminating.'

When they were on their own, Sir Robert turned to Mac-Gillivray.

'Who have we got out there?' he asked.

'In Cairo? No one we can spare. We borrowed a man from the DNI in Beirut. We've used him quite a bit before – Richard Mass Parkington.'

'Where is he now?'

'He shuttles between Beirut and Damascus. We can easily put him into Cairo from either of those places.'

'What's his cover?'

'A salesman in fabrics and canvas generally. Also selling greetings cards. Trying to get the Muslims to show an interest in Father's Day or cards for the prophet's birthday.'

Sir Robert grunted. He was unimpressed.

'An uphill task, no doubt,' he said dryly. 'No one else?'

'No. Apart from a crowd of general practitioners who are holding one of those conventions Cartwright mentioned. They're in Damascus for a few days, and then swanning off to Jordan with their wives.'

'Anything else known about this man Ronald you haven't told me?' asked Sir Robert, piercing the end of his cigar.

'Yes,' said MacGillivray gravely. 'One thing. His wife says he's a very ill man. If he doesn't get cortisone regularly, he'll die.'

Chapter Four

Damascus, Syria, June 28th

'Where to now?' the taxi driver asked Love brightly. This was one of those rare, hitherto only dreamed-of days, when it seemed he would make as much waiting as in driving. And look at the petrol and effort he was saving! Also, this fare obviously knew nothing about Damascus, and had no idea he was being taken the longest way to each destination. Yes, Allah was very good; just like the mullahs always said.

'The hotel,' said Love, and leaned back wearily against the cushions, his mind spinning as quickly as the car wheels. He would have lunch, then return to the Embassy and tell Jackson that there had been the most fantastic mistake. The Embassy people could sort out the mess. They would probably cable Colonel Head with the good news; or if they didn't or wouldn't, then he'd telephone him direct.

Love lit a Gitane. They were going along the Aleppo Road, past the new post office, where the pavements were so wide that cars parked on them; past trees wearing metal guards. In the distance, scrubby poplars rimmed the empty brownish-grey of the desert. He leaned forward to the driver; might as well see what Clarissa's car looked like.

'I've changed my mind,' he announced. 'Take me to the Atlas Service Garage, Hassan Boulevard. You know it?'

The driver nodded.

'Five minutes' journey,' he said as he turned the car. 'But the other way.'

The garage was like a hundred others in the Middle East: a concrete forecourt with three coloured pumps, their glass globes already lit, under a striped metal awning, and, at the back, a whitewashed building. Through its wide doors, Love could see a Chevrolet up on a ramp. The taxi stopped.

'Wait here,' Love told the driver, and climbed out.

A Citroën DS was being filled with petrol. The concrete was blotched with patches where other cars had bled black oil. Up against the side of the building stood an old Mack army truck, painted bright yellow, with a crane and lifting gear on a platform. Near this, two barefoot children played with a Mini wheel, twirling it like a top.

A man was trying to tighten a shock absorber on the Chevrolet, with a spanner too large for the nut. It kept slipping and he kept cursing. Another man, younger, in oily overalls, an unlit half-cigarette in his mouth, was cleaning his hands with Swarfega. He ran them under a cold tap into a cracked basin; the grease melted away. He looked at Love

61

questioningly, dried his hands on a paper towel.

'Do you speak English?' Love asked.

'Of course,' the man said instantly. 'What's your trouble?'

'No trouble,' said Love. 'Back in England I run what I think is the last supercharged Cord roadster over there, and I collect car radiator nameplates. I simply wondered whether you might have any nameplates or badges from cars that have been crashed and written off?'

The man nodded slowly, a mild gleam of interest in his eyes.

'An enthusiast, eh? I'll see what I can do. There aren't many exciting cars left now, of course. But when I was a boy, and the French were here, it was a different story. Isotta, Bugatti, Delage. We had them all. I've one or two badges left from those days. Come into the office.'

He led Love into a small room, not much larger than a telephone booth. On the walls hung calendars from tyre manufacturers showing well-stacked girls in unlikely poses, a list of telephone numbers to be rung in various emergencies, odd piston rings, a pair of wind-tone horns, a green and black Corps Diplomatique number plate. Beneath a desk lurked an old-fashioned Chubb safe. He opened it, pulled out a Lindt chocolate box, lifted off the lid. Inside, on oily cotton wool, rested half a dozen radiator badges.

'This is all I've got,' the mechanic said, almost apologetically. 'You may already have them in England, or not?'

'Not,' said Love.

He picked up the nearest; a circle with red and yellow stripes, the colours of Spain, and beneath this the white cross of Switzerland and two gold wings. The badge of the Hispano-Suiza. Of course, the literal translation simply meant Spanish Swiss, and the name had been chosen because the designer, Marc Birkigt, was Swiss, and his backers, Spanish. But the result of this collaboration had been one of the greatest cars of the vintage era. Each wore a magnificent silver-plated stork emblem on the radiator above the badge, in memory of a French first world war pilot, Captain Georges Guynemer, who used the stork of Lorraine as his personal insignia when he flew SPAD fighters with Hispano engines.

Such was the Hispano-Suiza's legendary reliability that, in the thirties, to demonstrate the quality of workmanship, one was driven flat out from Paris to Nice, then back to Paris again, and left in the showroom with a sheet of white paper under it to prove that no oil leaked from a Hispano engine. And not a drop did.

On what magnificent barouche had these golden wings once flown? What sort of people had driven behind them? And where were they all now?

As if answering his thoughts, the mechanic said, 'A French count here, when my father ran the garage, owned that car. He was killed in it. In those days, they hadn't the value they have now. It was broken up. I took the badge as a souvenir. Pretty, isn't it?'

Love nodded, picked up the next badge, another pair of wings – how odd that so many car manufacturers had chosen wings to emphasize the speed and grace of their cars – Bentley, SS, Austin, Kissel and a dozen more. These were the blue and red wings of the Invicta, a car that reminded Love of his Cord, with its outside exhausts and the fact that it had not been built down to a commercial price, but up to an idealist's dream.

It had begun life in the garage of Sir Noel Macklin's country house in Surrey, in the nineteen-twenties, and came to maturity in the year of the slump, when too few people had a thousand guineas to pay out simply for a bare chassis.

What young blade had sat behind the square bonnet with its long lines of rivets that this badge had graced? What girl had been kissed for the first time behind this badge? And where was she now?

This sort of endless reminiscence, this going back into time and imagination, was one of the pleasures of collecting anything, Love thought, as he held the two badges in his right hand, turned over the others. There was nothing much he hadn't already seen and rejected in England: Hillman, Ford, Morris, and other work-horse cars, worthy, but not rare. The mechanic watched him.

'You will take any?' he asked.

'These two,' said Love. 'How much?'

'Ten Syrian pounds.'

About a quid. Love pulled a note from his pocket before the man could change his mind.

'I'm sorry to see them go. I've had them for so long. But there it is.'

The mechanic pulled out an envelope from another drawer, handed it to Love. Love dropped the badges inside, put it in his pocket.

'Anything else that's rare?' he asked.

The man shook his head.

'Nothing.'

'Do you get many wrecks here?'

'A few. We've got one little English car at the back now. It was in a crash a couple of weeks ago. Your British Embassy is waiting for some news about insurance, I think.'

'What sort of car?' asked Love, as though he didn't know.

'Come and see for yourself.'

The man led the way through the garage into a space of waste land behind, where empty shells of cars lay like metal husks, their paint dulled by sun, splashed white with bird lime. Under a tarpaulin he could see the frog-eye headlights of a Sprite. The mechanic pulled off the cover.

'Girl got killed in it, apparently. Probably a head-on collision.'

The left-hand headlamp and the radiator grille had been pushed back, the bonnet buckled up to the windscreen which, oddly, had not cracked. Love glanced in the cockpit. A few splashes of blood darkened the white leather of the passenger seat, under a patina of desert dust.

'She was alone?' asked Love.

The mechanic nodded.

'Must have hit her head on the windscreen or something, for the driver's side of the car's hardly damaged.'

'What hit her?'

The man shrugged.

'Something blue. You can see the streaks on the side. Must have gone on. That's usual here in case of trouble. The mob will drag drivers from their cars and lynch them, after accidents. There's a lot of violence about. Maybe it's politics. Or the climate.'

Love bent down, ran his finger along the blue streaks. A

64

small fleck of blue paint was embedded in the base of the door-handle. He picked it out, turned it over. The back of the paint was dull grey undercoat. He split the fleck between his finger-nails. There was no third colour sandwiched between the grey and the blue. This showed that the car which had hit Clarissa's Sprite had not been resprayed; the paint was original. But did that get him anywhere?

'I'd better be going,' he said. 'Thanks for the badges.'

'Always pleased to meet an enthusiast,' replied the mechanic.

Love turned suddenly, as though on the impulse.

'Have you any colour charts here?' he asked. 'A friend of mine at the Embassy is thinking of having a paint job done.'

The mechanic went into the office, brought out a clip of metal colour cards. Each was about three inches square, all linked together at one corner with a piece of cord.

'We can get you any of these in a couple of days. Please put them back in the office when you've finished.'

He went under the ramp. Love turned the cards until he found the shade that matched the fleck of blue paint. The card was stamped: Mercedes Original, Midnight Blue. He put the cards back on the desk.

'I'll bring my friend in,' he called to the mechanic, and walked out to the taxi.

'The hotel,' he told the driver.

Outside the New Omayad, a young bootblack crouched on the pavement, polishing the shoes of an American tourist. The driver held open the taxi door. Love went up the entrance steps, across the dusty carpet, to the reception desk. The clerk glanced back at the hook that hung above the pigeon-hole for room 247.

'Your key is already upstairs, sir,' he said. 'Your room has just been cleaned.'

'Thanks. No calls?'

'No, sir.'

'I can't read your telephone books,' Love went on. 'They're all in Arabic script. Could you please give me the number of the local Mercedes agent?'

'Certainly.'

The man thumbed through the book, wrote down a

number on a telegraph form, handed the paper to Love.

'The operator can get it for you,' he said.

Love turned towards the stairs.

A group of doctors were having drinks in the lounge. One waved cheerfully to Love as though he knew him. Maybe he did; Love couldn't remember and he didn't care. He waved back mechanically, walked slowly up the stairs to the second floor, along the corridor to his room. Questions chased unknown answers in his mind. He did not want to cope with a flood of small talk; about merit money in Northern practices, the difficulties of parking in Birmingham. There might be a time for everything, but in his view, there was never a time to waste – least of all when he was so perplexed about Clarissa and this unforgivable mistake.

The key was in his door, as the clerk had said. He turned it, pushed open the door and stood for a moment thankfully in the dim hall, glad to be out of the sunshine, to be alone. He needed a drink before he could face lunch. He'd have a quick wash and go straight down to the bar. He kicked the door shut behind him, opened the next door into his bedroom.

The curtains were drawn against the heat of noon, as is the custom in Middle East hotels, but a reading light had been left on. Its shade was tilted, so that it was shining towards him. Behind this, in shadow so that his face was in virtual darkness, a man sat in the only easy chair. He was smoking, and he must have been there for some time because, in the ashtray at his elbow, a pile of cigarette stubs had already been pressed out into a cone of grey feathery ash.

He wore dark glasses, but it wasn't the glasses or the cigarette that caught Love's eye. It was the .38 Mauser that was aimed unswervingly at his stomach.

'Well?' the man asked softly, as though he had said something that needed an answer.

'Well, what?' replied Love. He wished he had not shut the door so decisively behind him. As he stood, framed in the narrow passage, there was no room to manoeuvre, no chance to escape. His heart beat blacksmith's hammers in his head.

'Are you Dr Jason Love, once in Teheran?'

The man's voice was deep, with a hint of Australian drawl.

He had broad shoulders, a hard, pale face.

'I have no brothers,' said Love.

The man smiled, lowered the automatic, spun it easily on the forefinger of his right hand by its trigger guard.

'I was there as well. Remember me?' He pulled off his glasses, stood up.

'Richard Mass Parkington,' said Love in amazement. He had met him once before in Persia. Parkington was a professional British agent, and they had both been trying to find the same man, a university professor who had disappeared. When Parkington fell ill with jaundice, Love had continued the search on his own – a journey that had taken him from the heat of Persepolis to the cold of Baker Lake in the North West Territory of Canada.

'Is this how you usually pay calls?' he asked him now, his voice hoarse with relief.

'There are no set rules, Doctor. But I saw in the hotel register you were here, so I thought I'd surprise you. I play it all by ear.'

'You want to watch how you play,' retorted Love, sitting down weakly on the end of the bed. 'You might get one of your own bullets in your ear-hole.'

Another surprise on top of the one he'd already had and he'd be a cot-case. He needed that drink more than ever, and a second and a third after that. 'What brings you here, anyway?'

'Business,' said Parkington vaguely. 'Trying to make life hard for people who might make life hard for me.'

'The way you go on, that could include me,' said Love.

'Never,' said Parkington. 'You lead too pure a life. You'll die in your own bed, never in someone else's.'

'Don't point that thing around,' said Love, nodding to the Mauser. 'It might go off.'

'It can't. It isn't loaded. I just carry it for fun.'

'I don't have your sense of humour,' said Love. 'Where have you been since we last met?'

'Oh, moving about. In the Bahamas briefly. I saw in the *Nassau Tribune* that you'd been there, too. You must have left about the day I arrived. Now I'm based in Beirut dealing with the Middle East.'

'What's the cover?' asked Love. How easily he fell back

into the old jargon again; he might never really have left it. You were never unarmed, you were clean; you were never discovered, you were blown. You didn't carry a friend's new telephone number in a distant city but a meaningless number. Then you subtracted the meaningless number from 9,999,999 – and, miraculously, what was left was the exchange number you had to ring. You never had an enemy, only the Other Side. And, having them, you had no need of other enemies.

Parkington's voice scattered his thoughts.

'Salesman,' he was saying. 'Fabrics for uniforms, canvas for tents, webbing for belts, anything to help the growing armies of Arabia. Not much market for boots, though. When they run, they like to run barefoot. It's quicker that way. And, as a sideline, I'm trying right now to interest Syrians in sending out greeting cards on Muhammed's birthday and other unlikely anniversaries. That's really why I'm here. Are you going to offer me a drink – seeing that I'm your guest?'

Love picked up the telephone, asked room service to send up a bottle of Bacardi, another of lime, a bucket of ice. Parkington slipped the Mauser back into its shoulder holster.

'How did you get into my room?' asked Love.

'Through the door. Like anyone else. Told the chambermaid I was an old friend. But you didn't look too pleased to see me. Your security's bad, and your nerves don't seem so good either.'

'They're not,' admitted Love. 'Odd thing happened to me today on the way from the graveyard. I'll tell you about it when we've had a drink.'

They sat in silence while the waiter wheeled in a trolley, poured out the drinks, then bowed himself away through the door.

'What were you doing at the graveyard? Saying goodbye to a patient?' asked Parkington. 'And what sort of odd thing, funny ha-ha, or funny peculiar?'

'I'd call it peculiar,' replied Love, and told him the reason why.

'You're sure this is the same girl?'

'Positive. I've known Clarissa since she was fifteen.'

'So who do you think is buried in her grave?'

'God knows,' said Love irritably. 'What's that got to do with it?'

Parkington shrugged.

'Perhaps everything. Perhaps nothing.'

He poured himself another drink.

'No one saw this car accident?'

'Apparently not. I've also been to the garage and had a look at Clarissa's car. It's got blue paint scratches from whatever hit her. The only car to use this colour new is a Mercedes. I've got the number of their agency. Thought I'd ring just to see if they know who owned a Merc. that colour.'

'Do that,' said Parkington approvingly. 'Meanwhile, back in the bedroom, I'll mix us both another drink.'

Love picked up the telephone, asked for the number the porter had given him. A girl answered in French; Love replied in English.

'I'm a visitor here,' he explained, wondering suddenly how many different stories he would tell to how many different people, and how embarrassing it would be if they should all meet. 'I've just seen a blue Mercedes which I rather liked. Only thing I'm not quite sure about is the colour – midnight blue. I don't know how it stands up to this climate. Could you possibly let me know any people to whom you've sold a car of this colour?'

'I'll have to check,' she said in English. 'Please wait one moment.'

Love heard car horns sounding distantly on the telephone, voices speaking in other tongues, and then the girl was back.

'We have sold three,' she said.

'Could you tell me who bought them?'

'Certainly. I have the file here. One was to an attaché in the Belgian Embassy, I think he's been posted home. The second was sold to a merchant in Aleppo. It was bought by his firm, El Adamah Securities, so I can't give you the name of the actual owner. The third was sold to the Monastery of the Sacred Flame at Yacanda, about twenty miles north of Damascus.'

'Thank you,' said Love. 'You're very kind.'

He replaced the receiver. Parkington handed him a drink.

'So what have you learned?' he asked quizzically.

Love told him. Then he told him about his visit to Suleiman. Parkington sipped his drink.

'This Suleiman character,' he said casually. 'How did he strike you?'

'Pleasant enough. A bit oily. But in a foreign country, almost anyone can look sinister, according to how you feel yourself. Said he's married the wife of the hospital superintendent, which may or not make him popular.'

'Depends on the wife,' pointed out Parkington.

'He's certainly a smoother doctor than we have in Bishop's Combe.'

'That's not very difficult to believe. So, in fact, apart from him, the only person who actually saw this girl was this fifth secretary, Jackson, who presumably just looked at her, but didn't examine her? There are drugs that could slow the breathing, so that someone would appear to be dead if they only had a quick look?'

'Certainly,' said Love. 'Phenobarb would do it – a really enormous dose. But why with Clarissa?'

'Suleiman may have married an expensive wife. Perhaps he needed money – and signed. Unless he was taken in, too.'

He paused.

'Well, the only thing to do is find out.'

'How?'

'We'll try to have a gander at Suleiman's bank account, in case he's had a lump sum paid in after the seventeenth. If he has, then we'll take it from there. If he hasn't, well, we'll still take it from there, for we've no other starting point.'

'And how do you propose to find out what an Armenian doctor has in a Syrian bank – when you don't even know the name of the bank?' asked Love sceptically.

'You, my learned doctor, are going to help me.'

'Thank you very much. This is all I need. This, and my head examining.'

'All you need are results. That's all we both need. How busy are you now?'

'I had plans to eat.'

'Forget them. We'll have to start right away, for it's no good after lunch. Everything shuts down then. It's siesta time here for banks and almost everyone else except visiting doctors – and legmen like me. Come on, I've a car outside.'

Parkington's car was a green, rear-engined Renault. They drove through the streets, over the intersection by the public gardens, down the hill under the wall of the mosque, behind a cinema where a strip of waste land opened on to the river. Parkington stopped beneath the high wall of a concrete building. Its porch was crammed with brown cardboard cartons of Japanese electrical equipment. They walked up two flights of stairs to a frosted glass door. A boy was carrying out a tray of empty coffee cups and half-empty glasses of water. Parkington knocked on the door and went in.

A fat man sprawled back in a swivel chair behind a plastic-topped desk. He was playing with a child's metal puzzle, the sort where two bent nails are linked together. He did not even glance up, but Love saw the slight flicker in his eyes that showed he had seen them. Parkington shut the door.

'Hamid,' he said. 'Here's an English friend of mine. Dr Love, from Somerset.'

Hamid stood up, extending a hand with soft brown fingers like a bunch of over-ripe bananas, but warmer and with sharper nails.

'Pleased and honoured to meet you, Doctor,' he said. 'A friend of Mr Parkington's is a friend of mine. Are you also in the greetings card export business?'

'No,' said Parkington hastily. 'He's over here with a group of English doctors. A convention. He's also interested in business. It's that we'd like to see you about.'

'But not currency, I hope?' said Hamid, and smiled knowingly. His yellow eyeballs were round stained glass windows in his head.

'No, my dear Hamid, nothing like that,' Parkington improvised easily. 'Three Syrian doctors are probably meeting him at another conference in Cairo this summer. He was asking me questions about them that I couldn't answer. I thought you might be able to help me?'

'Depends on the questions,' replied Hamid. He folded his hands closely across the enormous bubble of his stomach as though he feared it might escape and soar away.

'Simply a matter of credit,' said Parkington so plausibly that he almost convinced himself. 'You know how things are in England. We can only get so much money to take abroad, and it's much the same here. These chaps have all asked my friend for a loan. Can you find out discreetly what banks they use?'

'But of course. We only have half a dozen banks in Damascus. I know the managers of them all. I have got an account in one in my real name – and in the other five in different names, so I should. Who are the doctors?'

'Dr Hanania,' said Love, mentioning the first name he could think of. 'Then, the superintendent of the hospital, and a third chap, a Dr Suleiman.'

Lucky that Parkington hadn't said he knew four doctors, or he would have been stuck; as it was, he couldn't think of three names.

Hamid wrote on his blotting pad.

'It may take a few minutes,' he said.

'We'll wait,' replied Parkington, and lit a cigarette. Hamid scooped up the telephone, pushed it under his left jowl against his shoulder, dialled with a pencil. As each number replied, he spoke rapidly in Arabic. For one, a joke; for another, commiseration; for a third, a conspiratorial approach.

Outside, the river ran sluggishly, and across it, beneath the wall of the mosque, country buses waited for trade. The clock on the wall ticked away the minutes. At last Hamid replaced the telephone, threw his pencil down on the desk.

'There,' he said. 'Set me something more difficult next time, Mr Parkington. Now. The superintendent doesn't bank here but with the British Bank of the Middle East in Beirut. Your Dr Hanania is with the Bank of Aleppo, and Dr Suleiman has an account with the Bank of the Revolution, here in Damascus. I'm sorry I can't tell you what their accounts stand at. You'll have to go through the usual business of asking your own bank to see if they are trustworthy. You can probably do it all on the phone.'

'That part of it is easy,' agreed Love. 'Thanks for doing the hard bit. There's only one thing more, Mr Hamid. The names of the managers. It would help me a great deal if my manager could go direct, person to person.'

'Of course,' said Hamid immediately. 'The manager in Beirut is Dr Wazid. Mr Kahn is manager of the Aleppo

Bank, and Mr Usouf manages the Bank of the Revolution.'

They stood up, shook hands. Mr Hamid went back to his steel puzzle; how did the makers ever expect a child to cope with such a toy when he, a grown man – an overgrown man, his wife said, looking at his figure – found it so very difficult?

Outside, in the shade of the building, where beggars squatted in their filthy rags, and blind men stretched ulcered hands for alms, Parkington turned to Love.

'Now what?' he asked. 'I've done my bit. Any suggestions from you for turning up Suleiman's account?'

'Yes,' said Love. 'Not a very good suggestion, but the only one I've got. That's why I wanted to know the manager's name. I tried this once when a man paid me a dud cheque for an old car, and I didn't know whether he really was broke or only pretending. It worked then. It should now. Mr Usouf's office is bound to be on the ground floor. I'll go in and see him. You wait outside, and when you see me at the window, you run into the front of the bank, shouting for Mr Usouf by *name*. That's the absolutely urgent bit. And loud enough for him to hear. You have to get him out of the office for half a minute, which should be all I need.'

'What do I say when he comes out?' asked Parkington. 'That I've read one of his adverts about the advantages of having a bank account and couldn't wait another minute?'

'That's up to you,' said Love. 'But obviously we don't want to appear to know each other.'

'Obviously not. After this, we may not want to know ourselves.'

They drove slowly along the wide Avenue of the Revolution. Workmen were hanging more orange flags from the lamp posts; a delegation of Arab solidarity or some such thing was due in town. They always seemed to be arriving or leaving.

The Bank of the Revolution was in a stone building in an intersection, its marble steps cluttered with sweetmeat sellers and stalls of overcoloured postcards.

As Love went through the revolving doors into the entrance hall, a closed-circuit television camera watched him from the far corner. The floor was tiled in black and beige squares, like a gigantic chess board. A customer at the far end of the long counter was collecting blue bags of coins, and handing them to a messenger in khaki uniform. Love went up to the counter marked 'Foreign Exchange', because here he was most likely to find someone who spoke English. A clerk behind the vertical brass grille totted up figures with a ball-point pen.

'Excuse me,' said Love, pushing his passport under the grille. 'I wonder if I could see the manager, Mr Usouf?'

The clerk looked up as though he had made an improper suggestion. Why the hell did people interrupt when he was halfway down a column? He swallowed to conceal his irritation.

'You have an appointment?' he asked.

'No,' admitted Love. But I think this could be important to him.'

'Your name?'

'Dr Jason Love.'

'Please to wait a moment.'

He walked away, between tables where other clerks in white jackets pecked at Oliver typewriters, and whispered something to one of them. Together, they went into a room with a plain oak door. If that was the manager's office, the window would directly overlook the street. Luck was with him so far; Love hoped it would stay that way. The clerk came back, lifted a flap in the counter.

'Please to follow me,' he said.

Love's heart began to beat a little faster. Now that he was inside the bank, the whole scheme seemed far more complicated than it had appeared previously. If the oak door was as thick as it looked, how would the manager hear his name being called? Then he saw a fanlight open above it, and some of his doubts left him. After all, what was the worst that could happen? Simply that they could discover nothing at all about Suleiman, and that a few bank clerks would think that Parkington was a noisy, loud-mouthed Englishman and he was a nut. And, who knows, they could be right.

The clerk showed him through the door. The manager was tall, and thin. Half a dozen hairs loyally stretched themselves across his scalp. He stood up, eyebrows raised inquiringly.

'You wish to see me, Doctor?'

Love nodded. The door shut behind him in its pneumatic stop. Love sat down. He hoped that Parkington was in position.

'Yes, I do, Mr Usouf,' Love began. 'I'm a doctor over here briefly, with an interest in a greetings card firm in London. I don't think that this initially American idea of sending greetings on Father's Day, and on Holy Days and so on, has ever been exploited in Muslim countries, and my directors are considering opening a branch here.

'A friend of mine, Mr Hamid, mentioned your name to me. If we can do any business, I would like to open an account at your branch.'

So far, at least, he hadn't told a lie, the truth was slightly bent, but that, even to his Presbyterian conscience, was a different thing.

'Delighted,' said the manager. He sat back, pressing his fingers together, because he had nothing else to press. And Mr Hamid was a rich man. This could be interesting.

'What sort of facilities would you be requiring, Doctor?' he asked.

'Initially,' said Love, taking a deep breath. 'We would work on something pretty nominal. Then I have in mind a float of perhaps the equivalent of £100,000 sterling.'

The manager became more attentive. He leaned forward in his swivel chair, his lips pursed in the way bankers have when discussing other people's money.

'And,' added Love, 'this could easily lead to two or three times that sum. In credit, of course.'

'Of course,' agreed the manager. 'I appreciate that.' The idea of such a sum being overdrawn was not quite so pleasant to appreciate.

'Which brings me to the object of visiting you today, Mr Usouf, without any notice – and I need hardly say how much I appreciate your kindness in seeing me without a prior appointment.

'We have been given the names of some people in Damascus who might invest money in our company here, and naturally, since large sums can eventually be involved, we would want to take up banker's references.

'Not all of them bank with you, but one does, and

although I will obviously ask my own bank in England to check with you in the normal way, it would help me a great deal if you could say, strictly off the record, of course, whether you think this person is a man of substance – as I have every reason to believe he is.'

The manager nodded. His little head jerked up and down like a metronome: the message was coming through, but now it was his turn to show he was discreet. He had a part to play and he intended to play it.

'But that is against banking practice, Doctor. We cannot, naturally, as you will be aware, divulge details of any of our clients' financial situation. Except to other banks. You do appreciate that?'

'Of course I do, Mr Usouf. I am not asking you to divulge any details. I would not consider such a thing – any more than you should question me about a patient's health in detail.

'However, if you, as a business associate of the patient, asked me in general terms – because great issues hung on the answer – whether I thought his health would stand up to a particular job or not, then that would be a different matter. And, in very general terms, I would tell you. Now, all I ask is for you to give me a *general* indication of a man's financial health, without, of course, divulging any figures.'

'That might be possible,' allowed the manager cautiously. 'I am glad you see my position. Who specifically did you have in mind?'

'The man who banks with you,' said Love, as casually as he could, 'is a doctor like myself. Dr Suleiman.'

'Oh, yes. An old customer of ours.'

'Well, I need hardly ask any more. The amount of money he would be asked to invest would be around the equivalent of £15,000.'

The manager's eyebrows flicked up and down again as though they had a mind of their own – and as an unconscious indication of his thoughts.

'That is quite an important investment for a professional man, doctor.'

'I see we are on the same side, Mr Usouf,' said Love with a smile.

Usouf pressed a button, spoke into an intercom. A clerk

brought in a pale blue statement sheet. He placed it face down in front of the manager. Usouf picked up one corner, glanced at it. Then he put it back on his blotting pad, blank side uppermost.

'This is my client's last statement,' he said. 'I think he would be good for the amount in question. But, of course, I say that off the record.'

'Of course.'

Love stood up, walked towards the window.

'Now, Dr Love, would you like to open an account today?'

'Today?' Love repeated the word as though he had never heard it before. Where the hell was Parkington? He could not see him; only a woman in black carrying a child, and men in shirt sleeves, and the sweetmeat sellers voicing their continual ritual to buy. Then he suddenly saw Parkington across the road, watching the wall, not certain at which window Love would appear.

Love pulled out his handkerchief, took his sunglasses from his breast pocket, began to polish the lenses. Parkington saw the white movement of the handkerchief, began to walk towards the bank. Love sat down again at the table.

'That would be an idea,' he agreed. 'But I wonder whether you could give me the same information about the gentleman who recommended me to come here – which makes it rather embarrassing even to ask.'

'You mean Mr Hamid?'

Surprise painted wrinkles on Mr Usouf's forehead. And then, before he could clothe his thoughts with words, through the fanlight they both heard a hoarse shout: 'Mr Usouf! Mr Usouf! Quickly! Oh, my God, *Mr Usouf*!'

The two men glanced at each other in surprise, then at the door. Feet pattered on the tiles outside; other men were shouting unintelligibly in a tongue Love could not understand. The door burst open and a clerk rushed in, without knocking. Mr Usouf stood up, mouth wide open in amazement and alarm. The clerk spoke to him urgently.

'Excuse me,' Mr Usouf said to Love, and ran out with the clerk. Love leaned across the desk, flicked over the statement. On June 18th, an amount of 10,000 Syrian pounds had been credited by cash to the account of Dr Suleiman. Love replaced the paper, sat back in his chair, lit a Gitane. There

77

was now no need for haste. He had discovered what he had set out to find. QED.

Outside, in the bank, voices filtered through the fanlight; voices shouting, then voices petering out. He hoped they hadn't been too rough with Parkington, but maybe Parkington could look after himself. Mr Usouf came back into the room. He dusted the pockets of his jacket with his palms.

'Please excuse me, Doctor. A ridiculous disturbance of some kind. Somehow a compatriot of yours had discovered my name. I regret to say, Doctor, that he was drunk.'

'Drunk?' echoed Love. 'Disgusting. Sometimes I'm ashamed of my nationality, Mr Usouf.'

'Sometimes I'm ashamed of being a human being, Dr Love,' admitted Mr Usouf.

'Check,' said Love. 'Well, I am much in your debt. If you can give me a form to fill in about an account with you, I will take it back to the hotel. I will have to check with the Bank of England, because Syria is out of the scheduled territories, and you know how fussy they are with exchange control. But I hope we can do some business together.'

'I hope so, doctor. Most sincerely, I do.' Mr Usouf picked up the statement sheet, held it close to his body, shook hands.

Then Love was walking through the lines of typewriters into the hall, and out into the street. He had walked three hundred yards before Parkington caught up with him.

'Well?' asked Parkington.

'Ten thousand quid,' said Love. 'On the eighteenth. The day after he signed the certificate.'

'So. That leaves us with only one thing to do, apart from having a couple of drinks. Those clerks with their hot little hands like the claws of birds did their best to do me a mischief.'

'What's the only one thing?' asked Love.

'To find who's buried in that grave,' said Parkington, and guided him into a bar.

Chapter Five

The desert beyond Damascus, June 28th

He was not old, but sometimes he felt twice his age, and the soft ride of the air suspension on the 600 Mercedes always made him sleepy.

He folded his pale white hands together across his lap, like the soft petals of fleshy flowers, and dozed behind the white curtains. The car ploughed north from Damascus along the shimmering desert road in mirage after mirage of liquid heat, but shielded in its air-conditioned cocoon, he was already miles and years away in his boyhood.

He was the fourteenth gardener on the estate of Count Eckdorf von Heifenstaub some miles east of Brno, in Czechoslovakia. It was his first week at work, and he had been teased mercilessly by the others because of his strange accent, because of his slight build, because he found it so difficult to do what came so easily to them with their stronger, squat bodies, their broad shoulders and sinewed arms.

They seemed tireless as they carried the heavy lead buckets of water from the pumps, weeded the long gravel drives, bending down to pull out each tiny tuft of grass, or formed a gang to draw the lawn mower across the croquet lawn.

He did not like gardening, but then he had never liked working with his hands, using his muscles, smelling his own sweat, sour and stale, at the end of the day. Only fools worked like that. He had known this even then. He had been born with the knowledge, which those peasants never seemed to learn.

His mother's father said he inherited ideas like that from his father, but he had never even seen his father. All he knew about him he had learned from others, in asides, in sneering references; no one mentioned the man without half smiles or a disapproving puckering of the mouth.

He had been a travelling salesman, apparently, but no one

now remembered what he sold. He had been good looking, though; they remembered that; and he had lodged in the family house because it was cheaper than the inn and, of course, the daughter of the house was pretty. And, as events proved, she was also willing, which meant that the salesman was wisely off on his travels again, before her pregnancy began to show.

Jakob's grandmother was disgusted that her only daughter should have been foolish enough to fall into this ancient trap when she could have married someone with prospects. Instead, she had to marry anyone – quickly. This need for haste was in itself suspicious, and narrowed her choice.

Finally, the girl married a servant in one of the great houses; a dull, stupid man with mean eyes, too close together, and yellow teeth all broken and chipped and streaked with green. But then he would have had to be stupid to marry a girl already pregnant, or so Jakob's grandmother said.

As a boy, Jakob grew used to being taunted; if anything went wrong, it was his father's blood in him. He did not know why people always said this, and he was twelve before he discovered the reason.

Not surprisingly, his step-father did not like him; there were two other children of the marriage, both girls, both taking after their father in their bovine, crafty appearance. He was the odd boy out, the unwanted; a constant, living reminder of one act of folly. Even his mother resented him; he was the reason for everything she hated in her own life.

When Jakob was fourteen, he left the village school. His step-father knew an undergardener at the castle, and so Jakob started as a gardener's boy.

He found the work hard and monotonous to the point that sometimes he hid behind one of the potting sheds and wept at the futility of it all.

The others endured the endless drudgery of a formal garden, where the cycle of the seasons meant that as soon as you finished one sequence, you started on another, equally laborious, equally boring. Some of them had been Communists, of course, but even they had not railed against the monotony, the unchanging routine. He had. But what could he do to change things?

One year passed; a second, and then a third; and still the answer eluded him.

The only bearable times were the evenings, especially in the summer, after eight o'clock, when the head gardener in his dark suit with its four buttons on the jacket, the brass stud at the top of his collarless shirt, worn like a badge of office, had gone home. Then Jakob could imagine that he was not the lowest, most unimportant, most junior gardener; then he pretended that he was the owner.

Sometimes, on such summer evenings, as the dusk painted shadows on the lawns, Jakob would walk between the yew hedges, through the maze that took two weeks to cut, until he came to a gap in the hedge, and then he would stand looking at the enormous house with its verandahs, its porches, its balconies, hooded with striped red and green awnings like lacquered eyelids. He was always touched, not only by its size, but by its beauty, by the wealth and elegance and privilege it represented. How could he ever have a house like that? He could work for a thousand years at his wages and still not afford to buy a part of it.

His step-father would assure him, as they sat over supper in the kitchen, eating cheap sausage on a knife, drinking the sour local wine, that to everyone in life there came a chance, a moment of decision, when their choice could determine their whole future career. But, like most people, he had only recognized the chance after it had passed him by. He was never very explicit as to what this lost opportunity had been, but then older people never were; they preferred to imagine what frequently had never happened.

And then, quite unexpectedly, Jakob's chance came.

He was hoeing between rows of artichokes one morning when a shadow fell across the newly-turned soil, and all the robins flew away. He turned. A girl was standing watching him, with a parasol over her shoulders, twirling it slightly so that it spun like a coloured wheel, red, green, and blue. She was smiling at him.

He stood up and touched his cap in salute. He didn't know what to say, but he had been taught to say nothing until the nobility spoke to him, so that was easy enough. The momentum of the parasol slowed and stopped.

'How long have you been working here?' the girl asked him.

'Three years, ma'am,' he said, and looked about hopefully, nervously, almost desperately, for some more senior gardener to carry on the conversation.

He had never spoken to any of his employer's family face to face. They were always separated by distance, or by plate glass in their Austro-Daimler, travelling majestically down the drive behind a chauffeur and a footman.

'You don't know me,' she said. 'I'm Ingrid.'

He bowed.

'I'm Jakob,' he said, as though this was the most natural thing to say. He knew of her, of course, although he did not know her. She wasn't right in the head; she was mad, soft, wet, an idiot; but she was rich, and one day she would be richer. She was the Count's only daughter, and rarely allowed out of sight of the house because of what she might do or say.

'Do you like gardening?' she asked him.

He nodded. He didn't like it, but it was better than starving, and what else could he do?

'Tell me the names of the flowers,' she said.

'Which flowers?' he asked.

'This.'

She pointed at a lupin.

He told her.

'You know a lot about them?' she asked admiringly.

'It's my job.'

'Then you must show me all the flowers. Walk with me to the rose garden.'

He threw down his trowel, wiped his hands on the sides of his corduroy trousers and followed her, suddenly conscious of his dirty clothes, his boots cracked and split and unpolished, beside her elegance. They passed other gardeners, and, walking with her, he saw them suddenly not as his superiors, who tormented him, but as though he were their employer. He saw them suddenly bend over their hoes with false energy until they passed. Mad Ingrid, they were saying; but she seemed gentle and harmless, and after he had lost his initial shyness, Jakob could talk to her as though she were a village girl.

They had barely reached the rose garden before a nurse or some severe person in white uniform, her grey hair rolled in a bun like a ball of steel wool, came calling along the grass paths and took Ingrid away, and sent him back to his artichokes with a scolding.

He saw Ingrid again later that week. She showed him a book of flowers, with coloured pictures and directions for planting them. He thought she must like him, or why would she do this? He felt nothing for her, because there was nothing to feel; but then he felt nothing for anyone, only for himself.

She had said something about him to the Count, for he was promoted to work with two others in the flowerbeds around the house. Here, Ingrid would seek him out once or twice a week and talk to him, and he would try to match her silly, empty conversation with stories of the flowers which he had picked up, half listening, from old men about the village.

The other gardeners would jeer at him and made crude remarks about her, yet they envied him in a strange way, because she never talked to them, but only to Jakob.

Then, one afternoon, she came to him, excitedly for once, not wanting to hear his stories, but for him to hear hers. She beckoned him behind one of the laurel hedges cut to a perfect right angle. He followed her cautiously. Her father might get the wrong idea about them, and this could cost him his job.

'I've a secret to tell you,' she announced. 'My father.'

'What about him?' He looked around uneasily; also, he had two hundred seedlings to plant out before dusk.

'My father,' she repeated. 'He's hiding the pictures in the cellars.'

'Why?' he asked. 'What pictures?'

The only picture in his house was one torn from a calendar; a saint with a halo around his head, and two fingers crossed in the gesture of peace. And who would want to hide that anywhere? He had never realized that pictures could have value and so should be hidden.

'The Germans are coming,' she went on. 'He's put all the pictures in the cellar and he's going to block up the door so no one will know they are there. He says they're the best collection in the country,' she added proudly.

'The Germans?' he repeated. 'Why should they come?'

83

He knew nothing of politics, or frontiers and he was not interested in them. He only knew he had a living to earn, a chance to look for, that somehow he must recognize or for ever be a drudge, a cog in a wheel, instead of the power that turned the wheel.

Ingrid's brow puckered.

'I don't know,' she said. 'I did hear, but I've forgotten. But he's worried, and so is Mummy. They might leave.'

'Does that mean you would leave?'

'Yes,' she said. 'We would all go.'

She turned away from him. He put out a hand and, for the first time, he touched her on the arm. Her flesh was soft and warm and young, not coarse and red and rough from too many wash-tubs.

'Will you miss me?' she asked suddenly, unexpectedly.

He nodded. He would miss her. Ingrid's visits, unsatisfyingly brief and unexpected and intermittent, were still something to illumine the dreariness of his life. With her would go his only contact with the world of luxury he wanted so desperately for his own. Also, if her father left, what would happen to his job? He felt a sense of distant, but approaching alarm. The news was a trailer for future disaster.

'I won't have anyone to talk to about the flowers,' he said, thinking aloud. 'I'll miss you very much.'

She looked at Jakob as though she was trying to impress the outline of his face in her mind.

'I will, too,' she said gravely. 'I've had no one at all to talk to before. No one but nurses and maids. And you don't call them *people*. Not like you.'

Jakob looked into her vacant eyes, blue as cornflowers, empty as the wide summer sky. He looked and he heard his step-father's voice over the black bread and sour wine; everyone gets one chance in life. Watch for it, Jakob; take it, boy.

This was his chance. He realized it, although the plan was still only a vague, shadowy outline in his mind. For a moment, it was as though the whole world stood still; the birds froze like parentheses in the sky, leaves no longer moved. Time and again in the years ahead he would remember this scene and relive it with all its initial sharpness, the sounds and scents of a summer day.

'I don't want you to go,' he said. 'I love you.'

He didn't, of course. He loved no one else and nothing else; only himself. But it was as though some other person was speaking the words; he hardly recognized his own voice.

'What do you mean?'

No one had ever talked like this to her.

'What I say. I want you to marry me.'

Now he had said the words, their enormity almost overwhelmed him; he felt physically choked by them.

'*Marry* you?'

Her eyes clouded doubtfully for a moment. The thought was beyond her experience, beyond her dreams.

'Secretly,' Jakob said hastily, and her clouds of doubt disappeared.

'No one would know but us. It would be our own special secret. Then, no matter how far we were apart, we would really be together. We'd belong to each other, and no one else would ever know.'

'What about Mummy?' asked Ingrid practically.

'You could tell her – later.'

'Of course. So I could.'

It seemed so reasonable, so obvious, that she wondered why she hadn't thought of it before. But there were still questions.

'Where can we marry? We have to give notice to the church. I had a cousin who got married last spring. She had to tell the priest several weeks ahead.'

'We could marry in a lawyer's office.'

'A lawyer's office,' she repeated. 'What's that?'

He was not sure himself, but this was no time for insecurity or doubt.

'I'll find a lawyer,' he said. 'He would marry us.'

'Us?'

Ingrid's mind was drifting like one of the butterflies.

A bell began to sound across the lawn.

'I must go,' she said, almost relieved. 'It's lunch time.'

'Ten o'clock tonight,' he told her. 'I will be under your window. I know the one.'

'I'll be in bed.'

'You can get up,' he said.

She was easy to lead; her brain was feeble and simple and

trusting, and he knew then that all through his life he would be able to lead and sway weak people like her; and to a certain degree, most people were like her.

'Ten,' he repeated. 'And I hate to say this, but I have no money.'

He paused.

'I have a hundred korunas,' she said proudly.

'Bring them. The lawyer will want his fee.'

The bell clanged again. Ingrid reached out impulsively and squeezed his hand and smiled, her mind made up. Then she flitted away and Jakob went back to his plants.

At ten o'clock that night he was waiting beneath her window with his bicycle. After work, he had cycled the streets of Brno, until he found a lawyer's office above a shop that sold tin lanterns. The lawyer was a plump man behind a desk piled with papers.

'What do you want?' he asked without interest. What could a youngster want but a job, the chance to deliver a message, to carry a parcel?

'I want you to marry me.'

'To whom?'

The lawyer looked up now, half surprised, half amused. Was he making a mock of him?

'To someone I'll bring tonight.'

'This office shuts at seven.'

'How much would you charge to marry me at eleven?'

'It is difficult,' said the lawyer.

'Life is difficult,' said Jakob, realizing he was the stronger character, that he would always be the stronger character.

'Are you and the girl of age?'

'Yes. How much?'

'Fifty korunas, and I supply the witness, my clerk. I have to pay him.'

'Thirty,' said Jakob instantly.

He had never bargained before, but you had to begin sometime, and he was growing up fast. He had begun that day as a gardener's boy, and he would end it married to the daughter of a count –with a little money in hand.

'It is too little,' grumbled the lawyer.

'Then we are wasting each other's time.'

'No, no,' said the lawyer hastily. 'How can I be sure you will pay?'

'When you marry me, I will pay. Tonight.'

'Thirty korunas, then,' said the lawyer sourly, and dug his paper knife into the soft wood of the desk like a dagger.

He hadn't believed the boy would come back. He looked too young to marry and, anyhow, where could he get thirty korunas? But Jakob did came back, although the lawyer had nearly given up waiting for him.

At five past ten, Ingrid came out through a side door and joined him. He carried his bicycle so that it would make no noise on the gravel until they were fifty yards down the drive, and then he climbed on it and balanced her on the crossbar.

The wedding ceremony was simple and quick. Ingrid handed him the money, he peeled off three ten-koruna notes, pocketed the rest, and they cycled home. They did not even kiss as they said goodnight; Jakob did not know how to kiss a girl, and he was terrified in case he made a fool of himself, or in case someone saw him. Also, he was tired and hungry – he had eaten no supper – and still had his mother to face for being out so late. So he squeezed Ingrid's hand in his, watched her let herself in at the side door, and then cycled away thankfully.

After this, Ingrid and he met every day in the garden, but apart from touching hands, they had no physical contact; nothing appeared to have changed, but Jakob, with a copy of the marriage certificate folded in a newspaper inside the horse-hair mattress of his narrow bed, knew that everything had. If the Germans came, they would bring the chance which he had sought for so long, and for which he was now prepared.

It took all of eight months for him to know that he was right, because it took this time for the Germans to invade Czechoslovakia.

One afternoon, the roads around the castle were empty, the air filled with the hum of bees and the warm sleepiness of spring. By evening, these roads were churned and furrowed by the metal tracks of tanks and troop carriers. The castle, like all the other large houses, was seized. Troops camped on the tennis courts and the lawns; officers drove grey Mercedes and Maybach staff cars across the flowerbeds. At dusk on the day of the invasion, after the radio calls for cooperation, and the official announcement that all organized resistance was at an end, Jakob walked to the house which the German commandant had commandeered as his headquarters.

It was almost as though he was expected. An officer, wearing a grey uniform, unclipped at the throat, sat at the dining-room table, smoking a Turkish cigarette. He had pale blue eyes and the badge on his hat was a polished brass skull. Jakob came to the point at once. As he spoke, he wondered at his confidence, just as when he had first proposed marriage to Ingrid. It was as though someone else was speaking for him; as though he were watching the whole thing, taking no part in it.

'Sir,' he said. 'I've seen notices that say how information leading to assets that could be of value to the Reich, will be rewarded. I know where some valuable paintings are buried. What is the reward?'

The officer smiled. What could this country bumpkin possibly know? However, he would humour him.

'A quarter of their realized value,' he promised.

'Can I have that in writing?' asked Jakob.

'No,' replied the officer coldly. 'You have my word. That is enough.'

'I'll show you where this treasure is, sir,' said Jakob.

The officer called to a sergeant, who produced a reluctant corporal and a private soldier. Jakob led them through the back paths of the castle gardens, down into the servants' entrance to the cellars. He beat on the whitewashed walls with the flat of one hand until the blows sounded hollow.

'In there,' he told them.

They hacked a hole big enough to climb through, and then the officer arrived himself with a torch.

As they carried away the paintings to a truck outside, Ingrid tiptoed up to the edge of the group.

'What's happening?' she whispered to Jakob. 'I heard the engine and men talking.'

Jakob did not answer her. He turned to the officer.

'This girl is responsible,' he said. 'She and her parents.'

'Bring out the Count for questioning,' the officer told the sergeant. 'Take the girl now.'

Ingrid started to run as they turned towards her. The soldier tripped her, and the corporal seized her arms and held them, both wrists bent up behind her back. Jakob looked the other way. He could stand her screams, but he could not face her eyes. The Count recognized Jakob as one of his gardeners; he also recognized the paintings.

'They are my daughter's,' he explained frantically. 'I made them over to her some time ago. They were locked away as we have no safe and they are too large for the bank to accept them.'

'Your daughter is a traitor,' said Jakob. 'She hid them to keep them from the Germans who have come to liberate us. I claim the paintings and the reward for discovering them.'

'You,' repeated the Count in amazement. '*You* – a gardener? On what grounds are these paintings yours?'

'On the grounds that you have just said Ingrid owns them. I am Ingrid's husband.'

He produced his marriage certificate. The old man sat down on a stone bench, speechless. Then he began to weep tears of misery and bewilderment, tears of defeat.

Jakob was rewarded not with a quarter, as the officer had promised, but with a smaller proportion; after all, the officer had to show a profit himself, and they had nothing in writing. Also, Jakob was not in a strong position to bargain.

But from this beginning, Jakob's whole fortune changed. Because he appeared to be a simple country boy, few would suspect him. He could thus be enormously useful to the Gestapo. They moved him to another part of Czechoslovakia, then to Vienna, finally to Hamburg.

It was here that he changed his name to Steinmann, Man of Stone, for another plan was growing in his mind, but its potential profits were equalled by its dangers if too many people knew who he was.

All Jewish property was being confiscated throughout the Reich, but many of the Jews had relations in Britain, in America and elsewhere. These relatives often wrote pathetic letters to the Chancellery in Berlin and to local mayors, seeking information about uncle, brothers, sons and other relations who had disappeared. Jakob, now secure with a

Jewish name, intended to turn their distress to his profit.

He let it be known that he would like to see all such requests, and because he enjoyed close Gestapo protection, they were passed on to him.

The first deal he did as a result was with a Jew in Golders Green. His uncle, before his arrest, had owned a delicatessen in a street behind Hamburg railway station. The nephew wrote to the mayor, asking for information about his uncle – would it be possible for him to come to England?

Steinmann replied on notepaper of the Adlon Hotel, in Berlin. He explained that he had seen this request, but owing to political dangers, he was replying to it privately. He would be pleased to help as an individual, but help was expensive. He had bribes to give, to persuade other people to view the requests in a favourable way. Could he have more details of the man concerned and his delicatessen?

Back came a reply within the week. The deeds of the delicatessen were in a safe deposit in a certain bank; the nephew obligingly gave the number. Steinmann collected the deeds, had them made over to him by a Nazi lawyer, then telephoned the Central Registry in Berlin. He gave the full name of the man, his address, his age, the concentration camp where he was, and instructions that he should be liquidated, as an enemy of the State. The delicatessen was now under new ownership.

That was all there was to it; you had to recognize your chance when it came, just as his step-father had told him. But now he knew more; in addition to recognizing your chance, however disguised it might arrive, you had to use it. A chance on its own was nothing; a chance exploited could lead anywhere.

For Jakob Steinmann, his small delicatessen led on to apartment houses, garages, shops. Each month his little empire grew, and so did his personal danger, for his early value as an informer had dwindled, and by the second year of the war his wealth was becoming ostentatious. His success had outrun his usefulness.

It thus happened that he found himself unexpectedly drafted into the German Army, and posted after the briefest of basic training to the Eastern Front. He protested, he threatened, but no one seemed to care; the word had gone out that he was also expendable. Like thousands of others in Russia, Steinmann could easily have died, but his natural instinct for self-preservation was strong, and the thought of his property gave him added determination to survive.

During the retreat from Stalingrad, however, the engine of his half-track seized solid, and he was captured. Again, while others of his unit were left to freeze, or at best marched into Soviet captivity to work as slaves until death released them, Steinmann was able to use adversity as a lever to something better.

He claimed that one of the officers in his unit had served on the staff of Rudolf Hess, the Deputy Fuehrer, and so knew the real reason why Hess had suddenly flown to Scotland shortly before Germany invaded Russia. The officer was tortured, of course, but since he knew nothing, he could reveal nothing.

Steinmann, having made his number as one willing to co-operate, then became an informer against German guerilla groups which he claimed the retreating Wehrmacht had left behind in towns and villages.

These groups only existed in his own mind, but he was plausible, and he meant to stay on the winning side. At the end of the war, however, it was obviously impossible for him to return to West Germany to attempt to claim the property he had amassed. Too many people there knew him for a traitor; also, the Russians did not wish to lose him.

But, in 1947, while acting as a go-between for them in East Germany, he saw his opportunity when the train on which the delegation was travelling ran into heavy fog, and stopped. The Russians with him did not speak German well, and so, under the pretext of finding some official who could advise them of the cause and extent of the delay, Steinmann went out into the fog and did not come back.

He travelled to Italy, then on to Corsica, and there began another career.

He had heard the story of the wartime ship that had sailed from Italy laden with gold bars made from melted-down gold teeth fillings, rings and ornaments. It had been sunk off Corsica on its way from Civitavecchia to Marseilles. Many had searched the shifting sand for these bars; divers had gone down into the sandy seas after them, but without success. In

Bastia, Steinmann discovered that this gold, tarred to look like ballast bars, had already been found by local fishermen who lacked the ingenuity either to get the gold out of the country, or to convert it into cash.

In return for a promise of a share, Steinmann was able to suggest a scheme to make them all rich. At the end of the war, the American Army in Europe had shipped thousands of unwanted lorries, tanks and jeeps to Corsica where they wished to auction them – but with the strict proviso that none should be bought for use either by Jews or Arabs in Palestine. The British Mandate there was ending, and both Arabs and Jews were anxious for arms in the war that would result.

Steinmann travelled to Jerusalem and negotiated two separate deals with representatives of Arabs and Jews. To both parties he explained that if they would finance him, he would bid in his own name for whatever vehicles they wanted. He would then resell these trucks and tanks to them at a nominal profit, but there would be a rebate – in the form of gold bullion which he would smuggle out of Corsica in the vehicles, welded into jerrycans, in locked tool boxes and so forth. In effect, they would not only get their vehicles for nothing but a substantial bonus in bullion.

Steinmann suggested that they should split whatever this might be worth. This was agreed – as he guessed it would be. After all, this was a unique opportunity to buy what no one else would sell them – and at an interesting discount.

Both sides gave him letters of credit on Swiss banks, and he returned to Corsica.

After the sale, the vehicles were loaded on old Liberty ships, and tramp steamers, all the papers made out to such harmless destinations as Tilbury and Calais, where he declared that the tanks would be used as tractors and buldozers for clearing away bomb-rubble, and the trucks by civilian contractors. But as soon as the ships were out at sea, they all changed course for the Middle East.

This operation netted Steinmann a considerable sum, but still not enough to enable him to live in the style he intended. After all, he had to share it with the Corsican fishermen, and also the agents of the Corsican Fraternity, the local equivalent of the Mafia, who claimed a high percentage. Even so, he could keep himself without working for some years, and this led to other lucrative assignments, such as helping wanted men to escape to South America, for shares in various tourist enterprises and casinos operating as a front for Mafia money.

It was through one of these that he met a man on the run; a French scientist from the missile base in the Sahara. The scientist's son had been killed at Dien Bien Phu; his wife had left him, and in an agony of emotional conflict, the man felt unable to carry on with his job.

There was nothing whatever treasonable in his disappearance, but the news had leaked out, and it was at once assumed he had defected to the East, with his unrivalled knowledge of the new French rocket propellants, and their ingenious means for lowering the nose-cone temperature on re-entry into the atmosphere. In fact, the wretched scientist was on the edge of a mental breakdown.

Steinmann met him in a bar in Bastia, and as he sipped his pastis, it was as though he saw a whole rich new future revealed in the pale milky circle in his glass.

He poured all his knowledge of practical psychology, all his considerable personal charm and powers of persuasion into this new venture. Two weeks later, the scientist's body was discovered just south of Lyons at the side of the N7 in a wrecked car.

Some police surgeons were convinced that he was already dead when the car crashed, but since the whole case was highly involved and some important political personalities appeared interested, this view was never made public.

As one result of this inexplicable accident, the sum of 100,000 dollars was deposited in Steinmann's bank account in Geneva from an unknown source. As another, a Middle Eastern country, anxious to become a space power, but as cheaply and secretly as possible, found a way to save months of research and millions of money.

Shortly afterwards, Steinmann met a Bulgarian diplomat in Porto Santo Stefano, a man anxious to stay in Western Europe, where he had a delightful Italian mistress; a man who knew the key figures in the Chinese network of espionage and subversion that helped to keep chaos alive in Africa after the colonial powers withdrew.

Again, Steinmann operated his plan, slightly modified to changed circumstances, and once more he was successful – to the extent of a quarter of a million dollars from another, but also anonymous source.

The Bulgarian was less fortunate. The sea washed up his body on the beach one morning. The local doctor who made the autopsy was of the opinion that he was already dead when he had been put in the water – but who cared what a local doctor thought? As a result of this deal, an Iron Curtain country found new ways of insinuating its agents into Africa with almost total success.

There were other deals, large and not so large, with countries and with commercial concerns whose annual turnovers were greater than the budgets of many European countries. Steinmann's fortune grew once more, but this time it was in negotiable currency, and in such convenient financial centres as Hong Kong and Nassau, and Tangier, and through complicated banking arrangements in the Netherlands Antilles, with discretionary trusts in Panama, under pseudonyms and holding companies and investment consortia.

Step by cautious step, like a man climbing a glass mountain, Jakob had moved from what now seemed relatively uncomplicated deals to the matter that concerned him now. If he could bring this through successfully, with its overtones of irony, then even he would admit that he could retire. You had to recognize your chance, agreed, but you should never push your luck too far.

The green light of the radio telephone flickered impatiently. He hated sudden noise and so refused to have the buzzer or a bell in the car. He frowned at the interruption, reached out, scooped up the instrument. Khalif's voice spoke in his ear over the miles of baking desert.

'I thought I should report to you, sir, that an Englishman has been in to see the girl. Somehow he managed to get past the sentry. Says he's a doctor from the same part of England, and knows her father. I've checked him in the register. He seems genuine. At least, there is a doctor of that name – Jason Love.'

Beyond the windows of the speeding car, Steinmann could see the hills, grey as wrinkled firebricks, streaked at the top with snow, scratched with outcrop halfway up. He wondered what it would be like to be poor again, like the shepherds with their sheep, nuzzling those bare rocks for any scraps of green, Perhaps one of the shepherd boys out there felt as he had felt many years ago; discontented, planning to be rich and powerful. Perhaps so many things. He swung his mind back to the present.

'Have him watched,' he said briefly. 'And move the girl.'

Why was it that he had to attend to even the simplest matters himself? Why would no one accept responsibility? Why did so many people long to be led, and so few would be the leaders? Thank God all this involvement would soon be behind him.

'I just thought you should know,' said Khalif nervously, interrupting his thoughts.

'Of course,' said Steinmann, and put down the telephone. They had only a couple of days, and he would know more than Khalif could ever imagine. Two days, but with the elasticity of time, they could seem as many years.

He settled back against the leather seat, adjusted his headrest, closed his eyes. The car swept on and up towards the hills. Behind it, dust settled and shepherds and sheep turned their backs into the empty lonely wind.

Chapter Six

Damascus, June 28th

Parkington went up the stairs to his room. He walked slowly to conserve his energy. Outside his bedroom door he bent down to examine the two single hairs he had stuck across the lintel with saliva, but no one had been inside. He turned the key in the lock and went in.

He wasn't quite sure about Love. Was it entirely coincidence that he was there in Damascus, too, at a medical convention, or was MacGillivray using him again? He used amateurs for some things, partly because they cost nothing and partly because he controlled so few professionals. One of the results was that you never knew who was on your side fully or even partly, or even at all.

Parkington looked at his face in the big wall mirror, squeezed out a couple of blackheads under his right eye, opened his mouth, examined his tongue; it was coated. He was drinking too much, but then he always did, he always would.

He opened a suitcase, lifted out a false bottom, then a flat tin marked 'Bath Oliver Biscuits'. Inside it lay his Mauser automatic in a piece of rubber foam, cut to take its shape, a Czech silencer and fifty rounds of ammunition. He loaded the gun, slipped a dozen rounds into his cigarette case under the specially made spring clip, put the tin back carefully in the case, locked the case.

He carried the weapon shielded by metal because some customs posts in the more sophisticated countries had X-ray apparatus beneath the counters on which passengers innocently put their luggage for inspection. The outline of a gun was immediately seen – but who bothered themselves about a tin of biscuits?

He poured himself four fingers of neat whisky, drank it, took out two pills, one white, the other green – the booster to pour the adrenalin through his blood and keep him awake with no more bad effects than a slight headache and a dry skin, for twelve hours after he'd swallowed it; the stabilizer that would slow down his metabolism to normal.

This was like driving a car with one foot on the accelerator, and the other on the brake, but it was better than not driving. It did his heart no good at all, which was perhaps why he never ran upstairs, but it kept him in business. He'd take both pills before he met Dr Love that evening. He wasn't sure how busy they'd be, or for how long; and he wanted all his wits about him. He felt in his left lapel where two more pills were sewn into the lining. As he did so, he caught sight of himself again in the mirror. He *was* growing older. His face was fuzzed at the edges, like a photograph out of focus. His eyes were flecked with yellow. He was a hard and tough and efficient killer, but not quite so hard, tough and efficient as he had been, for now he sometimes imagined what the men he killed felt like, just before they died.

And what happened to him, when he grew too old – or too slow? He was like a gladiator, he thought, fighting a lion every day, twice with matinées, and the free list suspended. The only snag was that the same gladiator had to keep facing new lions; your enemies were always young. But if you owned the freehold of the arena, you could afford to sit out any fight you thought you might not win.

He would have to start looking for something else soon, while he still could. But what would it be? Some pensioned-off job in a remote, run-down British Embassy, examining passports, or giving lectures to black men on the Shakespeare country? That's if he were lucky. If he weren't, he'd end up in some unmarked grave that no one wanted to know anything about.

Like the one he proposed to dig up that night.

The reception in the Musée de L'Armée was fixed for three o'clock. Love had a horror of marching there in a kind of school crocodile, as Dr Plugge had proposed, and so walked on his own across the bridge, over the hurrying brown river, where the green and yellow and blue buses waited under the wall of the mosque. To the right lay the Archaeological Museum, with its empty green-tiled pool and rusty, bunged-up fountains, a statue without a head, stone Syrian lions beneath flapping Syrian flags.

Opposite it, the Army Museum stood in about an acre of garden. Inside, cases of ancient Arab swords, of muskets and mortars, and photographs of unidentified tanks in the desert adorned the walls. Outside, lay two aeroplanes with the black, white, and green roundel of the United Arab Republic on wings and fuselage stained by bird droppings.

To avoid the other doctors who filed through the dark building with obedient exclamations of wonder and interest, Love walked round outside looking at the old Panhard and Renault trucks which had been crudely sprayed khaki, even to the tyres. The sun beat back painfully from the gravel chips on which they stood. There were plaques in front of each vehicle, each ancient cannon, like tombstones in a cemetery of war.

The garden was overgrown, untended, shaded by fir trees; it all seemed rather sad, a monument to a martial ability that had fled away. Twice in recent years, in 1948 and 1967, the Syrians had been at war with the Israelis, and on both occasions they had worn more tread from their tank tracks in retreat than advance.

As Love paused, he felt a pluck at his right coat-sleeve. Beside him stood a young man in a white drip-dry raincoat, with dark hair above a friendly, pleasant face.

'Excuse me, sir,' he began. 'Are you with this party?'

'Yes,' said Love.

'Then I wonder if you could help me? I'm looking for a Dr Jason Love.'

'Why?' asked Love. Who was this character? A creditor? The man from the Pru?

The man paused.

'I am from the administrator of the Clinic. I understand that Dr Love was seeking him or the superintendent this morning, because he thought we have there one of his patients.'

'That's right,' said Love. 'I was.'

'You? Oh, then my search has ended. My name is Ahmed. I have a car outside. Perhaps you would come with me to the administrator?'

'Certainly,' said Love. 'Are you a doctor?'

'No. A student.'

'Of what?'

'Foreign affairs.'

'I see. Well, I'd better just tell them I am leaving.'

'It is unnecessary, Dr Love. We'll be back within half an hour. The next engagement in your itinerary is not till half past three, just across the road in the Archaeological Museum. I'll bring you back.'

'In that case, let's not hang about.'

They went out, past crowds praying in the mosque, with priests chanting extracts from the Koran. A blue Dodge, white curtains drawn over the rear window against the sunshine, waited in the street, its engine running.

Ahmed opened the rear door, and they both climbed in. The driver set off between sweetmeat sellers, and old men trying on second-hand clothes at the side of the road, past touts for the country buses that plied the desert as far as Beirut and Amman.

'Is this the way to the Clinic?' asked Love. He had a poor sense of direction, but he could not remember this road from his visit that morning.

'We are seeing the administrator at his house,' explained Ahmed. 'He is just now off duty.'

Love settled back against the cushions. There was a strong smell of sweat and oil from Ahmed's hair. Love felt drowsy; he would like an early night. Then he remembered what Parkington wanted him to do, and all thoughts of sleep left him. The car turned down into the bazaar and stopped.

'We will have to walk the rest,' said Ahmed. 'The road is too narrow.'

He led Love past the same shops he had seen that morning – or was it that they only looked the same? – and then up a flight of stone stairs, between a silversmith and a silk merchant.

Ahmed knocked on a door powdery with age and grey paint, and then turned the handle.

A man sat at a desk. He could have been any age from twenty-one to forty. He had dark hair, eyes the colour of melting tar and very white teeth, but then so had most of the men Love had seen in Damascus so far.

'Dr Love,' said Ahmed and went out silently, leaving the two men together.

'Are you the administrator?' asked Love.

The man inclined his head slightly and pressed the tips of his spatulate fingers together.

'Yes, Doctor. Your interest in the patient, in whose room you were found this morning, has been communicated to me, and I thought the best thing would be if we could meet. Please take a seat.'

He held out his hand. Love sat down in an armchair under the slow turning blades of the fan, took out a packet of Gitanes, offered one to the administrator, lit one himself, put the packet on the desk.

The room was sparsely furnished. A Persian carpet warmed the bare stone floor. The walls were colour-washed in pink. The administrator leaned back in his swivel chair that creaked with his weight, took up a letter opener in the form of a Damascus steel blade and began to pare his nails with it.

'As I understand it, Doctor – and I may be quite wrong – you used to be the doctor of a girl who looked remarkably like the patient in the room you entered today. Is that so?'

'No,' Love corrected himself. 'I know the girl in that room. Though she's never been a patient of mine, her father is. And I've known that girl for years. She's Clarissa Head. There's been some ghastly mistake.'

The administrator smiled. He leaned forward, threw the blade on the table, clasped his hands together and pulled as though he wished to extract his fingers from their palms.

'With all respect, Doctor, you are wrong. You have made the mistake, not a ghastly one, but a very easy one. Poor Miss Head did die. She never recovered consciousness. I know this, because Dr Hanania is a friend of mine, and he was very upset. She was a pretty girl.'

'*Is* a pretty girl,' said Love.

'*Please*, Doctor,' said the administrator in a more pained voice. 'You do not understand. The English girl, Miss Head, was buried on the seventeenth of June. There is a death certificate. There is a burial plot held in perpetuity by the British Embassy. There is no argument there at all. None.

'This girl in hospital, the one you have confused with the English girl, is in fact Armenian. She speaks English, but she is most certainly not Miss Head.

'Look, does *this* convince you?'

The administrator pushed a buff folder across the desk.

Love opened it.

A small passport-size photograph of Clarissa Head looked up at him from a page of medical notes written in French. Or was this Clarissa? *Could* it be someone else? Was it not possible that some other girl resembled her so closely that in his haste he had been mistaken? After all, he had not seen Clarissa for at least a year. Doubt showed in his face. Then he shook his head.

'I'm sorry,' he said, 'but you haven't convinced me.'

'It is regrettable that you should persist in the misapprehension, Doctor.'

The administrator sat back with a sigh, like a housemaster who has failed to extract a confession from a boy who he believed had smoked one Woodbine in the dormitory after lights out. Really, how obdurate some people could be.

'If you persist in this view, there is nothing more for me to say, Doctor. But it is quite wrong. All I can do is to repeat that.'

'Why is there a guard on her door?' asked Love.

'Her family have not always favoured the present government, and in view of the very considerable wealth and influence that they can exert, not only in Syria but in other Arab countries, it could be serious politically if anything happened to her.'

'Anything?'

'Anything. We live in strange times, Doctor. It is my duty to take precautions in a case like hers.'

'It's my duty to see her again,' said Love. 'I know she is Clarissa Head.'

But did he – or was he only trying to convince himself? Doubt dug blunt needles into him.

'I'm sorry, Doctor. That would be impossible. She is being moved shortly to a clinic in Geneva. She should have left last week, but we required to book the whole of the first-class compartment on an Air France Caravelle, and that is very hard to book completely without some notice. So we've had to wait, but I believe there is a plane this evening.'

'I could see her before she goes,' persisted Love.

The man smiled a sad, wintry smile as though at the prevarications of a particularly idiot child.

'No, Doctor, she is someone else's patient. I admit she bears some similarity to the unfortunate Miss Head, but that is all. I thought it best to invite you here to tell you, and so save you any false hopes that Miss Head was still alive. Now my colleague will take you back to the Army Museum.'

Love stood up.

'Look,' he began. 'I know as well as you do that this girl is not an Armenian. She *is* Clarissa Head. And I'm going to the British Embassy again to tell them.'

The administrator smiled.

'As you please, Doctor. You recall the Roman quotation – "They say, what say they? Let them say." If you wish to believe that, no one can change your mind for you. But your embassy will only corroborate what I have already told you.'

He held out one hand, and with the other pressed a buzzer on his desk. Ahmed opened the door.

'The doctor's ready to leave,' said the administrator. 'I hope you enjoy your stay with us, I have warm memories of my own time in London some years ago when I studied what we call Jewish engineering.'

'Jewish engineering?' repeated Love. 'What's that?'

'A Syrian joke. Otherwise, business administration. Now, good day to you. Or as we say here, go in peace.'

Love walked up through the souk, Ahmed bobbing at his side. Could he be mistaken? Was he making an idiot of himself? He climbed into the back of the Dodge, and the car pulled away from the crush of shabby touts who wanted him to see their damask, their silver napkin rings, their cedarwood carvings.

As they sped through the bazaar to the Archaeological Museum, he felt in his pocket for his cigarettes. Damn. He'd left them on the administrator's desk. Ahmed saw the movement, smiled.

'Here they are, Doctor,' he said, and handed over the familiar blue and white packet. 'I thought you'd forgotten them – and French cigarettes are too rare to lose.'

'Thank you,' said Love; really, these people were very friendly. Maybe he *was* wrong? He almost wanted to think he was, because everything would then be so much simpler, but inside he knew, still he wasn't.

He was late for the lecture, but that would not be the first time, or the last. And at least there wouldn't be a test afterwards to discover how much or how little he had heard. What hell to be a boy, back at school again, he thought, as he eased himself thankfully into one of the back benches near a case full of headless statues.

He sat through Dr Suleiman's talk, his mind many miles away. How could Clarissa have been involved in such a mistake of identity? A doctor had seen her body, so had the Embassy secretary – yet here she was, still alive. And why should the administrator of the hospital be so sure she was someone else? How could she be when Love knew who she was? And what did he do now? Go back to Jackson at the Embassy or approach Dr Suleiman after the lecture?

Dr Suleiman suddenly bowed and sat down. Love clapped

dutifully and mechanically. He couldn't remember a word the man had said. He stood up with the others and missed his chance of speaking to Suleiman, because he went out through a side door. Love walked back to his hotel on his own.

Was he winning or losing? He'd come with a very simple errand – to photograph the grave of a patient's daughter – and now, already, he was being drawn into a vortex of suspicion and intrigue. He wished he were back in Somerset where the greatest complication was that he might run over a rabbit in a high-hedged lane or disturb a nesting skylark underfoot if he took a short cut across the Quantocks. He almost expected some emissary from the hospital or the Embassy to be waiting for him in the lobby of the Omayad with their apologies for the mistake and a convincing explanation, but the only people were a deputation from North Vietnam, small men with Chinese faces and yellow skins, wearing identical fawn raincoats and silk scarves, and chattering in high-pitched voices.

He went up to his room, poured himself a double Bacardi and stood looking out at the hillside behind the hotel. Then he took off his jacket and shoes and lay back on the bed, hands folded beneath his head, the reading light switched off. Presently, he slept. He was more tired than he had realized.

When he awoke, the heat had deserted the day and lights were already flickering dimly on the far side of the road, like fireflies on the foothills.

He remembered a story he had heard of one of the rulers of the city in the twelfth century. This man had kept a lion as a pet, and one evening after dinner with his friends, he pushed a sheep into the yard so that his guests could see how speedily the lion devoured it. But to everyone's astonishment the sheep butted the lion – and chased it all round the courtyard.

Love hoped this was a propitious omen, for he had little liking for the task ahead. He looked at his watch; seventhirty. He swung his legs off the bed, pulled on his shoes and his jacket, splashed some cold water on his face, ran a comb through his hair and went downstairs.

As did not surprise him in a neo-Communist country,

there was no choice of courses for dinner, only the set menu; some surprisingly good shrimps in a creamy sauce, a tough steak, a sideplate of dried peas, then ice cream and coffee.

After dinner, he chatted briefly in the lounge to some other doctors, avoided an invitation to make up a four for bridge, and took the lift to the third floor. Then he walked down a flight, in case anyone was following him. I'm becoming as bad as all the rest, he thought. I'm getting in a state where I can do nothing straightforward. Soon I'll always jump off a bus to catch a taxi, change from one car to another – and yet who was chasing him? Was he only chasing himself?

He let himself into his room.

Parkington was already sitting in the easy chair, smoking a cigarette, with the reading light directed towards the door so that he was in the shadow.

'Don't you ever knock?' asked Love.

Parkington shook his head. The pills were working well; he felt keen and sharp and well-shaved. It was only as the effect wore off that you felt you were pushing a hundred and four with fallen arches and a cleft palate.

'I never waste energy,' he said. 'And what have you been up to?'

Love sat on the edge of the bed and told him.

'Now how do you propose finding out who's in that grave?' he asked, as though he had not already guessed Parkington's answer.

'We're going to dig it up,' replied Parkington briefly.

'You must be bloody mad,' retorted Love irritably. 'How can we possibly get away with digging up a grave in a public cemetery? Why don't we go back to the British Embassy? I'll see this fifth secretary fellow and explain there's been a balls-up, that I think the girl is still alive.'

'You only *think* now,' interrupted Parkington quickly. 'You *knew* before.'

'I know still,' said Love. 'Or, at least, I'm practically certain she is Clarissa. I haven't seen her for the last year, but I'll stake anything that Clarissa's the girl I saw in the hospital today. Despite what the administrator said.'

'But if you're so keen on going back to the Embassy, why didn't you go on your own?' asked Parkington. 'You could have done, but you didn't. Because you knew damn well what would happen if you did.

'The fellow would listen to you very politely and then say that this is not in his jurisdiction. He has the certificate of death for Miss Clarissa Head, and on what conceivable grounds can he request an exhumation? And how long would it take for some Syrian Civil Servant to agree to have a body dug up? By the time they did, there would be nothing but a coffin full of dust.'

'But digging it up is like Burke and Hare,' protested Love.

'Not quite,' corrected Parkington. 'They snatched bodies. We're just trying to see whether a body is in that particular grave.'

'How can you be sure we won't be caught?' asked Love. 'What's my excuse if something goes wrong? Here I am, a doctor, a guest in Syria, and instead of going to some reception tonight, with the Minister of Science, I'm helping a British spy to desecrate the dead. What kind of excuse can I give?'

'Nothing,' said Parkington. 'The only thing is that we won't get caught. I know it's against all your training. The Hippocratic Oath, what Aesculapius did at Troy and what Galen practised in Rome. The whole shooting match.

'But there are times when the only distance between two points is a straight line. This is one of those times, Doctor. Our only chance to find out quickly whether anyone is buried in that grave is to scrape away the earth and have a gander ourselves. When are you leaving with this convention?'

'Friday afternoon. If I'm not caught digging up a body.'

'At least it's not a Muslim's body. Only a Christian's. Funny thing. At school I was taught the Crusaders were the heroes and the Turks and Infidels and Muslims were the bads who wanted to despoil our holy places.

'But over here it's the Christians who were the bads. Just depends on whose side you're on, what history books you read.'

'And who wrote them,' added Love. 'How do you suggest we dig it up?'

'In the usual way. With shovels.'

'Have you got any?'

'Yes, two. But they're not things I carry about openly.' Parkington held up a briefcase.

'I had to saw off the handles so they'd fit in here. I also brought a sheet of canvas, which you can carry, and a few bamboo sticks, to make a wind-breaker. This will screen us from the road.'

'What are you going to wear?' asked Love, as though it were a social occasion.

'What I've got on,' said Parkington. 'Sweater, these old trousers, rubber gloves, so we leave no prints. I've also got a couple of pairs of special glasses.'

'What's special about them?' asked Love, remembering the electronic gadgets dear to MacGillivray's heart. 'Do they send messages or shoot bullets?'

'Nothing like that at all. But they are inflammable. Which can be quite useful if, say, we *were* seen and people started looking for two men with glasses. We could destroy them with a match. Also, if you throw them hard enough, the frames explode. Harmless enough, but they could give someone a surprise.

'They give a three-fold magnification, which makes them bloody hard to see out of. But equally it makes your eyes appear much larger, quite alters the shape of your face. Here's your pair. Wear them when we leave the hotel.'

He handed Love a pair of heavily rimmed glasses. They might come in useful if he had any small print to read; he hoped it wouldn't be written at the bottom of a charge sheet.

'Take your passport,' said Parkington. 'It's useful to prove who you are. Though I hope to God we don't have to.'

Love put his passport, his travellers' cheques, into a yellow oilskin pouch, unbuttoned his shirt, put the pouch next to his skin, buttoned up his shirt. He pulled on a pair of surgical rubber gloves – the only gloves he had with him – stuffed two handkerchiefs in his trouser pocket, a pencil torch in the inside pocket of his jacket, turned out the light.

'I've got the car parked under your window near the rubbish dump at the back,' said Parkington. 'I'll go out the front door. Give me five minutes and then come out after me. Don't forget to wear the glasses.'

'Check,' said Love and put them on. He felt like a goldfish peering through a bowl.

Parkington left the door open, so there would not be the sound of it slamming twice. His feet made no noise on the carpet. In the next room, someone was flushing the lavatory and then hawked noisily. Radio music played in another room; thin Arabic flutes, with the chords rising nervously. Love knew how they felt.

Love watched the minute hand of his watch move slowly round the dial. After five minutes, he went out, put the bedroom key under the carpet, walked down the stairs to the first landing. Two policemen in khaki uniforms, revolvers in black holsters at their belts, were speaking earnestly to the receptionist.

As Love watched, the man turned round as though to pick a key from a hook. But it wasn't there. Was it the key of his room? He felt his mouth dry with guilty apprehension. The policemen walked towards the lift. Love waited until the lift swung past him, then took off his glasses so that he could see the steps and ran down the back service stairs and out of a side door next to a shop that sold heavy machinery. He glanced in at the unlit showroom with its grey lathes and red oil lamps, but no one was reflected in the dark window from the other side of the road; so, presumably, no one had seen him leave.

Head down, hands in his trouser pockets, he walked around the building. Parkington's green Renault was parked with its lights off, one of half a dozen other cars, glistening with evening dew.

Love climbed in. Parkington said nothing, let in the gear. They took the road out towards the hills. He wasn't wearing his glasses either.

'Do you know where the cemetery is?' asked Love.

'I bought a street map in the souk when I got the shovels. It's only ten minutes. Once we're there, can you find the grave?'

'Easily – so long as I don't wear your bloody glasses.'

Sodium vapour street lights painted the night pale green. A few men sat drinking coffee in a café; at an all-night garage, mechanics were servicing a car on a ramp; otherwise, the city seemed deserted.

Soon the stucco houses fell away, and the road grew rough beyond the city boundaries. They nearly ran down a man jogging along on a donkey, and an old truck, with only oil lamps in front and none behind. Parkington turned right and left and right again, and stopped. In front of the car, the railings Love had seen earlier in the day marched away rigidly into the darkness.

Parkington backed the car until it faced the faint phosphorescent glow in the sky that was Damascus. He parked it beneath a cluster of cedar trees, switched off his engine, climbed out. From the boot he took a wide roll of thin black cloth, signalled to Love to take the other end. They unwound it over the car. Now no passing headlights would reflect on any bright paint or chromium.

'Now, on glasses, and no talking,' said Parkington, locking the car. 'Where exactly is this grave?'

'God knows,' replied Love, putting on the spectacles.

'But I thought you did, too.'

'I did – but I didn't come in this way this morning.'

He peered through the railings. Gravestones pointed white fingers out of the rough tufty grass, paths stretched out in neat rectangles, their gravel chips pale as teeth in a dead man's smile. Then Love saw a grave he recognized; an angel scantily clad, holding up a marble urn to catch the rain.

'It's over there,' he said.

Parkington opened his briefcase. The bright steel blades of the shovels glittered in the moonlight. Love held the roll of canvas and four bamboo stakes, while Parkington took out a coil of nylon rope, tied a loop and threw it expertly over a spike. They climbed up one side, over the top, and down the other, then walked hunched up, like men under fire, to offer the least possible target to any watcher, padding soft-footed through the grass, until they reached the grave.

Love unwound his roll of canvas, pushed the bamboo sticks into the ground, draped the canvas around them. They bent down by the edge of the newly-turned soil of the grave. Before they started to dig, Love looked across the tombs; there was no sign or sound of anything alive, not even a bird. Parkington handed him a shovel, pointed to one end, while he went to the other. He pushed the blade into the earth; it was surprisingly soft.

They worked in silence. A thin rain began to fall, mixing with the sweat that ran down their faces unchecked. The coffin was not so deep as Love had imagined it would be; possibly the earth was rocky underneath. His spade struck wood jarringly.

Parkington began to scrape away the earth from his end, until the lid lay bare. It was of plain, unvarnished wood, held down by eight brass screws. Parkington took a ratchet screwdriver from his pocket, bent over the first screw. He did not use a torch, but moved the screwdriver around the head of each screw carefully until it clicked into the slot. The screws came out easily. They had not been tightened.

They lifted up the lid a few inches from one side. Then Parkington took a quick look above the screen. The graveyard was still empty. He bent down again, took out a torch, flashed it briefly, under the half-open lid.

They saw an arm pale as wax under a robe, saffron coloured, thick and coarse, like fustian. Parkington moved the torch; it showed a strong and hairy hand, much browner than the arm, the palm ridged with dark lines. He snapped off the torch. What the hell was this? A monk in the coffin? Love levered desperately at the lid, but the earth still pressed down on it too heavily on one side for him to open it any further. He motioned to Parkington to scrape away more earth. They both stood up to ease their aching backs.

At that moment the whole cemetery seemed to explode into a giant circle of light.

A voice said quietly in English: 'Put your hands above your heads, drop the shovels and come out towards me.'

Love straightened slowly. The light, magnified by his absurd glasses, blinded him. If he moved quickly, he felt his back would break in two. He was still holding the shovel in his right hand, his eyes narrowed against the incandescent brilliance of the floodlight. Parkington threw his shovel down on the wet earth.

'Get moving,' ordered the voice behind the light. Love recognized it with embarrassment. It belonged to the administrator of the Clinic. Now what the hell could he say to him to explain his behaviour?

'As I thought,' the administrator went on. 'Two English-men. One, claiming to be a doctor, and the other man – well, we'll soon see who he is.'

He stepped into the floodlight blaze. In his right hand he held a gold-tipped cane. On the other side, moving with him, was a man in shabby battledress. He held a rifle crooked under his arm, rather like a gamekeeper. Lady Chatterley's lover. Well, he certainly wasn't his. Love looked at Park-ington. Parkington looked at Love.

Parkington's face was a mask, streaked with sweat; it held no recognition, no emotion, nothing.

'You get out first,' said Parkington, 'Age before beauty.'

'Pearls before swine,' ended the man with the gold cane. 'Dorothy Parker, I believe.'

'Correct,' said Parkington. 'I see you are well read.'

Love was out now, standing on the hard, firm earth near the grave. His eyes were more accustomed to the glare. Be-hind the dazzling brilliance of the floodlight, he could see the faint thin outline of the fence. Their car lay somewhere beyond that. So did their freedom.

Parkington turned and began to climb laboriously up over the mound of soft, yellow earth. Suddenly, he slipped and slithered forward, pushing out his hands to steady himself. He reached up, pulled off his glasses, threw them away in a gesture of defeat. As they hit the ground they began to crackle like a jumping jack.

The man with the rifle aimed wildly at them, fired. There was another crack like a stock whip and the light dimmed. For a second it glowed redly like a tiny sunset, then the dark-ness soaked it up.

'Run!' bellowed Parkington, ramming his Mauser back into its holster.

Love threw his shovel like a clumsy javelin in the general direction of the light. A cry of pain and the ring of a rifle, a bullet singing harmlessly away, and he was past them and running hard, bounding over the graves. He tripped over a loose stone and fell headlong on the gravel, got up painfully, ran on more carefully. He reached the railings and began to haul himself up and over. Parkington was doing the same thing about twenty feet to his right.

The railings trembled as they both jumped down on the

other side. For a second, the earth felt warm and moist to Love's spread hands as he landed. Then they were running to the Renault.

Parkington pulled out his keys as he ran, unlocked the driver's door, ripped away the black cloth, and they were inside. He pressed the starter. It was a second before the engine caught and Love prayed no one had attached a booby trap to the ignition. The prayer was answered; they hadn't.

The engine fired. Parkington threw in the clutch, and they were away, bumping over the rough ground to the right, without any lights. He waited until they were around the first roundabout and heading away from Damascus before he put on his headlights.

Love glanced through the rear window; nothing was following them. They overtook two buses both with roofs thick with carpet bags, tin trunks, baskets lashed with rope all wedged against drums of diesel oil, leaking slightly, for the long desert run to Beirut. Then the road stretched away into the blue night, towards the rim of hills waiting on the horizon.

'Where are we heading for?' asked Love.

It was obviously impossible to go back to the hotel, and yet what about his luggage, what about the convention? How could this behaviour be explained away, not only to the Syrians but to his colleagues?

'We're taking the yellow brick road,' Parkington announced cheerfully. 'Like the Wizard of Oz. Man, I'd thought they'd caught us. Lucky they were so sure they had. Lucky I'd got the glasses, too, that you were belly-aching about. Otherwise I couldn't have shot out that light.'

'But how does that help us now? We've made a balls of everything. Far better to have gone to the Embassy, as I suggested, than end up like this, on the run. That was the hospital administrator. I saw him in his office a few hours ago – and now he catches me digging up a grave. I'll be lucky if the General Medical Council don't haul me up for this. They will if they ever hear of it.'

'He must have guessed you weren't satisfied with his explanation. But why? And how did we slip up?'

'By ever imagining we could get away with this lunatic scheme of yours. That's how. So what's the next move?

What maniac idea have you got to get us out of this?'

'There's a place about thirty miles away. Maloula. It has a shrine of some sort in memory of St Tekla. Apparently she set off for Damascus to see St Paul, and her family chased after her to bring her back. She reached the mountains at Maloula and they split open and let her through. She was so impressed she didn't go any farther.

'There's a tiny hotel now, near where she died. I've been paying for a couple of rooms in it for the last two weeks, as a Professor Wilbraham.

'If we're rumbled there – and we will be eventually because all these villages have at least one police informer – we'll move on to Homs. I've also rooms booked there just in case. Name of Scarsdale, schoolmaster on sick leave.'

'You think of everything,' said Love ironically. 'Pity you didn't think it was a better idea to go to the British Embassy about the grave.'

'I did think,' said Parkington, 'but it was a bloody worse idea. Now at least we know who's buried there.'

'Speak for yourself,' said Love. 'He's no one I know. A monk in a saffron robe.'

'Well, we'll find out what kind of monks around here wear saffron robes. We'll build it up gradually,' said Parkington.

'All this takes time,' replied Love, 'and that's one thing we haven't got. I'm supposed to be listening to lectures, not digging up graves and chasing all over the desert.'

'So long as you're not *in* the bloody grave, you should worry. Now shut up moaning and keep an eyeball cocked to the rear. I want to know if we're being followed.'

Chapter Seven

Covent Garden, London, June 28th; the Syrian Desert and Maloula, June 28th–29th

MacGillivray polished his reading glasses with a Kleenex tissue, and undid the knot in the pink tape that tied the buff folder on his desk. Inside, lay a mass of flimsies typed in double space, all without any attributions. These were the summaries of the overnight Intelligence reports that had been decoded in the huge, air-conditioned decoding room beneath the Cenotaph in Whitehall, and then brought round in a sealed satchel by a dispatch rider, marked for his eyes only. To minimize the risk of any source being identified, none had signatures, or any addresses, only the dates.

The first confirmed that money earned through drug smuggling in Hong Kong was, in fact, being used to finance Communist-inspired so-called students' riots in the Colony. That was nothing new. The man who sent this must have been reading the Sunday papers; he should have saved the cable charges for a more worthy cause, such as getting drunk, thought MacGillivray sourly. The people he had to work with these days ...

He screwed up the sheet irritably, tossed it into the metal wastepaper basket by his desk. Every hour the basket was emptied, the contents incinerated, and the ashes shredded. All very sound security – but why, he sometimes wondered, were not more thorough checks made on the men who did the burning – and the men who sent the signals? This was a subject close to his heart, but always, when he raised it, he was assured that checks were made at regular intervals; it sounded almost medicinal to him.

He glanced at the second and third reports; nothing startling in either of them. Then the fourth caught his eye, and he read it through with mounting gloom and dismay. Irritation, and anguish at what Sir Robert would say, spread like indigestion through his stomach. He opened a drawer in his desk and took out a Digestif Rennie, but even this could bring no comfort.

The signal had come from the British Embassy in Damascus.

INFORMATIVE. Two British subjects disappeared, presumably together, from Damascus overnight in unusual circumstances. One, Commander Richard Mass Parkington, ex Royal Navy, has left the New Omayad Hotel without notice, also without paying his bill. Syrian

Rent-a-Car have further reported to the Embassy that a Renault Dauphine SL 27568 hired in Parkington's name on self-drive basis from them three days ago has not been returned to them today as agreed.

Second British subject, Dr Jason Love of Bishop's Combe, Somerset, attending convention of doctors at the New Omayad, has apparently only visited one lecture and is also missing from hotel.

Local police contacts claim both these characters were found allegedly interfering with a grave in Christian cemetery outside city. Police refuse to provide details which grave involved. Quick examination shows trampling in earth in north-east corner of graveyard where British subjects are buried.

Must further inform you that Dr Love visited Embassy, speaking to fifth secretary, regarding death in motor accident of British subject, Clarissa Head, also from Bishop's Combe, Somerset. Miss Head's grave is in British area of cemetery.

MacGillivray put down the paper, smoothed his blunt fingers over its rough crinkly surface. He knew Love; he had used him once, long ago, for a trifling affair when he didn't realize he was being used. He had used him more recently, when he had asked him to go as a delegate to a malaria conference in Teheran – and try at the same time to discover what had happened to a professor of classics who was also a British agent.

Their lives had crossed once or twice since – but what the hell was he up to now? And why the devil should he and Parkington be digging up a grave?

He looked through the double-glazed windows at the pigeons desecrating the Duke of Bedford's crest above the covered market-place; *Che Sera Sera*, whatever will be, will be. He had been long enough in the business to know that this was not necessarily so; it represented a simplification he could not always accept. He pressed a button on the intercom to connect him with the liaison bureau of the Foreign Office.

'Mac here,' he said when the voice he expected answered him. 'Just received that message from Damascus about the two disappearances. How long can you keep this out of the papers?'

'Depends on whether any wives are involved, or families. They may start getting agitated because they haven't heard from their husbands, or whatever.'

'There are no wives involved here,' replied MacGillivray. 'But it would help me a lot if you could pass the word to the Embassy in Damascus that nothing will be gained by premature publicity. For as long as they can stall. Say a minimum of forty-eight hours.'

'Will do,' said the voice and hung up.

MacGillivray screwed up the paper, threw it into the basket, skimmed quickly through the next half-dozen messages, and then read the last three more carefully.

The first came from a stringer, a part-time agent, a Eurasian police inspector in Karachi. He had been useful in the past with details of methods used by airline stewards to smuggle gold. Once, he had uncovered an ingenious attempt by a one-legged man with a completely false leg made of gold. Another case had concerned a suit of fourteenth-century armour being exported from a London antique dealer. This had turned out to be a suit of gold sprayed with metallic paint. But while his latest message had nothing to do with gold, it could still be valuable.

Attended village demonstration yesterday 22nd which possibly valueless but disconcerting here. At 12.00 hrs, our time, 20 to 30 men usually in coffee shop suddenly seized staves and sticks and set about three Belgians photographing building. The Belgians escaped by car but greatly shocked by experience.

Some anti-British manifestation that had gone wrong, thought MacGillivray, and yet he wondered why. He knew the village; he had passed it every day years before when he was living in Drigh Road in Karachi, near the enormous hangar built to house the airship R101, which had never flown farther than Beauvais in Northern France.

He could understand a demonstration against some class, such as money-lenders, or even when privilege was involved, but why beat up a handful of Belgians? He put the memo on one side and read the next, which had come from another part-time contact near Bahrein, in the Persian Gulf.

At 11.44 hours our time on 22nd, five British subjects were stoned as they passed through village, four miles north of Bahrein boundary. Attacked men were assaulted at traffic intersection. They reported that their attackers acted like sleepwalkers. Police here puzzled by outbreak which not in usual line of anti-British-American-imperialist demonstration.

The third report came from Mali, in the Maldive Islands in the Indian Ocean, where the RAF maintained a refuelling post at Gan. Here, at four minutes past twelve on that same day, six members of a gang of coolies engaged in digging a monsoon ditch had suddenly attacked the Australian surveyor. Then, apparently, they had been quite willing and ready to return to their work. None of them could give any explanation for their conduct.

Three unusual, uncharacteristic outbursts in three places, many hundreds of miles apart, yet apparently linked by time. He pressed another button on his intercom. His secretary, Miss Jenkins, replied.

'What is the time difference between Bahrein, Karachi and the Maldive Islands?' he asked her.

He heard her rustling through pages of a reference book, and then her Welsh voice spoke again.

'Taking Karachi as the central point, when it's noon there, it will be eleven forty-four in Bahrein, and twelve four in the Maldives.'

'Thank you.' MacGillivray flipped up the switch.

It was as he thought. Something must have happened at exactly the same moment in these three places, to act as a catalyst for these demonstrations. But what – and why? Could it be something to do with the sun? What other connecting link could join these outbreaks?

It took him a few minutes to think of the radio. He pressed the button again for Miss Jenkins. This time she appeared in the door of his office in her working clothes; a dark tweed skirt and white blouse, the papers of her shorthand notebook primly held back by an elastic band. The changing seasons

116

of the year seemed to pass her by; she appeared to wear the same severe clothes summer and winter. Or maybe it was only that they looked the same.

'Ah, Miss Jenkins,' said MacGillivray, as though he had not seen her already that day, 'two things. First, signals to the senders of these last three messages. Ask them to reply whether the rioters concerned had access to a radio. And, if so, what programme they were listening to.'

'That last part should be difficult,' she suggested hesitantly. MacGillivray shook his head. He didn't like people suggesting difficulties; they invariably argued for themselves.

'Not if we can find the station. If these fellows at the coffee house, say, had the radio going all day as is very likely, tuned to the Voice of Islam or some such thing, then it's simply a matter of just checking back what the station was broadcasting at that time. Oh, and ask whether these attacks were isolated. Were any other westerners involved in surrounding areas? Mark the signal most immediate, reply within the hour.'

After Miss Jenkins had left the room, he stood looking out over the lorries unloading fruit in the market outside. When the intercom buzzed on his desk he was so far away in his thoughts that the unexpected noise surprised him; he had to row his way back to the present. He pressed the button and Sir Robert's voice filled the room with indignation.

'I suppose you've read this thing from Damascus?'

'I was coming to see you about it, sir,' replied MacGillivray, not entirely truthfully. He wasn't, but now he would have to.

'What about the girl?' asked Love. 'Clarissa.'

'What about her?' said Parkington, changing gear.

'We can't leave her on her own.'

'Why not?'

'Don't be a bloody fool,' said Love angrily. 'How can we? I've been recognized by the hospital administrator. He already knows I'd been to the Clinic, in her room – and yet he claims she is officially dead. Can't you see we've put her life in danger now?'

'Don't mind her life. Think of ours.'

'I am. But she's the reason I got mixed up in this at all. We must take her to Maloula.'

'How can we?' asked Parkington practically. 'How are we going to get her out of the hospital, for one thing?'

'Easily,' said Love. 'Turn the car round.'

'Balls,' retorted Parkington.

'They're useful on occasion,' agreed Love. 'But not now. Turn the car.'

'You like this girl?' asked Parkington.

'I like all girls,' countered Love. 'Turn the bloody car.'

'OK. Have it your way, Galahad. But don't blame me this time if we do end up in the cells.'

Parkington swung the car round in a wide arc, their tyres skidding and spitting out small stones like gunfire.

'Now where?' he asked.

'The People's Clinic, off the Aleppo Road.'

'Can you remember where she is, inside the building?'

'Surely. The administrator told me she was being moved tonight.'

'Do you think she'll still be there?'

'I don't think anything,' said Love. 'I only hope.'

They were back in the outskirts of the city now, the cedar trees unexpectedly green in their headlamps. The Clinic loomed to their right, beyond a rash of tin huts, and the big concrete houses with their folded metal shutters. Two oil tankers were parked off the road. Beyond them, Love saw a wooden trellis structure like a miniature Eiffel Tower, topped by a metal box.

'That's our card of entry,' he said suddenly. 'The air-raid warning.'

'You may be right,' said Parkington. 'You can only be wrong.'

He stopped the car, switched off the lights. Dust swirled over them and was gone; the air felt cold and damp. A February evening in a Salford sidestreet.

'If we set off that alarm,' said Love, nodding towards the trellis, 'they'll think there's an Israeli air-raid. The radio's always talking about Israeli planes flying over Syria, so they're half ready to believe it. All the guards are bound to turn out, anyway, if only for a few minutes, until they realize it's a hoax. Which might give us long enough.'

'Do you think it will work?' asked Parkington dubiously.

'Like I said, I only hope,' retorted Love, and grinned.

He opened the cubby-hole of the dashboard, rooted about for a pair of pliers and a few odd lengths of wire. He snipped off the plastic insulation at each end, got out of the car, and climbed a barbed wire fence that surrounded the wooden tower. Two metal conduits containing electric cables were clipped to one end of the uprights. One led to the siren, the other to an inspection light with a wire netting grille around its globe. Halfway up this second conduit was a throw-over switch on a fuse box. Love turned back to Parkington.

'The siren's probably controlled from a police station somewhere, and the cable will be dead until they switch it on. But if we join this other wire from the light to the siren, you can simply switch on and the siren will sound.'

'Seems simple, the way you tell it.'

'It is. Well within your intellectual capabilities.'

'Mine?' asked Parkington, surprised.

'Yours. Because I suggest you do this now, while I go into the Clinic and see if I can find Clarissa. At least I know her, and where she was. It'll take you about five minutes to fix the siren which should be long enough for me to find her – if she's still there. Then turn on the siren and bring the car round to the back. I'll try and be waiting with Clarissa.'

'It's a bloody risk,' said Parkington dubiously.

'So's life,' replied Love. 'If you knew the number of terrible things that could happen to you with every breath you take, it's a wonder you breathe at all.'

'I'll take your word for it,' said Parkington. 'Into the Clinic, then, and do your best. Have you a gun?'

'No.'

'Well, take mine.'

He handed his Mauser to Love. As Love's hand closed around the comfortingly serrated feel of the butt, he suddenly remembered the advice in Murray's *Handbook to Syria* about the wisdom of carrying a gun.

He pushed it into his jacket pocket, began to walk smartly towards the Clinic. Half a dozen military ambulances were huddled together under a cluster of trees.

He walked past them, then round to the back of the Clinic, and up the metal fire escape; this seemed safer than risking the front door. That porter might remember him.

On the second landing, he pulled the fire door towards him, went in through it, closed it quietly. He was in an empty corridor that smelled of wax polish. Domed ceiling lights reflected from the polished brown lino. Somewhere a generator was humming, and the whole building trembled slightly like a great ship about to leave shore.

He walked along to the main landing, and the lino snapped at his heels with every step he took. The sentry had gone from outside Clarissa's room. Love turned the handle, pushed open the door. The room was in darkness, but sufficient light filtered through the curtains from street lamps outside for him to see that the bed was empty, and made. So she had been moved. But, where?

For a moment, his mind seemed to stand still as it does in nightmares, when you dream you are wading near the shore in a shallow green sea, and suddenly you turn and see a huge curving wave roaring in from the horizon to overwhelm and submerge you.

Love fought down a rising tide of alarm and despair, forcing himself to imagine what he would have done if he had been required to hide a patient in a small hospital. Where would he choose? She could be in any of the rooms, but equally he could not try all of them; he had no time, for one thing; and, for another, someone would be bound to question him.

The safest place would be in the operating theatre – or would it? She might find her way outside, or some surgeon who didn't know she was there might need the theatre.

No, that was no good. If he were trying to hide someone in a hospital, he would choose a psychiatric ward – or a mental ward, if he could find one – because people accepted what psychiatric patients said with latent reserve.

They might claim they were Napoleon, or a poached egg, the Emperor of Barbados or Nelson's Column; therefore, when they spoke the truth, they also received as little respect. The very fact of placing her in such a ward would discredit anything she said – and the more sensible her story seemed the more reluctant would everyone be to accept it.

Love glanced at his watch; two minutes until the siren

sounded, if Parkington were keeping to his timetable, and then she would almost certainly be under guard and any rescue attempt would be impossible.

He felt panic grow within him like a plant. He ran down the stairs, and then slowed when he saw a soldier outside a door on the landing. He nodded to the man, who saluted. Now he had barely ninety seconds left. On the wall hung a board with Arabic and English notices, listing the names of wards and private rooms. The third name down sounded the most promising.

LA SALLE NUMERO CINQ. RESERVEE A L'USAGE DES MALADES PSYCHIATRIQUES

Room Five. Where the hell was that? It must be a waiting room on that floor somewhere. He walked along the corridor; the numbers on the doors were 25, 26, 27. He was going the wrong way. He turned back. This seemed more hopeful: on one side the numbers read 24, 23, 22 and on the other, 1, 2, 3. He opened the door with the numeral five on it, switched on the light, closed the door carefully behind him.

Clarissa was sitting in a chair, asleep. She half struggled to her feet, blinking her eyes in the sudden glare.

'What's the matter?' she asked. 'Why, Dr Love!' Her face lit up with surprise and amazement as she recognized him.

'I've come to fetch you,' said Love.

'But how did you know I was here?'

She seemed to have no recollection that they had already seen each other earlier in the day.

'It must be at least a year since I last saw you – at that party Daddy gave. What are you doing in Damascus?'

'Right now, trying to get you out of here,' said Love. 'Don't ask me why, but grab your shoes and a coat and anything else you need. You're coming with me. You're not coming back here.'

'But why the hurry? What's happened? The doctor said I was going to another hospital. I've been waiting for him.'

'This doctor says you're moving. I'll tell you why later. Now, get your gear and come.'

Something in Love's urgency infected her. She was wear-

121

ing khaki slacks and bush jacket, like those issued to the Syrian Women's Army. She picked up an airline bag, and turned towards him.

'I'm already packed,' she said.

At that moment, the ululation of the air-raid siren trembled through the building and all the lights went out.

'What's that?' she asked, her face puckering with surprise.

'Nothing,' said Love, 'but it means we're too late to use the door. We're leaving by the window.'

Already, he heard feet in heavy boots drumming along the corridor, orders being shouted, doors opening and slamming shut.

Somewhere a child was crying, and fear sharpened women's voices. He locked the door, seized a cane-bottomed chair, jammed it under the door knob to give them another few seconds if the lock was shot away, turned out the light, and opened the windows. Cold night air blew in, heavy with the smell of oil.

'Do just what I say,' Love told her. 'We're going down the fire escape. There's no risk if you don't panic. Now – follow me.'

He vaulted over the windowsill, landed on the metal platform of the fire escape. Clarissa jumped after him. He caught her. She was heavier than he had imagined, and the platform trembled as they struggled for balance. Then, together, they were racing down the stairs, their feet ringing on the metal, diamond-shaped treads.

Suddenly a searchlight exploded on them like the sun, dazzling them. It was so close they could feel the heat in its rays. There was no hope of concealment now. Clarissa hung back, bewildered.

'Run!' Love shouted, and pulled her after him.

Men were shouting orders down in the darkness beyond the circle of blazing light. He pulled out Parkington's Mauser, fired down the beam, once, twice. The light went out, leaving a red glow from its carbon arcs.

Love blinked in the sudden blinding darkness, pushed the automatic back in his jacket pocket. He would have to run by feel until his eyes grew accustomed to the night. Ambulances were starting up, with dimmed blue headlights. On one a siren was wailing. Behind them, came a sudden bang-bang of anti-aircraft gunfire. Clarissa flagged.

'Don't go so fast,' she gasped. 'I'm dizzy. It's my first day up.'

Ahead of them in the darkness, Love could hear the ominous rattle of rifle bolts. Someone was shouting orders excitedly. A bullet ripped past them and blew dust out of the cement wall above his head. He pulled Clarissa back against him. Another bullet nicked the metal platform, making it ring like a huge gong.

Love had been surprised that she had no guards outside her bedroom. Maybe this was because the back of the building was adequately covered by sentries. It was obviously impossible to leave that way; they would have to go back inside the hospital and find another way out.

He felt for a doorhandle, pushed Clarissa in through the door and shut it behind him. They were on a landing of some kind; a blue emergency bulb burned dimly in the ceiling.

'What's happening?' asked Clarissa, leaning weakly against him. 'Why are the lights out? What's that banging?'

'Later,' said Love. 'Save your breath now for running.'

He looked around him desperately for a weapon other than Parkington's Mauser. He didn't wish to shoot again, unless he had to, for a bullet was the ultimate answer to any argument. Also, he had no quarrel with the guards, no quarrel with anyone. He was a doctor, dedicated to lengthening life, not to shortening it; all he wanted was to escape with Clarissa with a minimum of pain and commotion to anyone, including himself.

He moved forward into the main corridor and bumped into something cold and hard, hanging shoulder high on the wall. He felt a leather horizontal strap grip, a vertical metal cylinder. A fire extinguisher; well, this could be better than nothing. Not a lot, but a little.

Love unbuckled the strap, pulled down the cylinder, turned the nozzle away from him. There was a round, flat knob on the top to punch, held in place on its plunger by a split pin. He pulled out this pin, and, holding the extinguisher across his body, with Clarissa hanging on one arm, he walked along the corridor, and down the main stairs.

They were in darkness, and in the hall, under blue night lights, he could see shadowy figures in white, possibly orderlies, and three soldiers with rifles slung on their shoulders.

Concealment now was useless, but in the dimness and confusion Clarissa might just not be recognized until they were actually on the ground floor. He paused for a moment, for the soldiers were unslinging their rifles, rattling their bolts in an unwelcoming way.

What a ridiculous situation to be in, he thought, and for a moment the absurdity of it almost made him smile. Transfer this scene to Somerset, and what would he think if a Syrian doctor climbed up the fire escape into Minehead Hospital, set off an air-raid alarm and then attempted to kidnap a patient? At the very least, this would surely be a complicated question of ethics. At the worst, it would provoke some rather cold remarks: 'After all, old man, these are foreigners.' 'I mean, what can you expect? Eh?' All right, so he wasn't exactly upholding the traditions of Hippocrates and Galen. But what else could he do? And what would they have done in his place?

One of the men in white coats flashed a pocket torch up at them. At once, the man began to shout excitedly in some language Love could not understand. Even so, the message was hard to miss. Two soldiers raised their rifles to their shoulders and aimed at them. Love knew what a pheasant must feel like, looking down the barrels of the guns.

He kept on walking, for the same reason as the pheasant keeps on flying; there was nothing else he could do, and it was harder to hit a moving target. Surely they would not shoot without a further warning? Worse, he had to be nearer for the fire extinguisher to be of any use.

The first soldier fired.

The bullet hit a window behind them. Glass splintered in a mass of tinkling triangles. Love sniffed the once-familiar smell of burned cordite. That took him back a few years. Obliquely, he thought, that soldier will have to pour boiling water through his barrel to clean it. He should have held his fire. Then he was down on the bottom step.

'Wait!' he shouted. 'There's been a terrible mistake!'

His voice sounded thin and dry, like someone else's. The man in the white coat called up in English.

'Stand right where you are. If you move, you will be shot.'

'What the hell is this?' asked Love, in as brusque and authoritative a voice as he could manage. As he spoke, he punched the release knob of the fire extinguisher. A great fan-shaped jet gushed out, hitting the crowd on the stairs, blinding the soldiers. Two more shots sang themselves harmlessly into the brickwork.

'Run!' Love shouted to Clarissa, and dragged her past the crowd, out through the swing doors.

He threw down the extinguisher so that it jammed the door shut, and then they were in the courtyard in front of the Clinic. Was it really only hours before he had been there in his taxi? So much seemed to have happened, it could have been centuries ago.

The lawn was milling with people. Engines raced, men shouted orders, doors banged, and behind them all rumbled the renewed thunder of the anti-aircraft guns; hundreds of window panes rattled like loose stones at each barrage.

Where the hell was Parkington?

Of course, he was expecting them at the rear of the Clinic. Love began to run, holding Clarissa's hand. A figure detached itself from the darkness and ran with them.

'Thought you were never coming,' panted Parkington. 'The car's here at the front, without lights. I couldn't get round the back. It's thick with troops. Like the Royal Tournament.'

They passed soldiers at the double; ambulances with engines running; a Jeep laden down to its springs with anti-aircraft shells; and then they reached the familiar outline of Parkington's Renault, and piled inside.

Fifty yards down the street a road block had been set up with a Jeep and a telegraph pole thrown across the road. Parkington slowed; people began to run towards the car. Someone was flashing a lantern. If they stopped, they would be caught.

'Duck your heads!' shouted Love. 'Drive on!'

He pulled Clarissa down behind the front seat, shielding her body with his own. Parkington dropped into third gear and accelerated. As the car hit the boom, he threw his body horizontally across the seat. The car rocked, dizzily veered to one side, and then he was up behind the wheel again, and in control.

'Lucky we've got a rear engine!' he shouted back to Love above the roar of the engine. 'You couldn't have done *that* in your Cord!'

On the edge of the city, Parkington switched on his headlights. Only one was working; the other had been smashed by the pole. Ahead of them stretched the desert, a deeper darkness than the night sky. The road dipped, clouds of evening fog billowed towards them.

A Shell station, ablaze with little neon curlicues of Arabic script and a rash of fairy lights, came and went; a silver Nairn bus and trailer refuelled under a BP sign for the long run to Baghdad, and then once more there was nothing but the empty darkness. Love glanced back through the rear window. In the far distance, he saw two lights, like animals' eyes, very small and far away.

'There's someone behind us,' he told Parkington.

Parkington glanced up into the driving mirror.

'One of those buses,' he said.

They drove on in silence, neither entirely believing it, but yet wanting to desperately, because the alternative was too gloomy. The lights slowly grew brighter.

'Can you drive in the dark?' asked Love.

'If I have to.'

'You'll have to,' said Love. 'Those lights are gaining on us.'

They were approaching a little village now; mud walls beige beneath the moon, a few prowling dogs, a camel and a donkey tethered under a dusty tree. A handful of women in black still drew water from an ancient well. Out in the desert again, clumps of trees grew at intervals on either side of the road.

'Hold on to your seat,' warned Parkington. 'I'm going into one of these to cut my lights.'

He swung the wheel suddenly to the right. The car lurched and bumped, springs bottoming as they hit rocks with a clang of metal, and then they were running across a flat field rutted by furrows, dried in the sun, like a giant's washboard.

Ahead of them sprouted an outcrop of rock about thirty feet high. Parkington skirted this, flicked off his lights, came back to the main road. He drove on more slowly by the moonlight filtered through the scudding clouds.

'They're gaining,' said Love, looking over his shoulder. 'And there's a second car with them. Seems like a busy bus route.'

Parkington said nothing. He held out his hand silently. Love put his Mauser in it. Parkington cocked the automatic with his right hand, laid it carefully in the open cubby-hole lid in front of him.

'You're not armed?'

Love shook his head.

'My strength is as the strength of ten because my heart is pure,' he said, trying to convince himself. He felt absurdly cheerful because he had managed to bring Clarissa out of the hospital. All the ethics and arguments about whether there had been a genuine mistake could wait. He had the girl – and what good news he would be able to send her father!

He glanced behind him.

The lights grew larger; they now sat with their heads and shoulders silhouetted against the windscreen and dashboard.

'If you put your own lights on again, could you beat them?'

Parkington shook his head.

'No. I've turned the wick up as far as it'll go. I don't greatly like the look of this.'

'I like it even less,' said Love.

'What exactly is going on?' asked Clarissa suddenly; she had been so quiet in the back of the car, they thought she was asleep.

'A good question,' said Love. 'If we knew we'd tell you.'

'You said you would tell me. Later. Well, later's now. So what's happening, Doctor? And why are *you* here? And who's driving this car with the gun?'

'Richard Mass Parkington, at your service,' said Parkington, holding a hand over his shoulder. 'You must be Clarissa Head?'

'Obviously,' replied Clarissa. 'Who else did you expect?'

'I don't quite know,' said Parkington. 'You may not realize

it, but you've been posted as dead. In fact, your father has been told you were killed in a car crash.'

'You're joking.'

'Never been more serious.'

'Is this true, Doctor?' she asked Love.

He nodded.

'But how *could* such a ridiculous mistake happen?'

'That's what we're trying to find out,' said Parkington. 'But no one seems very anxious to help us. Dr Love here saw the hospital administrator, then the doctor who signed your death certificate, even the secretary at the British Embassy who informed your father. All assured him you were dead.'

'Are you mad?'

'It's all a question of degree. You've also got a grave with your name on it in the local cemetery. And Dr Love and I looked inside that grave just to see who *was* buried there.'

'And who was?'

'A man of middle age, dressed in a monk's robe.'

'My God. So you *are* serious. Was he a Syrian monk?'

'I've no idea.'

Suddenly Love gripped Parkington's arm.

'He wasn't Syrian. His skin was too pale. Only his hands were brown. He was European.'

'So what?' replied Parkington. 'There are plenty of European monks. Even if their number has been diminished by one.'

'I don't understand what you're talking about,' said Clarissa. 'All I remember is driving north out of Damascus in my Sprite and suddenly I saw a car coming right at me. Then I woke up in hospital and they told me I'd had an accident. And nothing else.'

'What sort of car?'

'I don't know. But it was big and blue.'

'And you were driving out of Damascus?'

'Of course. I told you. I'd spent the night there.'

'Then whoever hit you was coming into Damascus from the north?'

'Obviously. Why do you ask?'

'Because we were told it the other way round. You were hit going into the city.'

'Does it make any difference?'

'I don't know,' said Love slowly, 'but I'm beginning to think it does.' Like the flakes in a child's kaleidoscope, tiny, isolated unconnected facts were beginning to settle, starting to make a complete picture.

A European with brown hands in a newly-made grave; a collision between two cars, one blue coming south into Damascus, one white going north out of the city. What if the monk had been in the blue car – perhaps the blue Mercedes registered in the name of the monastery whose habit he was wearing?

Now why should a man with pale skin have brown, lined hands? He was thinking of a patient in Bishop's Combe who had died that Easter. His hands had been the same colour, for he had died of Addison's Disease, which affects the suprarenal glands, and brown, deeply-lined hands is one of its outward symptoms. This man could have died from the same cause – if he hadn't died in a car crash. He suggested this to Parkington.

'Now why has no one claimed that monk's body?' he asked, thinking aloud.

Parkington looked at him, a new respect in his eyes.

'How would you treat Addison's Disease?'

'Cortisone,' said Love.

'My God,' said Parkington slowly. 'You've given me my first break in this case.'

'This case?' repeated Clarissa. 'Are you a doctor, too?'

'No,' said Parkington, 'a sort of Civil Servant.'

'That explains the gun,' said Clarissa dryly and lit a cigarette.

Love glanced behind them.

'There's a third car following us,' he said. 'How long before we reach Maloula?'

'Never, if they catch us,' replied Parkington.

'Where's Maloula?' asked Clarissa.

'In my particular branch of the Civil Service,' explained Parkington, 'it's always best to have more than one escape route. I'm too old to play the wandering nomad, where my caravan has rested, that sort of thing, so just in case of need I book rooms in the name of Wilbraham – a good old Muslim name – in this village of Maloula, about thirty miles from here.

'There's a tiny hotel, used mostly by people who come to visit a shrine. It's out of the tourist season, so they're quite glad to rent any rooms at all. Next question?'

'How to shake these characters off our tail,' said Love.

The lights behind them were closer now, at times obscured by dust, so that they appeared as six swirling gold circles. Then the haze cleared and six white eyes blazed at them over the empty desert.

The road ahead was a dim ribbon unwinding grudgingly, marked by milestones like a giant's buck teeth.

'There's one thing in all this that puzzles me,' Parkington said, breaking into Love's uneasy thoughts.

'Only one? What is it?'

'How they knew we'd take this road. I deliberately didn't drive north when we left Damascus. I went east first and cut back, yet those characters were on to us almost at once.'

'So?'

'So either someone told them where we'd be. Or we were followed all the while.'

'How?' asked Love. 'There was no one on the road.'

'You don't have to be there in person to follow someone,' pointed out Parkington, 'not nowadays.'

'What do you mean?' asked Clarissa.

'What I say. You use science. You clip a magnetic bug underneath a car if you want to know where it's going. That's really a tiny transmitter that sends out a signal, a sort of bleep-bleep, every two minutes for as long as the battery lasts – about seventy-two hours.

'Then you need two RDF – radio direction finding – sets a mile or so apart, and you move their aerials until the signals come in loudest. Then you draw two lines on a map along the path of the signals and where they cross, there's your car.'

'You think someone's doing that here?' asked Love.

Parkington nodded, glanced back uneasily at the following lights.

'I think they must have,' he said. 'But I can't stop to find out. Because if the car *is* bugged, they'll have hidden it away pretty securely. Maybe inside a headlight, or in the spare tyre. It could take hours to find it.'

The car bumped over a rutted part of the road. Parkington swore under his breath; a sheep scuddered to safety twenty yards ahead. Clarissa's bag slipped across the seat. Love turned round to help her push it away and barked his hand on a hard corner of metal.

'What have you got in the back?' he asked Parkington irritably.

'A portable gas ring,' Parkington replied. 'Put it on the floor if it's in the way. It's clipped on top of a metal bottle of gas. I use it to make myself an early morning cup of tea.'

'Hurrah for the Civil Service,' said Clarissa. 'Everything stops for tea.'

'Never mind all that chat,' said Parkington. 'What worries me is this bug.'

'It worries me, too,' said Love. 'But what can we do about it?'

'Nothing, if it's in the car already. Tell me, did anything odd happen to *you* today?'

'Apart from digging up a grave, being chased by Syrian police, setting off an air-raid alarm, maliciously causing a city to black out, shooting a searchlight, kidnapping a hospital patient, and discharging an offensive weapon, to wit a fire extinguisher, at a fine body of men who tried to stop me, and then breaking through a road block, absolutely nothing.'

'When you saw that administrator, did anything happen?'

'I told you,' said Love, 'sweet F A.' And then he remembered he left his cigarettes behind him in the administrator's office.

'Well?' said Parkington quickly. 'You're not so sure?'

'It's so small, it's not worth saying.'

'Say it.'

'Only this. I left my cigarettes on his table and the fellow who'd taken me there gave them back to me in the car afterwards. That's all.'

'Let's see the packet,' said Parkington.

Love pulled it out of his breast pocket.

'There's a torch in the cubby-hole,' Parkington told him.

Love flicked on the torch inside the cubby-hole, which shielded its glow.

'Take out each cigarette and shred it,' said Parkington.

'But this is my only packet.'

'This is our only chance.'

Love pulled off the rubber gloves he had worn to dig up the grave, shook out the twelve cigarettes remaining, looked inside the blue and silver packet: it was empty. He picked up a cigarette, broke it, shredded the tobacco between his thumb and forefingers: nothing but tobacco there. He did the same thing to a second, a third, half a dozen with the same result. Then he picked up the seventh cigarette, and, even before he broke it, he felt a faint and pliable resistance inside.

'There's something in this one,' he said, rather like a child at a party who feels the outline of a folded paper hat, a lucky horseshoe charm, inside the cracker.

'Let's have a look,' said Parkington.

Love picked away the cigarette paper and the curly tobacco shreds, and laid bare a thin blue ceramic cylinder about two inches long, slightly thicker than a match. From one end a piece of silver wire protruded and had been bent back close to the shining blue surface. Love held it in the palm of his hand, shone the torch on it so that Parkington could see.

'Ah,' he said with satisfaction. 'So now we know what's giving our position away and how they got on to us so quickly in the cemetery. We might as well have rung them up and told them what we were going to do. So, we're up against pros, whoever they are.'

'We use the same things, so I know. I've stuck them in putty in a window frame, one even inside a soft centred chocolate. The fellow who swallowed it sent out his own radio message to us for the next twenty-four hours.'

'How are we to get rid of it?' Love asked him.

'Throw it out of the window,' suggested Clarissa.

'No,' said Love. 'It will still keep transmitting. And they'll guess we've kept on this road instead of cutting across the desert.'

Love flexed his fingers; they still felt soft and sweaty after the rubber gloves. Parkington glanced at him in the dash-light glow.

'I've got it,' he said suddenly. 'We'll use one of your gloves.'

'For what?'

'Lean over in the back and grab that butane gas ring, and I'll tell you.'

'You don't mean to say you're going to brew up now, for God's sake?'

'Of course not. Just find the thing.'

Love leaned over the seat, gripped one of the stumpy plastic legs of the cylinder, pulled it on to his lap. He had a similar one in his surgery for boiling water in an emergency. But what use could it be to them now?

'If that transmitter started to send its signals from half a mile away, they'd follow it,' said Parkington.

'Obviously,' agreed Love. 'But how the hell do we move it that far?'

'Drop it in one of the fingers of your glove and fill the glove with gas. There's a bit of string in the cubby-hole. Tie up the ends, and we'll push it through the window.'

'The glove's too heavy to rise very high. It's not a balloon. Also, butane's heavier than air.'

'No matter. We just want it to bob a few feet up, so the wind carries it for half a mile. We don't want it to soar away altogether. But hurry. We've only got minutes.'

Love slipped the transistor into the thumb of the glove, pulled the wrist opening over the gas cylinder, turned on the tap. Gas hissed, and the glove swelled like a pale, ghostly hand under the green dash lamps. Love turned off the gas, tied the string twice round the end of the glove as tightly as he could.

'Ready to go,' he said.

Parkington swerved to the right for fifty yards. Love opened the window and threw out the glove. For a moment it bobbed as though on an invisible sea; then the wind took it, and it moved slowly to the west, dipped once slightly and was gone.

Parkington swung back on to the road, accelerated away. Love swivelled in his seat and watched the six headlamps behind them through the swirl of dust. For a moment they still kept after them, and then slowly they swung to the right. Their beams carved long white tunnels through the dusty darkness.

'They're turning,' Love shouted.

'And the best of British luck,' said Parkington.

Love glanced back, but the lights had disappeared altogether. Parkington switched on his one headlamp. The desert rushed at them through the windscreen, grey and empty. Milestones came and went too quickly for them to read the miles. They passed a broken-down truck stacked with sacks of flour, with stones behind the wheels, a flock of sheep huddled together for warmth, turning terrified eyes at them. Once, a hawk flapped ahead of them for a while, and then was gone.

Soon they began to climb; the road was built above the level of the desert now, like a dyke. Under it, the ridge of hills wore a thin dusting of snow, like white hair on an old man's head. The half-moon was a Muslim crescent in the sky. As the road began to wind and bend its way into the hills they could see square houses with blue doors and blue around their windows.

'Blue's the lucky colour out here,' explained Parkington.

'Hope it's lucky for us,' said Love.

He felt himself dozing against the seat. Clarissa was already asleep in the back, with Parkington's raincoat pulled over her for warmth. The car grew colder as they climbed. Parkington turned on the heater, and the windows misted up; it was nearly freezing on the other side of the glass.

Houses with Moorish arches stared like empty eye-sockets at them. They passed a derelict coach up to its axles in mud at the left of the road, a row of poplars naked as stripped bone, bending in the wind that swirled around the car. A string of orange, red, and blue fairy lights swung across the road, glittering like some unreal stage decoration for a play that would never begin. The little village was empty as a begging bowl, apart from prowling cats that pressed themselves against doorsteps, their eyes reflecting the lights as they went by.

'Maloula,' announced Parkington. 'We're here.'

The hotel was a squat square building with a flat roof, built close up to a vertical side of rock. Parkington stopped at the door, woke up Clarissa. All three went into an entrance hall, cold as a catacomb. Through an open window the night air felt damp with water that streamed down the rock face. An old woman wearing wooden-soled sandals and a black dress, a black shawl around her head, lips sunk in over a toothless mouth, showed them upstairs. Their breath hung like fog under the naked electric bulbs. Altogether, Love would have preferred the Ritz.

'You wish to eat?' the woman asked in French.

'What is there?' asked Love without enthusiasm.

'Lamb stew.'

'We'll wait for breakfast,' Parkington told her, and when she had gone and the door was shut, 'I've a couple of bottles of Scotch in my suitcase. They'll be a better nightcap than lamb stew, eyeballs and all.'

They drank the whisky neat from tooth glasses. Then Clarissa went to her room, and the two men sat on the edge of Parkington's bed; there were no chairs. The floor was bare unvarnished boards under a threadbare rug, abrasive with trodden-in sand. There was no running water in the room, only a ewer in a bowl on a marble-topped table. A picture of a saint looked down on them from the wall; perhaps St Tekla, perhaps not.

'What now?' said Love, pouring some more whisky.

'Bed,' said Parkington. 'Tomorrow is another day. Never put off today what you can put off tomorrow, as the strip-tease girl said.'

'And if we're no nearer then?'

'Then we think again,' said Parkington, and poured another drink for himself.

Love was asleep. The sound of sobbing woke him. He sat up, groping for the bedlight that wasn't there. His fingers closed around the slim barrel of his fountain-pen torch, switched it on. Someone was crying in the room next door. Clarissa.

He swung his feet out of bed, put on his shoes, pulled on a shirt, a pair of trousers, went in to see her. The room, with moonlight filtered by the curtain, seemed identical with his own. He closed the door softly.

'What's the matter?' he asked.

'I'm frightened,' she said.

She sat up.

'Why?'

'It sounds silly, but I can't say exactly. I know I should be more specific but I'm all confused. Maybe it's just bewilderment. I can't believe Daddy was told I was dead when anyone could see that all that I'd got was mild concussion at the worst. I mean *why* should anyone do that? Have you cabled him to say I'm all right?'

'Not yet. I meant to this evening – after we'd been to the cemetery. But I didn't have the chance.'

'Poor Daddy. He must be so lonely. Tell me, how do you think such a mistake was made? I mean, how could it be?'

'Perhaps someone had a special reason for wanting to be rid of someone else, and they couldn't think how, and then there was a convenient car accident. No witnesses, only a girl knocked out. They could pretend she had died, get a bent doctor to issue a death certificate, and then bury the man they wanted to be rid of in her grave. That's a possibility. No more.'

'But what sort of people would do such a thing? And why should they want to kill a monk?'

Love sat down on the edge of the bed, one of her hands in his.

'I don't know, Clarissa,' he said. 'Maybe it didn't happen like that. Maybe that man in the grave wasn't a monk. Maybe it just suited some people to dress him like one. I don't know any of the answers yet, but I will.'

'I hope it doesn't take too long. Tell me, what sort of Civil Servant is your friend Parkington?'

'Not wildly civil. He's a spy.'

'For us?'

'Yes.'

'Do you trust him?'

'I trust very few men,' said Love. 'When you're a doctor, too many people tell you too many lies. You hear so much of the twisted side of human nature that you're rarely quite sure of anyone. But I've seen Parkington before in a tight spot. Yes, I think I do trust him. Anything else?'

She shook her head.

'How is your head?' he asked her.

'Fine. No strain at all.'

He moved his hand under her hair. Her forehead was bruised and scratched, and high up on the base of her skull he felt a small plaster patch. The irony of his situation suddenly amused him. He smiled.

'What's so funny?' she asked.

'I was just thinking. With everything I've done out here so far, digging up a grave, setting off an air-raid alarm and so on, I deserve to be struck off the Medical Register. But, oddly, the thing they'd probably get me for, if they wanted to, would be for being in this room with you.'

'But I'm not your patient,' said Clarissa. 'That makes it legal, surely?'

'The oddest thing of all,' said Love, 'is they'd never believe I was just sitting on the edge of your bed.'

'Well, if they don't want to believe that why give them the chance?' asked Clarissa practically. 'Anyway, you must be cold.'

'I'll survive. Now you try and sleep. I'll stay here with you until you do.' Slowly, her breathing grew more regular; then, she slept.

Love returned to his room. At some time between night and morning he awoke for a second time. He thought he heard a movement but there was nothing, except the roar of the water outside. He started up on his elbow listening to it, feeling a sudden sense of alarm, and then he sank back and lay looking up into the darkness seeing nothing.

What would it be like to have her always there, next to him, a part of him, her life shared with his? At first thought, it appeared a golden prospect, but then, like a mountain that beckons to be climbed, there was the other side you couldn't see until you'd reached the peak: the long, slow fall into the foothills of acceptance and boredom, perhaps eventual indifference.

For a long time he lay thinking, eyes open. Then he slept.

Love lay in the grave in the Christian cemetery, and sharp, bright spades were removing the comforting warmth of earth from his body.

The walls of the grave felt cold and hard and steep and dark. A rusty agony of rheumatism racked his joints, and water cascaded all around him.

He moved in desperation and woke up. He was in his narrow, rope-mattress bed, pressed hard up against the damp concrete wall, and his throat felt sore and swollen. He raised himself on one elbow, glanced at his watch. A mist had formed on its steel case; seven o'clock. This must be how fish felt all the time, cold and wet and raw. Thank heaven he hadn't got fins.

He sat up. The room in daylight looked no more prepossessing than on the previous evening. Through the open window, he saw water streaming like black tar down the side of the rock. Moss and bright green flowers grew on either side. He shuddered; he didn't envy them a bit.

He stood up, unlatching the shutters of another window that opened out on to the village itself. It was built halfway up a long gentle hill and suddenly ended with the sheer rockface. The hotel opened on to a wide empty square. To one side was the tomb of St Tekla with its chapel, and a courtyard, also hewn out of the mountain, where the faithful could sit and drink icy water; a zinc cup was carefully chained to a metal peg in the rock.

Love washed in the ewer of water on his plain, unpainted wooden dressing table, then dressed. He wished he could shave, but he had no razor with him. He stroked his stubbly chin, rough as sandpaper. Then went out into the corridor and down the stone stairs to the dining-room.

This, like his bedroom, was simple to the point of crudeness; wooden chairs, a bare wooden table set with a plain linen cloth, cheap metal knives and forks. Parkington was already at the table drinking black Turkish coffee. The woman who had greeted them on the previous evening came in carrying a tray with two plates of tiny fried eggs, and a loaf of bread, porous as a sponge, cut into slices.

'Where's Clarissa?' Love asked.

Parkington shrugged.

'You should know better than me,' he said.

'She was all right last night,' said Love.

'I bet she was,' said Parkington. 'Lucky you're not married. Marriage, my friends tell me, is the tomb of love.'

'It won't be mine,' retorted Love. 'You spell that word with a small "L". Where d'you think she is?'

'Probably putting her face on.'

Some of the unease Love had felt when he awoke after leaving her room was returning, and with it a fear of things going wrong; danger signals flashed amber in his mind. He put down his knife and fork on the tatty cloth, ran up the stairs, knocked on Clarissa's door. There was no answer; he went in. The bed was made, but the room was quite empty. She might never have been there at all. He came down the stairs three steps at a time.

'She's gone,' he told Parkington.

'Gone?'

Parkington repeated the word as though he hadn't heard it before.

Love turned to the old woman.

'A girl arrived with us last night. Have you seen her?'

'She went out early.'

'Why? Where to?'

The woman shrugged. How could any man ever appreciate a woman's reasons for doing anything? She was drying a plate with a cloth. She carefully put the plate in an old-fashioned wooden rack, folded up the cloth neatly, hung it over a string, pulled the two sides until they were level before she spoke.

'She did not say,' she said.

'Where could she go from here on foot?'

'There's nothing to see here except the shrine,' explained the old woman. 'Do you wish to visit it? I have the keys though it is not open yet officially.'

'Thank you, but later,' said Love. 'First we must find our friend.'

Perhaps there was an easy explanation? Maybe Clarissa was just enjoying the morning sunshine in the village? Parkington followed him to the door of the hotel. A few children played in the dust, and an old dog with red-rimmed pouchy eyes and torn ears growled feebly at them, and then beat the ground with its tail. But Clarissa was not there.

'Oh, my God, this is all we need,' said Love irritably. 'I was mad ever to get involved with you digging up that grave.'

'Too late now,' said Parkington cheerfully, 'as the birth control man told the pregnant woman.'

Love turned back into the hotel.

'Did you see which way she went?' he asked the woman.

She shook her head. 'There was an early morning bus south. Maybe she went on that.'

'Where does that go?'

'Eventually, to Damascus. From the foothills here it goes to Aimaltimaih, the Eye of the Fig.'

'What's that?'

'A village.'

'And then?'

'Then there's nothing but the desert. The bus stops at the monastery, and after that nowhere else till it reaches Damascus.'

'What monastery?'

'The Brothers of the Sacred Flame.'

'Sounds like the Mafia,' said Parkington.

'What sort of brothers are they?' asked Love.

'They worship the Lord in their own way,' said the old woman cautiously.

'So do we all,' said Love thoughtfully; remembering that the Abbot had ordered a blue Mercedes, and a blue Mercedes had crashed into Clarissa's car.

'It is a Muslim shrine now, but once it was Christian. It is said that the prophet Muhammed was hungry and alone in the desert. He struck the nearest rock with his stick and water poured out. Then he struck another rock and fire came forth. And then a ram caught its horns in a bush, and since he had fire and water he could cook and eat and so he was refreshed. So a monastery was built on that spot.'

'How far is it from here?'

'An hour in your car,' said the old woman. 'Longer, of course, by bus or by donkey.'

'If I'd any sense,' said Love, glancing at his watch, 'I'd be now listening to a lecture – the incidence of hypnosis in painless childbirth among the Armenian middle classes.'

'If either of us had any sense, we wouldn't be here at all,' said Parkington wearily. 'Let's pay our bill, and get the hell out.'

Chickens from outside came clucking into the kitchen for scraps.

'What sort of robes do the brothers wear?' Love asked the woman as she counted their change. 'We met a holy brother in Damascus who wore saffron robes.'

He did not add that the holy brother had been wearing his robes in a grave.

'Then he was a brother from this monastery.'

'How do we find the place?'

'From Aimaltimaih, follow a small road to the west. When it ends, you will see stones mark the rough direction.'

'How will we recognize the village?' asked Love. 'Even if there is a sign, we can't read Arabic.'

'You will see a garage with a red, white and blue globe on the petrol pump, and, nearby, a tinsmith. Go in peace.'

'Thanks,' said Love. He felt he could use the peace.

She gathered up her money and left the room.

'Who do we say we are at the monastery?' asked Parkington.

'Tourists, pilgrims, anything. Someone there's bound to speak French, and I can get by with a little better than Laplume-de-ma-tante stuff. Then we'll take it from there. Never cross your bridges before you come to them.'

'It helps if there's a bridge when you need it,' said Parkington dryly.

'Check,' said Love.

As they went out, Love was surprised at the chill in the air; they must be higher up than he had realized. Behind the hotel, a fissure floored with brown stones ran through the rocks, possibly a relic of some earthquake split. This was the route that the Romans had used to march through Syria nearly two thousand years before. This was also the way through the rocks that had so miraculously helped St Tekla.

Overhead electric wires led to naked bulbs, still burning; someone had forgotten to turn them off. Lovers had carved hearts on the rock faces; others had written initials and dates with felt pens. High up on either side were arched recesses, each the shape of a heel, shelters for shepherds in the rainy season.

Beneath the village lay a cluster of blue and white houses, some with spirals of smoke from their squat, square chimneys, and then the desert stretched into a grey infinity to meet a sky, equally empty, equally desolate and unfriendly.

They climbed into their car. Parkington took a tape cassette from his pocket, slipped it into the Philips tape recorder beneath the car radio. Then he plugged a small plastic box with a long lead into the aerial socket, moved over a circular graduated dial, switched on the radio.

'What's all that?' asked Love, watching him.

'Transmitter,' Parkington explained. 'Ultra low frequency. It's a pack I carry that plugs into any car radio. I recorded the message in my room, then I can play it at four or five times the speed of speech – backwards if I want, changing the speed up and down. All sorts of tricks to make it more difficult for anyone trying to monitor it.'

'Who's it to?'

'We've got a few people over the border in Lebanon, with a repeater station. It's for MacGillivray, eventually.'

'Give him my love. In a small letter. But what can he do to help us?'

'Sweet nothing. But at least it tells him where I am – and you can bet that someone in the Embassy's already sent a screed of indignation about the grave bit.'

'My God,' said Love in an anguished voice. 'So that balls-up is known at home, too, then?'

'Only to a very select audience. Now shut up while I hear if this thing works.'

Parkington pressed a button on the box and a jumble of sound poured from the speaker.

'It does,' he said thankfully.

He unclipped the wire, carried the box and cassette back to his room. Love sat looking out at the cold sunshine on the rocks. Parkington returned, started the engine.

They drove down the winding road, scattering indignant chickens, while children paused above spinning tops to watch them go by. Within ten minutes they were on the plain, where the snow still lay in ditches, just out of the sunshine. The wind beat at the car so that it rocked from side to side.

Love glanced behind at Maloula. On the mountain peaks some shreds of brown rock, darker than the rest, gave the impression of soldiers standing close together watching them. The effect was so real that he shivered. Colonel Head had been right in thinking what he was proposing was too much to ask. He was an idiot ever to have agreed – and yet who could believe that such a simple request could become so complicated?

Parkington drove fast and in silence. The sun came out more strongly, and under it and around them, the grapes lay pale on the vines. A single bird flapped slowly from nowhere, keeping pace with the car, and then wheeled away. A signpost, Homs 131; a broken-down truck, stones jammed behind the rear wheels, a rock beneath its sump; three men levering with crowbars at the front of an old Chevrolet that had gone off the road into the soft sand.

They reached Aimaltimaih, saw the red, white, and blue sign of a Sun petrol station; then more mud shacks, a pyramid of old motor tyres outside a vulcanizing shop, a tinsmith already at his furnace making kettles; a crowd of cycles gathered under the shade of a tree, all chained together by their front wheels. At the roadside old women with black shoes, black stockings, black cloaks, black hoods over their heads, patiently waited for some country bus, like figures stepped out from the stream of time.

The road turned left between two mud houses, under a criss-cross of electric power cables, and then the tarmacadam ended. A shepherd, wrapped in rags against the wind, watched them with an expressionless face as they slowed down. Large stones now marked the direction the road should take, and soon even these fell away.

The desert lay liquid ahead of them, a constant baking, shimmering mirage. There were no animals, no birds, no people. The wind had dropped and heat baked the metal roof of the car. It was impossible to open the windows because of the dust and grit that would pour in from the front wheels, so they sat, sweating and silent, each with his own thoughts and wishing they had someone else's.

They drove through a cluster of small, box-like houses, where palm trees leaned long trunks over the roofs, and then ahead of them they saw the monastery. A wall twenty feet high, perhaps ten times as long, and without any windows, bisected the horizon. Here and there, it had fallen into decay, and been patched with mud bricks, burned brown by the sun.

Behind and above this wall two round mosques soared like huge stone breasts, and by each one stood a minaret, ornamented with fine stone tracery and variegated marble, and small diamond shapes in red and green and blue ceramics. In the centre of the wall was a high gateway with stone pots either side, and a cluster of trees. In their shade crouched a forlorn collection of shabby people; men in dirty rags, women in black clothes, with black scarves around their heads; a few dejected children with running noses, playing in the sand.

A man had set up a crude stall with a packing case, on which he had laid out melons with ribbed green skins like Turkish turbans and full of pink seeds; grapes on vine leaves, a pile of polished oranges. Parkington stopped the car fifty yards beyond the gate, locked the doors carefully, walked back with Love beside him. The sun felt pleasantly warm through the backs of their jackets; grasshoppers and crickets whirred in the scrub. Parkington put a Syrian pound on the board, picked up an apple, threw one to Love. The man smiled. Truly Allah was kind in sending two such rich *effendi* when business was so poor.

'I believe there's a country bus that runs from Maloula to here and on to Damascus?' Parkington remarked conversationally in Arabic.

The man bowed his head.

'That is so,' he replied. 'It left here half an hour ago.'

Parkington clicked his fingers in simulated annoyance.

'Did anyone get off?' he asked.

The man nodded.

'That woman with the withered arm,' he said, pointing to a woman in black who crouched beneath the shade of a tree, as though asleep on her haunches. 'She comes to drink the water of the holy spring in the hope of a miracle.'

'What holy spring?' asked Parkington.

'The fountain of Charki – the fountain of the sun – in this monastery. Prophet Muhammed was once wandering in this desert and was overcome by thirst. He knelt down and prayed to Allah, the one true God, to deliver him from his anguish. And the rocks split and water poured forth in abundance, and he arose refreshed. This water still pours from the fountain at certain times of the year. Then other rocks opened and fire came out, so he could cook and eat.'

'Is this one of those times?'

'It is the will of Allah, whether the water flows or whether

144

it stays within the bosom of the earth. This woman has been coming for weeks in the hope that she can bathe in the waters and be cured.'

Parkington translated some of this to Love.

'In the Bible, the pool of Bethesda near Jerusalem also had therapeutic qualities,' said Love. 'Look it up. St John, Chapter five. Incidentally, according to the Apocryphal Gospel of Nicodemus, this pool had a link with Syria, for a part of the original Tree of Life, which could cure any disease, was removed from the original site of the Garden of Eden and planted near Jerusalem. Then Solomon was told that the Saviour of the world would be hanged from it, so he cut down the tree and buried the trunk. Long afterwards the pool was dug near this spot, and the tree gave the water its curative powers.

'And then Moses was also in the desert, and suddenly he saw a bush on fire with some sacred flame. Exodus. Chapter three.

'From a scientific point of view, I think that was caused by the vast quantities of oil there must be under this sand. Gas from the oil forced out water – like that cataract at Maloula – and sometimes the gas also escapes and burns.'

'How do you know all that?' asked Parkington.

'The benefits of a Presbyterian boyhood,' Love replied.

Parkington grunted. This scientific chat from the past had no meaning for him; his problems were in the present, and they were bad enough. He turned back to the man behind the stall.

'Anyone else get off the bus?' he asked.

'One other person. A girl. Perhaps she was English?'

'Where did she go?'

'Into the monastery.'

'Has she come out?'

'I have been here all morning. No one has come out through this gate.'

'Is there any other way out?'

'No, this is the only gate.'

'Thank you.'

Parkington translated this to Love.

'Looks like she's still inside. Let's go in and see for ourselves.'

They walked through the arched gateway, into a courtyard flagged with stones and surrounded by palm trees and jasmine and bushes with thick fleshy leaves. The air suddenly felt colder. Love guessed they must be very near water, possibly an underground river, or a lake. This could be the source of the water that gushed at intervals through the ground.

To one side of the yard stood a well, ringed with a stone wall. On an ancient pulley hung a lead bucket. At the far end of the yard, double doors opened into some place of worship, where the walls were smooth with ceramics and mother-of-pearl inlays.

At the centre of the courtyard, in a kind of grotto made by rocks laid one on the other, lay a smooth stone. From a cleft in this, like a dimple in a giant brown apple, a flame three feet long burned soundlessly, a trembling golden leaf of fire. All around it were piled tributes; faded, withering flowers, newly baked loaves of bread, glass beads, a stone flagon of wine.

To their left were other buildings with cedarwood doors dried by centuries of sun and studded with black bolts. A few chickens clucked their way across the warm flagstones, and a yellow dog sleeping in the sunshine opened an amber eye and growled, and then began to beat the stones with his tail, as though ashamed of his rough welcome. As they stood, a bell began to boom in one of the minarets. Was this a warning that strangers had arrived – or was it simply to mark the passage of time, the approach of eternity?

A man wearing saffron robes, his hands folded in front of his paunch, walked slowly across the courtyard. The soles of his sandals, made from strips of old car tyres, flapped on the stones as he walked.

'Good morning,' called Love.

The man paused, turned as though he had not seen them, and then began to walk in their direction. Under the deep cope of his robe, his face seemed curiously pale. As he came nearer they saw that it shone with an unhealthy patina of perspiration. He stood still, turning his head this way and that. Love and Parkington saw that his eyelids sank over dark sockets; he was quite blind.

'We're tourists,' Love explained. 'We heard that you had some sacred relics here.'

It was a guess, but surely there would be something; Love had yet to visit any shrine or monastery in the Middle East that could not produce some convenient evidence of its own importance: the mosque of Omar in Jerusalem contained finger-prints of the angel Gabriel, plus Muhammed's footmark. He remembered and shared Sir Thomas Browne's opinion of such things: 'That Miracles have beene I doe believe; that they may yet bee wrought by the living I doe not deny: but have no confidence in those which are fathered on the dead; and this hath ever made me suspect the efficacy of reliques.'

The monk bowed.

'You are English?' he asked in English.

'Yes,' said Parkington.

'Please to wait a moment,' he replied slowly. 'I only speak a few words.'

He walked back into the shadowy recesses of the mosque.

'What do we do now?' asked Love.

'I leave that to you,' said Parkington generously. 'After all, you know the girl.'

The monk returned with a colleague, also in a saffron robe, and a tasselled rope around his waist. The skin on his face was brown and hard, his eyes bright as black beads.

'What do you wish to see?' he asked.

'I understand you have some relics,' said Love.

'That is so,' said the man, 'But they are not on view this week. We are repainting the room where we keep them.'

'We've come a long way,' said Parkington.

The man glanced at him, as though calculating how far they had come.

'In that case,' he said, 'if you will excuse the state of the room, please to come with me.'

They crossed the yard into the cool dimness of the outer chapel. Love could see wooden scaffolding poles and horizontal trestles, a five gallon oil drum with its top sawn off, full of whitewash. On the floor lay two crude brushes made of blades of grass roped together. The monk pressed a switch; a light glowed beneath the glass top of a case.

'Here you will see a sacred hoofprint of Muhammed's camel. It travelled, says the legend, from Jerusalem to Mecca, in four great leaps. Now it has a place in Paradise with Borak, the Prophet's horse, and Tobit's dog.'

They stared at the brown slab of clay with the round hoof-mark in it, and said nothing. After all, what was there to say?

'And here is a part of the spear with which Jesus Christ was given a sponge of vinegar as He was crucified. At first there was a Christian foundation here, then a Muslim one,' the monk explained. 'Then the Crusaders raised it and finally the Muslims rebuilt it. But both religions have much in common. After all, St John the Baptist is buried in the Great Omayad Mosque in Damascus. St George also has his tomb within the city.'

As he spoke, he flicked over another switch and they peered dutifully through a glass case at a corroded piece of metal, just recognizable as a sharp edge – but whose? Was it possible that the blade of which that had been part had ever belonged to a soldier who had watched Christ on the Cross nearly 2,000 years ago?

'These are the only relics we have,' said the monk and reached for the light. 'They are very sacred.'

'So I see,' said Love. 'Tell me, a friend of ours, a girl, came here early today. Did she also see these things?'

'A girl? There's no girl here.'

'The old man at the door said a girl came in half an hour ago,' said Parkington easily.

'There are men out there who will tell you anything for a few drachma,' retorted the monk. 'They will tell you what you want to hear because then they think you will tip them more. They have no faith, no honour. They are like dung-beetles.'

'But the man didn't know what we wanted to hear,' Love pointed out.

'Many of the monks from this shrine are in Mecca paying a pilgrimage, and the few of us left, apart from our blind brother, who greeted you, are engaged in decorating these rooms. There is no one else here.'

'Is there any other place she could have gone to?' asked Love.

'That I could not say. But there is certainly no woman here.'

'What about behind those doors?' asked Love nodding towards the main building.

'Not there, either. This monastery is built on a holy spring,' the monk explained. 'From time to time the water rises into this well outside and into another well behind those doors. When it does so, we lower a wooden tray with small earthenware vessels to gather up the water, which has healing properties. We send bottles of it all round the world. I believe that Christian monks do much the same thing in their monastery in Jerusalem, near the Garden of Gethsemane?'

Parkington nodded; he had seen them doing it.

'We must have made a mistake,' he said, as though that disposed of the whole thing.

He led the way out of the mosque.

'Has one of your colleagues died recently?' asked Love, when they were back in the courtyard.

'No,' said the monk slowly, shaking his head in a puzzled way, 'At least, not to my knowledge. Why do you ask?'

'I heard from Damascus that a monk in a saffron robe had died. I wondered whether he was one of your order?'

'As I said, most of the brothers are in Mecca. I would have heard, I think, if one had died on the way. Even though we have no telephone communication, we do have visitors. People bring us vegetables from Maloula. Others take away our bottles of water. I think you are mistaken.'

'How do you get into Damascus?' asked Love.

'We have a car.'

'A blue Mercedes?'

'I know nothing about these things,' the monk replied with a smile. 'It is something small and serviceable. Why do you ask so many questions?'

Love shrugged.

'I'm interested in cars,' he explained lamely.

'You come from England?'

'Yes.'

'Then, may I ask you a question? What brings you so far afield on your own? We have Americans who come from even farther away, I know, but usually they come on what I believe you call a package tour, in tens or twenties.'

'I'm a doctor,' Love explained. 'I was in Damascus at a convention.'

'Ah, yes. I see.'

The monk held out his hand.

'Go in peace,' he said.

Love took his advice. Parkington was waiting impatiently at the gate. They walked out to the car, climbed in. He started the engine, lowered both front windows against the heat.

'What do you make of that?' he asked.

Love shrugged.

'What do you? We seem to have caught them in the off-season when they are tarting up the place for the next bunch of tourists. The only thing that struck me as odd was the fellow at the door who said he saw the girl go in, without any prompting from us.'

'Anything else?' asked Parkington.

'No. Why?'

'When I left you in that mosque place, I had a gander around outside. On one of those minarets, the lightning conductor had been cut about three feet from the bottom. Sawn through.'

'So?'

'In the war,' Parkington went on, 'when we had to transmit from occupied France, it was always hard to find suitable aerials. We could receive using a spring mattress as an aerial, but it was damned hard to get a message off until someone hit on the idea of using lightning conductors on certain buildings, such as chimneys, which are made of brick or china clay and so were naturally insulated from the earth. Those minarets are covered in ceramic – the best insulator in the world.'

'But what would monks transmit from here?'

'Certainly not "Housewives' Choice",' said Parkington, 'but the top part of the wire was scratched, as though someone had put a clip on it.'

'So what do we do?' asked Love ingenuously, resigned already to what they would have to do.

'We'll go back,' said Parkington. 'That's what we do. Only this time, when it's dark.'

Chapter Eight

Covent Garden, London, June 29th

It was eleven o'clock in the evening, and MacGillivray was tired. His dinner jacket hung on a wooden hanger from a hook behind his office door, and he wore a loose Paisley sweater over his dress shirt because (a) it felt more comfortable, and (b) at that hour, at his age, despite his rigid military upbringing, he thought he owed himself any such aid to relaxation that he could find.

He had been at the Royal Opera House with his wife that evening; Sir Robert L— had unexpectedly offered him two tickets at short notice for he couldn't use them himself because he had to fly suddenly to Bonn for an Interpol conference. During the second act, the transistor receiver MacGillivray wore in his breast pocket had sent its tiny buzzing message through the lining of his suit. This meant he was wanted back at the office urgently.

He gave his wife some excuse for leaving early, picked his way across the knees of those sitting alongside him – usually he managed to get himself a seat at the end of the row, but this evening he had been unlucky – and walked through the market to his office.

It had been raining, and the air felt cool and damp, as the air always used to be when he was a boy in Perthshire. Lorries lined the streets, shining with dew, the black tarpaulins above their loads of fruit glowing like glass under the lamps. The pub doors were wedged open, and the bars busier than they were during the day, for Covent Garden only really came to life at night.

He let himself in to Sensoby and Ransom, through a side entrance, threw back the dead man's lock on the door, in case anyone should try to follow him, and walked up the stairs. A dim blue night-light burned on the landing, and Miss Jenkins was waiting with a thermos of coffee and a tin of his favourite biscuits. As he hung up his jacket, she handed him a sheet of flimsy. He sat down, read it without a word, nodded, broke a piece of shortbread in half, dipped it into his coffee, read the message again.

He recognized the code number at the beginning without having to check; the signal was from Parkington, and purely routine. It gave his present map reference on the War Office grid system, the radio frequency he was using to receive reply signals, the time he would try to be on the air; at five minutes after every hour, from eight in the evening until eleven in the morning, Parkington's time.

MacGillivray turned the dial of the automatic time calculator on his desk. Eleven in London; that meant it was after midnight in Syria.

He read on:

Informative Stop temporarily retreated above reference Stop Dr Jason Love inquiring Damascus on behalf father condition new grave of daughter Clarissa Head ex Bishop's Combe Som Stop He believed Clarissa still alive Stop Accordingly up-dug grave together found body European male fiftyish wearing monastic saffron robe Stop Male's hands deep brown and furrowed Stop Love says this symptom Addison's Disease requiring cortisone to cure Stop Advise disease Dr Ronald suffered Stop No sign girl Stop Surprised by armed intruders Stop Escaped to Maloula check your reference with Love and Clarissa who was patient Peoples Clinic Damascus Stop During night 28/29 Clarissa Head left our custody believed proceeding Monastery of Sacred Flame approximately 40 miles SSE Stop Visited Monastery but most monks absent in Mecca Stop Those remaining deny arrival of any girl Stop Unsatisfied Stop Intending investigate interior tonight Stop Endit

And the best of luck, thought MacGillivray, as he pressed the buzzer on his desk. Miss Jenkins, as imperturbable at eleven at night as eleven in the morning, appeared in the doorway.

'Anything else?' he asked her.

'Something from Karachi and another from Bahrein,' she said.

'What about?'

He could not for the moment recall having sent signals to either station.

'Those anti-European riots.'

'Oh, yes. What about them?'

'I have the messages here, sir.'

She handed him a folder. He skimmed through the flimsies. The riots didn't appear to be so much anti-British as just simply against white people. Two Belgians had been attacked in Karachi; two Dutchmen and a German in Bahrein. Their ages and names were given, but that meant nothing to MacGillivray. Why should they be their real ones?

'Nothing's in from the Maldives yet,' Miss Jenkins continued, 'but there's been an electrical storm over the Indian Ocean which could have delayed it.'

MacGillivray nodded, skimmed through the signal from Karachi. Across the road from that incident, three English women had been alighting from a taxi, and yet they had been shown no hostility whatever.

He read on. Rioters arrested in both Karachi and Bahrein said that they felt as though voices inside them were urging them to attack all people with pale skins. One claimed he actually thought it was the voice of his dead father telling him to act like this. None of the arrested people knew any of the victims personally, but all laid stress on the strength of their feelings that they had to attack them.

Slight traces of LSD had been found in their bloodstreams. All denied taking the drug – which they said they had never heard of – and in their poor financial circumstances this was quite likely. In the home of one an earthenware phial had been found. The rioter said it had contained holy water drawn from some sacred spring. Chemical tests showed faint traces of LSD, larger deposits of RNA acid, plus other substances, as yet unidentified.

This water had a wide circulation among primitive Muslim communities in the Middle East and Asia, much as water drawn from the River Jordan at the place where John the Baptist had christened Jesus, was exported to various Christian countries. Healing qualities were claimed for it, also, the power to give visions; this could be attributed to the

LSD which appeared in its natural state in several such holy springs.

Samples of water from other identical phials in nearby villages showed similar percentages of LSD, but no RNA acid and no traces of this other unknown substance. In both cities, the radios in the coffee shops had been tuned to the Voice of Islam. At the time stated this had been broadcasting a serious talk on the Koran; nothing politically inflammatory whatever. But three minutes before the violence began, some other transmitter had cut across the Voice of Islam's wavelength with Persian music and a man's voice speaking. This had lasted for only a very short time; no one could remember who he was or what he had said. It was probably a freak of atmospherics.

If it had happened once, MacGillivray would agree, but not twice, and perhaps three times. He would know when he heard from the Maldives. He lowered the paper, his mind miles away. Intelligence was, in essence, a matter of piecing together unrelated items, like bits of a jumbled jigsaw, and making a mosaic picture of something else from them. Here he had two facts, apparently unconnected – a pirate radio talk, some acid in so-called holy water – that had somehow ended in violence.

He had produced results with less, but not much less. He remembered especially one occasion when it had been imperative to know the physical size of Soviet missiles, especially the Vostock launcher, and those used by the Egyptians against the Israelis, so that their performance could be approximated.

But how to find their length in a short time? Then it was discovered that the editor of Jane's *All the World's Aircraft* knew the exact distance between white spots on the ground of Red Square, in Moscow, where the annual military parades were marshalled. With this one known fact, he compared the dimensions of the huge missiles from photographs taken as they went through the Square – and was accurate within inches.

MacGillivray sipped his coffee again, broke another piece of shortbread. Then he picked up his telephone.

'Get me Professor Cartwright,' he told Miss Jenkins. 'And Sir John Dean. Urgently. And wherever they are.'

Then he sat back and waited for the calls to come through, chewing his shortbread, wondering whether his wife would get a taxi on her own or whether she was still waiting for him. Also, what convincing explanation could he give her for his behaviour tonight? He could think of nothing, and his unease spread again, like a miasma of doom.

He was reaching in the drawer of his desk for another indigestion pill when the call came through.

Chapter Nine

Maloula and the Monastery of the Sacred Flame,
June 29th–30th

Parkington locked the door, left the key in the lock and motioned Love into the middle of the room. He picked up his suitcase, opened it on the table. Love watched him, interested, and yet somehow not involved, as though he had no part in all this, as though it did not concern him at all. He should be back in Damascus, at a lecture on child psychology and the results of corporal punishment on parents. And he wished to heaven that he was.

'Right,' said Parkington, like an army instructor addressing a dim squad. 'I suggest we leave about eleven, which means we should reach the monastery after midnight. We'll hide the car and then get over the wall.'

'And if we're discovered?'

'We won't be.'

'You said that about the cemetery,' Love reminded him.

'All right, all right. If we *are* discovered, we say we wanted to photograph the place by moonlight. I've got a camera.'

'And what's in the camera beside a film?' asked Love dubiously. 'Something that shoots gramophone needles or gas or whatever?'

Parkington shook his head.

'Unfortunately, not. That would be a bit too obvious. On

155

the other hand, old MacGillivray has given me something that may or may not be useful.'

'Such as what?' asked Love sceptically.

'Such as some pep pills sewn in my left lapel.'

'That's a load of rubbish,' said Love angrily. 'What possible use can pep pills be? Here we are, already on the run from the Damascus police for digging up a grave and, no doubt, they know now who set off the air-raid alarm and kidnapped Clarissa who also has disappeared. And you talk about pep pills! God knows what the doctors at the convention think. This is serious for me, Parkington, if it isn't for you. You may make a living larking about in this way, but I don't. What would my patients think back in Somerset if they heard what I'd been up to?'

'I'm not concerned with what your dreary patients think, because that's entirely academic. I'm not concerned with what anyone thinks, but what they do. I'm concerned with facts. You got yourself into this, Doctor. You insisted on rescuing this girl from the Clinic, when I said, leave her alone. Now she's disappeared, you want to duck out. But it's all too late for that. I'm certain that girl's inside the monastery.'

'Maybe,' said Love more calmly, 'but how do we get her out? Certainly not with a couple of pep pills.'

'They could keep us going.'

'We've been going long enough, and made no progress,' said Love sourly. 'What do you think's happening there?'

Parkington shrugged.

'If I knew, we'd save ourselves a journey,' he replied soberly.

Love said nothing. It all appeared unconvincing and inconclusive to him, and yet there seemed no other way to discover what had happened to Clarissa Head, except to go back to the monastery and see for themselves whether she was there. Perhaps she had lost her memory; maybe she was suffering from the after-effects of concussion and had just wandered away, caught a bus because she was near when it stopped, got out when it stopped again. He had known people involved in accidents do stranger things.

If they returned to Damascus and threw themselves on the mercy of the British Embassy, it was conceivable that somehow they might be smuggled out of the country, before the police caught up with them. But then they would leave without knowing what had happened to her, and why, or even where she was. He took a deep breath. Parkington was right, if for the wrong reasons. He would have to return or not be able to live with himself.

'O.K.' he allowed grudgingly. 'You win. Now what do we know about this monastery?'

'Damn all, except what's in the tourist handbook.'

Parkington opened a beige leaflet written in French, English and Arabic, with two blurred photographs of the monastery. On the back was a sketch map, showing the distance in kilometres between Damascus, Aleppo, and Homs. Rivers were blue wriggly serpents.

He opened a large scale map of the area that showed the monastery as a square dot with a dotted line around it to mark the wall. Several small rivers or canals converged on the site.

'There must be a great lake under it,' said Love thoughtfully. 'Maybe the water overflows during the rainy season, or, as I said, underground gas pressure builds up and blows out a water spout – and the flame.'

'Could be. Now, let's get our bearings and see where north is.'

At ten past eleven that night, by Love's Juvenia wristwatch, they set off for the second time along the road to the monastery. Under the moon, the desert stretched into a misty infinity. Eyes of wild cats or wolves glittered like green glass in the gloom. Here and there a tiny flame trembled in a window as a mother kept vigil by the bedside of a sick child, or an old person lay with a candle by their bed, a stranger to sleep and fearful of the dark.

A couple of miles from the monastery, Parkington switched off his lights, and then two hundred yards from the clump of trees where he intended to leave the car, he accelerated, turned off the engine and coasted the rest of the way. The only sound was the swish of their tyres on the soft, silica sand, and the faint creak of springs.

He turned into the clump of trees, pulled on the handbrake. He slipped a Philips recording cassette into the tape recorder under the radio, switched on the set, checked that the ancillary equipment was working. Now any messages that arrived would be recorded automatically on the tape; Parkington could play them back later at the speed of speech.

They shut the car doors carefully and tested the silence. The moon threw long shadows from the mosques, and the minarets pointed stiff ceramic fingers against the sky. The night was cold and a wind was blowing down from the hills in the north, sad and chilly, without comfort, without hope. Involuntarily, Love shivered; he had little confidence that they would succeed in rescuing Clarissa, and no enthusiasm whatever for the attempt, and yet what else could they do but try? He pulled the black sheet over the car so that none of the bright parts would reflect the moonlight, and tried to forget his forebodings.

For a few minutes they both waited under the trees. The trunks groaned against each other in the wind; leaves rustled silkily. Gradually, their eyes grew more accustomed to the dim light. Somewhere, in the distance, a dog was barking, faint and faraway, and once an airliner droned overhead, its tiny red and green lights flickering like stars down the sky.

Parkington looped a coil of thin nylon rope, with a four-headed hook at one end, over his left shoulder, his camera over his right. He wore his Mauser strapped by two elastic bands to his right leg, just below the knee.

Love had his pencil torch clipped in an inside pocket of his jacket; he had left his passport and cheques in his room at Maloula.

They set off from the trees, walking at right angles to the monastery wall, so that they would approach it through the comforting shadow from the mosques. Under their rubber soles, the sand felt fine as fluff, and despite the cold, Love was soon himself perspiring with the effort; it was like walking through a thick fog.

They came into the cone of darkness of the nearest mosque, silhouetted against the moon, went on for a few more paces, and were under the wall. The bricks still felt warm after the heat of the day; the ancient stones and mortar had stored up the warmth and now slowly released it. They felt between crevices of the rocks and stones for any toe or hand-hold, but there was nothing.

Parkington slipped the rope from his shoulder, laid it carefully in a coil at his feet. From his jacket pocket he pulled out what looked like a plastic starting-pistol. Then he took a small steel rod, the size and thickness of a pencil, pushed this down the muzzle of the pistol, attached the four-headed hook to the end.

He pointed the pistol up into the air, towards the monastery wall, and squeezed the trigger. With a pop like a champagne cork being drawn, the rope whipped up past Love and over the wall. Parkington scraped a small hole at his feet with a stone, buried the compressed-air pistol in it, then stood up and pulled gently at the rope.

The hooks scraped on the rough stones on the other side of the wall, and then one gripped. Parkington wound the rope around both wrists and gave a sharp tug. The hook held firm. He nodded to Love and began to climb up the rope, hand over hand. When he reached the top of the wall, he peered over carefully, then rolled over the top to minimize the risk of discovery, and jumped down inside.

Love followed.

Parkington pulled the loose end of the rope over the wall behind them, coiled it up, pushed it under a corner of a loose paving stone; they might need to use it on their way out. Then they dusted their hands, smoothed down their jackets and looked about them.

The courtyard was empty. A few chickens clucked disapprovingly from some unseen overhead roosting place, and then settled down to sleep.

Still keeping in the shadows, Parkington and Love began to move around the edge of the building until they faced the well. Suddenly, a bell boomed above them twice, and they both jumped, their muscles tightening at the unexpected noise. It seemed harmless enough; perhaps a call to prayer? Love remembered how the bell had rung when they had been in the monastery that morning and it had apparently signified nothing.

The yard was empty as far as he could see. They moved on more slowly now, for they were approaching the corner of the building, and once round it they would be in full light of the moon.

Parkington took a small mirror from his breast pocket, the sort and size that dentists use on a metal probe, and moved it slowly around the edge of the brickwork. The yard was also empty on that side. In the far corner stood a small, brass ceremonial cannon, richly scrolled, that glittered dully in the moonlight. It stood on four solid brass wheels, with the barrel pointing slightly upwards. Behind this were the double wooden doors, with a huge locking beam across them, that led into the main part of the building.

There seemed no other way into the monastery, yet presumably there must be, because if there weren't, how could the monks move the beam in position once they were behind the door? This problem puzzled Love.

He was still thinking about it seconds later when a generator began to hum somewhere like a heavy mechanical heart, and the entire courtyard glowed in an amber, throbbing light.

Love and Parkington straightened up; there was no point in trying to hide now; they had nowhere to hide, in any case.

Three monks stood alongside the far wall. A door was open behind them, the outside carefully painted to simulate raw rock. So that was why they hadn't noticed it. Ah, well, it was too late now. The centre monk approached them. He was the one they had spoken to earlier in the day.

'So,' he began pleasantly. 'You have returned. Evidently we must have something here to interest our English visitors. What relics do you wish to see at this time of night?'

He stood a few feet from Love, and only his eyes belied the friendliness of his voice. Parkington swung his camera around to his chest.

'I want to take some moonlight pictures,' he explained.

'Really? And to do this you throw a rope over the wall, climb it, bury the rope, and then creep around the side of this building? Why? When you could so easily have come through the main gate, as the other people do – as you did this morning?

'I don't think that's a very good explanation. You've come here with something else in mind.'

'No, really,' said Parkington.

'Save your words. A friend does not come like a thief.'

The other two monks had moved up close behind the speaker. They now stationed themselves one on either side of Love and Parkington. For a moment, Love thought of making a wild dash for freedom – an uppercut to the jaw of one, a quick heel back against the shinbone of another, and then a leap for the door.

But to do this would immediately admit their guilt. And, after all, these monks had some right to be suspicious. The boy who was only suspected of stealing apples was proved guilty the moment he started to run. It would be wiser to brazen things out.

'Walk,' said the monk and jerked his head towards the open door.

They walked. The door shut behind them and they were standing in a well-lit corridor paved with stone and with stone walls, damp to the touch. The air felt so cold that their breath hung in it like fog. Long crystallized stalcatites pointed white fingers at them from the ceiling; moss grew, soft and soaking, between joints of the streaming flag-stones.

The leading monk opened a door on the right of the corridor, stood to one side as Love and Parkington went through it. He followed them, closed the door, which had a square spy-hole with a hinged wooden lid. The other two monks waited in the corridor.

The room was small, with a stone floor, stone walls, and a rush mat. On the wall facing them hung a framed page of the Koran, under a tattered flag with the crescent and star of Islam. Two candles burned in brass sconces on either side of the flag.

To the right, a shabby maroon curtain hung from an ancient brass rail, and trembled slightly in the draught from a door behind it. An electric light bulb with a cheap china shade lit up the room with a fluctuating, feverish brilliance. That generator, Love thought inconsequentially, must be very old. The room felt slightly warmer than the corridor, but not much; the difference between cold and very cold.

'Who are we going to see?' asked Parkington.

Before the monk could reply, the curtain was pulled to one side. Behind it, stood a man in a dark suit, and heavy walking shoes. His face was sallow, his shoulders unusually broad. He shut the door behind him, pulled the curtain across it, came into the room, lit a cigar. The monk spoke to him in German, explaining what had happened in the courtyard.

'So you are English,' the man said, as though he might have known it all along. His white teeth glittered in the trembling candle flames.

'Yes,' replied Love. 'Who are you?'

'A guest of the Abbot,' the man replied smoothly. 'As I believe you know, many of the brothers of this monastery are in Mecca. We are their guests in their absence. And now it seems that you are our guests, if uninvited. Why are you here?'

He smiled with his mouth, but not his eyes.

'We wanted to take some photographs,' said Parkington.

'Of what?'

'Of this place, by moonlight,' said Parkington.

'But you have no flashgun. And, is it usual, for anyone wishing to take photographs of a religious institution, to fire a rope over a wall from some clever little gadget that you immediately proceed to bury? You even hid the rope afterwards. Come, come, you must do better than that.'

'How do you know about the rope?' asked Love. There seemed no point in carrying the absurd cover of photography any further. He hardly knew a shutter from a frame, and he would be surprised if Parkington was much more knowledgeable. The man opened the door of a cupboard. Inside it, the blue radar screen of a portable Sony receiver glowed luminously, like a huge electronic eye.

'That's how,' he said. 'My colleagues then went out to meet you. We also examined the place you had climbed over the wall. Now, why are you here?'

Well, why were they here? Was it too late to tell the truth, or at least part of the truth? They had really nothing else to tell.

Love said, 'There's an English girl, the daughter of one of my patients – I'm a doctor – and I believe she came into this monastery today. She is ill, perhaps seriously. We would like to find her. She needs treatment.'

The man smiled.

'Ingenious, but unconvincing,' he said. 'Also, there's no girl here.'

'She may be here without your knowledge.'

'I don't think you're looking for any girl, either ill or well,' replied the man. 'I think you have come to steal some of the relics. Well, you are not the first to have that idea. They would fetch a great sum from many museums in the West. Just imagine what people would pay to see the spear of the centurion who was on duty at the Crucifixion, at a side show at Coney Island, or in one of your English stately homes!'

He chuckled briefly at the thought.

'Anyhow, it's too late to discuss this matter tonight.

'You will stay here in one of the monks' cells until the morning, and then I'll inform the police in Damascus. They can take over the matter.'

He half turned, as though remembering something.

'You say you are a doctor. Are you Dr Love, by any chance? Dr Jason Love?'

Love nodded.

'Then the police will be extremely pleased to see you, Doctor. I have just heard over Damascus radio how you and someone else – possibly your colleague here? – are both wanted for desecrating a grave, for shooting at police officers, and I believe there's also a charge that you started a false air-raid alarm?'

'You never heard that on any radio,' said Love. 'Who the hell are you?'

The man's eyes narrowed momentarily.

'My name is Jakob Steinmann.'

He turned to the monks.

'Take them away,' he said.

'If you can,' retorted Love, and dug back with his right heel against the shins of the monk who had moved in close behind him. The monk gave a grunt of agony, but he recovered sufficiently, before Love could turn, and drove his fist into the small of Love's back, above his right kidney.

Love reeled forward and collapsed over the table. The legs splintered with his weight, and the table slithered to the ground with him on it. Through a red mist of pain he saw Parkington's right hand whip in a scything blow to hit the monk's throat. The man toppled like a melting candle, and then Parkington was standing to one side, his Mauser in his hand. Steinmann went on smoking as though all this was no concern of his. He had not moved; he glanced from the monk on the floor to Parkington's Mauser, and tapped some ash from the end of his cigar.

'A very interesting performance,' he said, 'and all the more unexpected coming from two harmless photographers anxious to take moonlight pictures of an ancient monastery. It is more than unusual, it is totally unnecessary.'

'I'll give you three,' said Parkington, 'and if you don't tell us where the girl is, I'll shoot.'

'You will give me nothing,' Steinmann told him, 'because you have nothing whatever to give. Except your life.'

Love raised himself on his elbows.

'The spy-hole!' he shouted hoarsely. 'Duck!'

But he was too late. He heard a faint phut from behind the thick door. For a second, Parkington stood, the Mauser still in his hand, and then his fingers opened and it toppled out and fell on the stone floor. He sank at the knees, staggered, reached out to clutch the table that wasn't there, and fell. Steinmann bent down, picked up the Mauser. The door opened. One of the monks was holding an air pistol; he had fired through the open aperture in the door.

'Take them away,' ordered Steinmann, slipping the Mauser in his pocket.

Love crawled to his feet, fighting back the urge to vomit, as waves of nausea made the floor writhe under him. He knelt down at Parkington's side, rolled him over to examine his wound. A small tufted dart stuck through his right shoulder, over the nerves that controlled his arm. Love pulled out the dart, helped Parkington to his feet.

'It's not a proper bullet,' he said. 'Just something to numb you. You'll be all right.'

'I wouldn't take your word for that,' said Steinmann, tapping ash on the mat. 'My friends here don't like people who attack them. After all, monks are brothers of peace, aren't they?'

He gave an almost imperceptible nod. The monk with the air pistol slipped it in his belt, and hit Love in the solar plexus as he straightened up. As Love went down, the monk's knee came up. Love instinctively jerked his head to the right, his judo training, his habit of teaching it in local British Legion classes in Bishop's Combe, making the motion a reflex action; the knee missed his nose and teeth.

The other monk picked him up, and hit him across the face with the back of his hand. As he staggered, trying to ride the blow, the monk hit him again, this time in the stomach. The walls folded and the floor swam up to meet the ceiling. The rest was merciful darkness.

When Love awoke, he felt so cold that his teeth chattered uncontrollably. He tasted dry blood in his mouth; his nose was also crusted with blood, sore and raw. He moved his hands carefully across the floor; the stone flags felt gritty to his fingertips.

He moved his body gingerly because it was one enormous pain, throbbing with every beat of his heart. His fingers touched a wall, cold and damp, soft with moss and fungus.

Someone groaned in the darkness by his side; he felt in his pocket for the fountain-pen torch, flicked it on. Parkington blinked his eyes painfully in the sudden unexpected light.

'Where are we?' he asked weakly.

'In that monk's cell, I should think, like the man said. But without the monk.'

'That's one mercy.'

'It's about the only one, then.'

Love stood up, shining the torch around the walls. Blocks of stone were laid on each other without cement. The wooden door, thick as a tree, was studded all over with iron stars. Above him in one corner, a small opening, bisected by a metal bar, let in a pale rectangle of light. There was nothing else in the room; no bed, no chair, no mat. Nothing for their comfort, and nothing with which they could arm themselves.

'What happened?' asked Love. 'I don't remember much.'

'Just as well,' said Parkington. 'After you went down, the monks set about me.'

He stood up slowly, shook his head to rid himself of the dizziness that accompanied the act of standing.

'Now what?' asked Love, thinking aloud. 'We wait for the Syrian police to pick us up? Or for that character Steinmann to turn his trained monks on us? In fact, is there a choice?'

'Listen,' said Parkington urgently, gripping Love's arm. Together they stood in the silence and heard the flap, flap of slippered feet pass outside the cell. Love moved to the aperture, stood on tip-toe, peered out. In the corridor, a monk paused at the door, felt a bolt on the door that Love could not see.

Blue night lights glowed in the roof. The monk's breath hung beneath them like fog on the damp air. Then he walked on and out of sight, the flap, flap of his feet growing softer. Love flashed his torch briefly across the corridor. Its tiny beam lit up a square ante-room or hall, with ropes coiled on the stone floor, a wooden frame packed with small stone flagons. He flicked off his torch and turned to Parkington.

'The monk's doing the rounds,' he said. 'We seem to be near the well where they draw up this holy water. There must be *some* way out.'

'There is,' agreed Parkington. 'Through the door.'

'But how do we open the bloody door?'

He beat on it with his fists. It was so thick and heavy, so swollen with dampness, that the wood soaked up the sound like a sponge. Love glanced at his watch – it had been removed and put back on his right wrist, presumably when they saw that it contained nothing more lethal than the usual Juvenia alarm. Half past four – but was that morning or afternoon – and of what day? How long had they been in this cell – and how long had they left before they would be removed, either by the monks or by the police from Damascus?

The sound of approaching footsteps grew louder. Listening behind the door, they heard the muted breathing of the monk as he paused to test the bolt, and then his footsteps faded for the second time. Love pressed his hands over his face to try to force his tired brain to concentrate. Was the whole thing a nightmare? Would he wake up screaming? He opened his eyes to reality; the small square cell, the raw dampness in his throat, pain in his bruises. He was awake, and screaming wouldn't help him.

'If that monk is on some kind of sentry-go and passes here regularly, we might be able to intercept him,' he said slowly, an idea forming in his mind, changing shape, amoeba-like, even as he spoke.

'You take off your belt,' he told Parkington. 'I'll join it to mine, and then get up to this breathing hole, or whatever it ᵎ in the corner. If you can beat on the door and make him pause just for a second, they might just reach around his neck.'

'Then what do we do? Hang him?'

Love shook his head.

'Not at first. But threaten to if he doesn't hand over the key to this door.'

Parkington slipped off his belt, looped it around Love's, tested them for tightness, handed it to Love.

'We'll try a dry run first,' said Love.

He went back to the aperture and dangled the leather loop out into the corridor. It was not nearly long enough to reach the door. Hope dwindled like a dying candle flame, and then was suddenly rekindled. He turned back to Parkington.

'I'll drop my watch out,' he explained. 'He must see it, he's almost certain to stop and bend down and pick it up. Then – let's take it from there.'

'You can take it from anywhere,' said Parkington gloomily. 'I still don't think we've got a hope.'

Love unbuckled his watch. He dangled it through the window, and then let it drop. It fell, face down, the stainless steel back glittering bluely under the night lights. The ticking, magnified by the stone floor and walls, sounded loud as a metronome.

The footsteps they waited for came faintly, then more strongly, from the darkness behind the wall. Love stood on the tips of his toes, holding his breath lest the monk should hear him breathe and look up.

He could see the man approach, his cassock swinging as he walked. The blue lights glinted on a ring of keys at the rope around his waist. There was a sudden intake of breath as he saw the watch. He bent down slowly, picked it up, held it up to his ear, then looked at it in the palm of his hand. His head moved as he began to turn to look up towards the aperture, the only place from which it could have fallen.

At that moment, Love slipped the belt over his head, under the chin, and pulled back sharply with all his strength. The monk's skull crashed against the stone wall. He gave a sharp hoarse cry of pain, and fear, dropped the watch, clawed frantically with both hands at the leather thong that threatened to throttle him, his breath beginning to bubble at his lips. He scrabbled with his hands, kicking out his feet. Love, leaning out, saw he was the monk who had hit him in Stein-mann's room. The knowledge encouraged him to twist the belt tighter.

'Listen,' he whispered through clenched teeth. 'If you move now, you'll kill yourself. Stay still and you'll live.'

He loosened the belt for a fraction of a second to allow the monk to take in some air into his lungs, and then jerked it tight.

'Hand up the keys.'

The monk shook his head, clawing again at the strap. Love pulled it tighter, and then loosened it.

'Hand them up.'

The monk gave a gasp and filled his lungs with air once more. Love gave the strap another jerk.

'For the last time,' he said. 'Those keys. Otherwise we'll kill you and take them ourselves. You can't win, but you could live.'

The monk's left hand went down blindly to the folds of his cassock. He held up three old-fashioned metal keys, each about five inches long, on their ring. Parkington put out his hand to take them. The monk smashed the keys against his hand, trying to spear his palm against the wall.

'Nasty,' reproved Love, tightening the strap. 'You should have learned better manners in your monastery garden.'

Parkington grasped the keys, pulled them in, ran to the door.

The first key was too small, the second one fitted, but the lock was so rusty he could not turn it. He pulled the third key off the ring, and jammed this into the handle of the key in the lock to use as a lever.

The key turned reluctantly, and then, with a creak of rusty mechanism, the lock groaned open. Parkington swung the door inwards on its ancient hinges, and he was outside. He had no time for finesse, nor was he disposed to gentleness. The monk was stronger than he was, and might be armed. Also, like Love, he recognized him. He brought up his right knee into the monk's groin, and, as he sank, Love let go of the belt. Parkington caught the man, staggered with him to the wide landing.

Love followed him, locking the door after him. He bent down over the monk, picked up his watch and put it on.

Then he slipped on his belt, handed Parkington's back to him. The monk was still unconscious. Parkington's hands felt expertly for any gun. He was unarmed save for a sheath-knife in his belt. Parkington removed it. The corridor was filled with silence, and then the sound of their breathing. Had their struggle been heard outside? Was this the only man on guard?

Parkington felt in a deep pocket in the man's cassock, pulled out two black plastic boxes, both flat and thin, as big as boxes of matches. One had a red circle painted on its side, the size of a penny; the other was plain. Both had small, spring-loaded plungers at one end. Parkington turned them over carefully in his hand.

'What do you think they are?' he asked Love.

Love picked them up.

'I'd say some sort of remote control signaller,' he said. 'We use much the same thing in hospitals. Surgeons on duty have one in their pocket, and when they're wanted urgently someone in a central office sends out a radio signal and this thing bleeps so that the wearer knows he's wanted in the ward.'

'Looks like that, I agree,' said Parkington, 'but I want to be sure. Wake up Charley Boy here and we'll ask him.'

Love straightened up, flashed his torch across the corridor. He picked up one of the small bottles, held it upside down, but it was empty. Near the rack stood a glass carboy, carefully packed with straw in a metal container. He pulled out the rubber bung, sniffed at the throat of the carboy, shook it. Liquid of some kind slopped about inside. He tipped over the carboy, poured some out over the monk's face. His eyelids fluttered like a moth's wing, and he sat up.

'Don't shout,' warned Parkington, holding the knife, sharp edge towards his Adam's apple, as an inducement to silence. 'Keep it in whispers or you die. Now – what are these gadgets?'

The monk's eyes flicked from one man to the other. Then his back arched so that the blade nicked his flesh and drew a bead of blood.

'What are they?' asked Parkington again, pressing the knife against his skin.

'I push that switch and it rings a buzzer in Steinmann's

office,' he said sulkily. 'Then he knows I'm on duty.'

'I see. Sort of electronic way of punching a time clock. And the red one?'

'That works the transmitter. Remote control. We can start it without being there.'

'What do you transmit?' asked Parkington, remembering the bare end of the lightning conductor.

'I don't know. I don't speak Arabic.'

'When's your next signal due to Steinmann?' asked Love.

'In an hour. I'd just made one when I saw that watch.'

Love slipped both boxes in his jacket pocket. The monk swivelled his head, trying to calculate exactly where he was. He saw the carboy, and instinctively wiped the back of his hand across his mouth.

'For God's sake,' he said anxiously. 'Not that stuff.'

'Why not?' asked Love, but the man was mumbling and ignored him.

'Let me go. Let me go!'

'We're all going,' Parkington assured him. 'And you're leading us out. Now.'

'There's no way out,' retorted the monk, suddenly sinking back weakly. 'Only the main door and that's guarded.'

'By whom?'

'The others,' he said. 'Also there's a cannon on the other side. It's used for firing a salute on the Prophet's birthday and holy days. You can't escape that way.'

'Where does the water in the well come from?' asked Love.

'An underground lake.'

Love remembered the blue rivers and canals that centred on the monastery in Parkington's map. It could even be connected to the water gushing from the rocks in Maloula; the same pressure of gas could force it out miles away.

He shone his torch briefly down the mouth of the well, but the beam was too weak to show more than the wet stones that ringed it. The inside was green with moss. Spongy white plants sprouted unhealthily, a strange fungus of darkness and decay. Then he saw the rusty horizontal rung of a ladder pegged into the wall of the well.

'There must be a way out,' he said. 'That ladder there's for climbing. We're going down, and you're going first.'

'No,' said the monk. 'No.'

'Yes,' hissed Parkington. He pressed the blade of the knife gently against the man's jugular. 'Now.'

'I don't know the way out,' mumbled the man in an extremity of terror, his eyes wide and white as marbles in his head. 'The lake stretches for miles.'

'Get up and no funny ideas about shouting for help. For even if it came, it'd be too late to help you.'

They were all standing now, the monk leaning against the low wall, his face still distorted with pain. He took a pace forward, tripped over the flagon, almost fell. Love kicked it over the edge, counted five before he heard the splash. The well must be deeper than he had calculated.

'Hurry,' said Parkington. 'We've not got all day.'

The monk began to climb, feeling cautiously with his slippered feet for the rusting rungs. He went down slowly and reluctantly, hand over hand, testing each rung before he trusted it with his weight, anxious to prolong the climb as much as he dared, for each second that passed could bring nearer the arrival of his relief. Parkington followed him, while Love shone the torch on both of them. When they were beyond the range of his feeble beam, he switched it off and climbed down himself.

With each step he took, the air grew colder until it seemed to numb his bones and lock his joints, so that suddenly every movement was a conscious aching, gnawing effort. The vegetation on the walls grew thicker. It brushed his face, clammy and puffy, like the soft, fat fingers of men long drowned. He shuddered involuntarily. Up above their heads the circle of the well opening grew dimmer and smaller. Beneath their feet they saw another circle glittering like a round mirror. This was the lake, but how deep would it be, and where did it lead?

The monk whispered hoarsely, 'I'm on the last rung.'

'Then jump,' said Parkington.

'No,' beseeched the monk. 'It may be deep. There may be currents. I can't swim.'

'Jump!' repeated Parkington.

'No!' the monk cried.

Parkington brought down one heel sharply on the man's

knuckles. With a moan of pain, he loosened his grip and fell. The mirror surface shattered as the boom of the splash volleyed up through the vertical shaft. Then the ripples stilled and the monk was staggering from side to side for balance, feeling blindly for the slimy walls, sobbing for breath as the iron chill of the water covered his heart.

Parkington climbed on down and jumped beside him. Love followed, holding his torch and the two plastic boxes above his head to keep them out of the water. The cold seeped through his trousers, gently at first, and then, as it reached his flesh, he had to bite his lower lip to stop crying out because of its sudden spreading numbness.

This cold was something he had never experienced or imagined; it made his heart labour, the breath rattle in his throat, his body shake in violent, uncontrolled and uncontrollable spasms. All feeling left his limbs; nothing was real, nothing existed but the hard agony of freezing alive.

Shining stalactites hung down almost to the level of the water which all around them stretched away into a glittering infinity of silence. The walls reached up into the roof of an underground cavern. It was impossible to say how wide and how long this cavern was, or from where it was fed.

They stood irresolute, in an agony of coldness that froze all sense of direction. To move was to feel the cold more fiercely. The loneliness, the darkness, the iciness of the water had drained all initiative from Love's mind.

Parkington ripped off the top button of his jacket, held it up out of the water, began to unscrew it into two pieces. Inside, embedded in the plastic, lay a tiny compass. He turned slightly to the left and then to the right until he had centred the needle.

'North's there,' he said, pointing with the edge of his left hand. 'According to that map in Maloula, Damascus is south-south-east. If we head in that direction we should strike one of those rivers.'

He turned to the monk.

'You lead,' he said.

'There's no way out there,' the monk said stubbornly, his voice thick and slurred. 'I told you, this lake stretches for miles. And there's another danger.'

'What's that?' asked Love.

'Every so often, gas collects here. The pressure builds up and forces water up through this well or the one in the yard. It's been like that for hundreds of years. The monks have copper valves that regulate the amount of gas they let out to control the level of the water. I tell you it's not safe to go on.'

'And I tell you it's not safe to stand here,' said Parkington. 'Get moving.'

The man took a pace forward, and then suddenly spun round and knocked Love's torch into the water with his right hand. As they staggered in the darkness he drove his left fist into Parkington's face. Then he jumped back and splashed towards the bottom of the well, shouting incoherently at the top of his voice. His hoarse animal bellowing echoed and re-echoed around the high roof of the cavern; down the long hidden aisles of shimmering, frozen darkness.

Love started after him, but his feet slipped on the slimy bottom of the lake and he almost fell, floundering beneath the water, gasping for breath at the chill which constricted his throat. He had lost his torch and one of the bleepers. He held the other up out of the water, his fingers locked around it, like a dead man's hand.

'Leave him to me,' said Parkington, his voice thick and hoarse. He turned the knife in his hand so that he gripped the point of the blade and its smooth curved back lay balanced between his thumb and forefinger. When he saw the monk reach up for the rung to pull himself free of the water, he threw the knife.

It hit the monk in the neck. He gave a sudden cry of agony and tore at the blade; blood began to pump in a viscous stream. Then slowly, and with a terrible finality, he slid down into the water.

Love heaved at him to drag his head above the surface, but with his robes waterlogged he was too heavy. He slithered from his grasp, a rash of bubbles broke at the surface, and then the shimmering mirror of the lake dipped and was smooth.

'He's dead,' said Love. Years in general practice had taught him that life was only a loan, redeemable on call. But sometimes the speed at which it was redeemed surprised even him; this was one of those times.

'Let's get the hell out of here before we join him,' said Parkington weakly.

'Can you see that compass without the torch?' asked Love as they took slow, agonizing steps through the water.

'No,' replied Parkington. 'We'll have to trust to luck.'

'It hasn't proved too trustworthy so far,' retorted Love bitterly, and then saved his breath for walking.

At first, the bed of the lake was slippery, and they slid and fell half a dozen times, spitting out water as they stumbled, hoping desperately they were not walking in a circle. Then they left the slime behind and were walking on what felt like gravel.

They walked for half an hour by the luminous hands of Love's watch, but even the exercise and the effort could not warm them. Love felt as though a steel cage was contracting round his lungs and heart; the cold was so intense he could hardly bear to breathe.

The angle of the floor changed suddenly, and they were up on a small island, out of the water. They stood shivering while Parkington peered at his compass, but it was impossible to see. Love held the luminous dial of his watch at right angles to the needle, which they could then just make out as a faint and tiny shadow. They reset it, set off for a second time.

The water grew deeper, and once or twice they heard splashes as though small pieces from the roof were falling about them.

'This lake must be fed from somewhere,' said Parkington, trying to convince himself as much as Love.

'Obviously,' said Love. 'But there could be miles of water under here. And it may not come from this direction.'

How long would it be before the blood congealed in his veins, until his heart could no longer pump it around his body, before the heavy, mortal, but almost welcome, drowsiness overwhelmed him? Would it be in ten more minutes or in twenty? Statistics he had learned as a student about how much heat and cold the human body could stand, danced in his brain. Sailors sunk in wartime Arctic convoys to Russia had lasted only minutes in icy seas. At the present temperature here, it could not be more than half an hour before their blood grew so thick and chilled that even to stand would become an effort beyond their abilities, and they would sink down slowly and almost silently. Half an hour, and then the end, lost in an unknown, subterranean sea. A sea. Currents. Of course! That was how they could find where the water came from.

'Have you got a match?' he asked suddenly.

'A match,' repeated Parkington, 'I've got a whole bloody box, but it's soaking wet. You'll never get one to light.'

'Give me a match, and for God's sake don't drop the rest.'

Parkington handed him a Brymay box of matches, sodden and about to disintegrate. Love opened it carefully, removed one match, threw it a foot away on the water, and a second close behind it.

'Now watch those,' he said. 'Tell me if they move.'

They stood silently, shuddering with cold, their teeth loose as dice in their gums, forcing themselves to watch the matches. They moved slowly, almost imperceptibly, past them to the right. Love waited, counting in his mind, until there was no doubt he was not imagining their movement. Then he turned to Parkington.

'If they're going to the right, then the current must be coming from our left. That means one river's over there. Let's head towards it.'

He crammed the box into his pocket and they set off. The shore sloped down sharply, and the water grew deeper until it was over their hearts, and they gasped for breath, their bodies arched, muscles standing out through their flesh like carved sinews in ancient Greek statues, like the muscles on corpses, taken from tanks of formaldehyde, that Love had dissected as a student.

After ten minutes, they stopped again. Love pulled out two more matches, threw them on the water. They moved past them now, at an angle, but more quickly. The current was increasing, but they were going slightly off-course. They turned until the matches were behind them, then, for the third time, they set off. They did not speak. There was nothing to say. Their thoughts were companions enough, and they needed all their energy to force themselves on.

The water grew deeper and Parkington, the taller of the two, suddenly bumped his head on the roof. He staggered, and Love steadied him.

The water was now up to Love's shoulders. For the third time, he threw matches on the water. Now they moved far more swiftly, and in seconds were lost.

The same thought bore into both their minds: they were coming to a tunnel where it would be impossible to walk and breathe, and they would have to hold their breath and push on in the hope that the tunnel would only be short. If it wasn't, they could either try to retreat, or they could drown, at whatever point they had reached.

'Wait a minute,' said Parkington suddenly, and felt in his lapel.

'What's the matter?' asked Love.

'Benzedrine tablets. I'd forgotten them. They'll give us a bit more energy.'

He tore open the stitching in his lapel, and then carefully removed two tiny capsules of edible plastic, each about half an inch long.

'Bite it,' said Love, as he took one from Parkington's soaking hand. 'It'll get into the blood quicker than if you just swallow it.'

The bitterness of the capsules, added to the cold, made them shudder and retch, but somehow they swallowed the grains, sour as wormwood, and swallowed again to keep them down.

'*Now*,' said Love. He led the way until the water rose up to his chin, and then he stopped.

'I'll go first,' he said.

'What if we can't make it?' asked Parkington.

'What if the floor falls in? Ask a stupid question, you get a stupid answer.'

Love took a deep breath and started to walk forward, letting out his air gradually, breathing in again slowly, feeling the benzedrine beginning to move in his sluggish blood stream. He paused again as the water came over his mouth, filled his lungs with air, through his nose, let it out slowly to try and control the pounding of his chest, and then took an enormous breath.

He pushed his hands, locked together, out in front of him like the prow of a vessel, to try and cut his way through the water. Then he began to walk.

They seemed to be in some kind of tunnel or venturi tube

through the rock. The current was moving more strongly towards them, cold as a wall of ice. At every step the power of the current increased, so that Love could have stood, leaning forward into the water, supported by its pressure against his body.

It was breaking over his head now, numbing his brain. He could feel his heart hammering against his rib cage and his eyes seemed to be bursting from their sockets.

Blue and red and yellow stars exploded and were gone; the blood thundered in his ears, roaring like an approaching train. He was not a living, reasoning person, any more, but an automaton.

He could not see, and soon he could no longer feel the beating of his heart. It might have been beating in someone else's body.

One step. Another. A third.

The stars merged all their colours into one blazing whiteness. It was like staring into a searchlight. Beyond this dazzle, whirling dark circles revolved in infinite complexity.

A fourth step. A fifth. He heard the blood in his ears again, but this time the sound was high pitched, the music of the spheres, the songs of eternity. He took one last step – and suddenly he felt the level of the water fall.

He jerked back his head and struck his skull on the roof, but he could breathe again, and he let the air out of his tortured lungs, blowing bubbles against the current. He breathed in again and the stars dimmed and went out. He walked on now, more confidently, his arms held out on either side, fingers stretched so that they could just touch the edges of the tunnel. The current grew weaker with every step, and soon he could see the level of the water glittering. He was through the tunnel and into another cavern.

Above him, the roof was arched and ribbed like the roof of some enormous mouth. He stopped and looked about him. To the left he saw, for the first time since he had entered the well, a faint, luminous archway.

'We're through,' he shouted. 'We're through.' His brain sent the message to his mouth, but his lips were too stiff to form the words. All he could do was to give a soft moan. He turned to see Parkington, but Parkington was not there. He must have fallen. Oh, God, was he dead?

Love plunged back into the tunnel, shouting unintelligibly, not words, but animal cries in the cold. Then he bumped and almost fell over something at his feet. He took a deep breath, bent down and pulled at Parkington's jacket. He dragged him through against the current, and then propped him up, back against the rocky wall. Parkington slipped limply to one side. Love leaned against him to hold him upright. Water, streaked ominously with red, ran from his nose, from a cut on his head; he must have knocked himself unconscious on the roof.

There was no chance or place for artificial respiration or the kiss of life. Love could feel no pulse on Parkington's wrist, soft and slippery with water, cold as fish scales. He drew back his right hand, balled it into a fist, punched Parkington lightly in the solar plexus, once, twice, harder when the gentle blows brought no results. He was almost fainting himself with weariness and cold; if Parkington fell, he knew he had not the physical strength to drag him up again.

Suddenly a gout of vomit poured from Parkington's mouth. His face contorted, contused with pain. A little colour streaked his skin. He staggered, breathed and opened his eyes.

'Don't speak,' gasped Love. 'Save your strength. Walk!'

Somehow, Love half dragged him, half supported him, through the shallower water towards the opening. With every step, the light grew stronger. Once, bending down, Love saw a patch of sky unbelievably, overwhelmingly blue.

The rocks glittered black on either side, like shining walls of coal, and the roof came down barely a foot above their heads so that they had to crawl on their hands and knees, beneath the jagged rock teeth. And then they were finally through and out into the unexpected sunshine. For a few seconds, they lay in the shallow water, too weary to move, blinking, trying to appreciate the fact that they were still alive – and free.

On either side of the small river grew clumps of bulrushes, and then there were grey rocks, with lizards on them, and the desert.

Love raised himself on his elbows. He still gripped the

plastic box, but now his fingers could open. He let it fall on the sand and the sun drew steam from it. A mist of morning heat shimmered on the horizon. Summoning all his strength, he dragged Parkington out of the river, and together they lay, water streaming from their clothes, but at least on hard rock, that grew warmer as the sun climbed up the sky.

Soon the strengthening morning sun felt hot on their hands and faces, then on their bodies, as their clothes began to steam. Still they lay, lost between sleep and waking, too weary to move.

A vulture clawed its way down the sky and stood, head on one side, watching them. Then it spread its wings in disappointment and flew away; they were not dead, but sleeping.

Chapter Ten

The Monastery of the Sacred Flame, June 30th

Steinmann sat in a polished oak chair in the monastery dining-room. The floor was of flags, dusted with silver sand. The table top, made from cedar planks joined with pegs, felt smooth and waxed beneath the tips of his fingers. He had a bottle of Poland water and a glass in front of him. Now and then he sipped gently; he never drank anything but Poland water. He had a weak stomach, and it was comforting to him. Also, it had associations with the past, with his impressionable youth. He remembered that Count Eckdorf von Heifenstaub had always drunk Poland water, never water from the tap; what was good for him must be good for Steinmann, too.

On the other side of the table, sat Krasna, eyes downcast, fidgeting, crossing and uncrossing his legs. He was on a bench with no back to lean against. A man in monk's habit stood, arms folded, by the door, and watched him. In the rope around his waist, he had a Smith and Wesson .38. No one spoke, and Krasna avoided their eyes. He did not know who these men were, or where he was. In its halo of china shade above their heads, the single electric light throbbed irritatingly, and increased the headache from which he had suffered since he had walked into his room in Damascus and found this man he now knew as Steinmann waiting for him.

Steinmann had long ago learned never to undervalue silence in any interview between superior and inferior; he always waited until he could see a sign that silence had been used to its full effectiveness before he spoke. In this case, he was waiting until a pulse began to beat in Krasna's right temple, until sweat showed on Krasna's forehead, and he ran the tip of his tongue nervously over his dry lips. Then he knew the moment would be ready for speech.

Krasna's eyes traced a vein in the wood, a knot in its hole. He wondered how old the tree had been, how strong the branches that had grown from this knot, who had cut it, and where and when.

He had to think of something tangible, something real, something away from the nightmare of the last few days, or he would scream and break down and weep as he had seen so many other men collapse under interrogation. But where was he? And where was his son, Issan?

After Krasna had been gassed in his room in the souk, he had been blindfolded, and then with his hands tied he had been driven across the desert with Steinmann and another man dressed as a monk. They would not speak to him, and so he had no idea who they were or how far they had travelled. After some hours, hunger and fear and reaction made him sleep. When he awoke, sick and weak, in the morning, he was in a room with a rope-mattress bed, a stool, and a rush mat on the floor. It was a cell of some kind, for the stone walls were bare and the door was bolted from the outside.

Steinmann came in with a monk who brought him a bowl of soup and a couple of slices of rye bread and some olives, but there was no spoon, no knife, nothing he could use as a weapon, or even in a last extremity to take his own life. His watch, his braces, even his shoe laces had been removed. The monk went out and left him alone with Steinmann.

Krasna sat dejectedly on the edge of his bed, and the soup grew cold on the stool.

'Where am I and who are you?' he asked Steinmann.

He was sure that he was back somewhere in Albania in one of the hidden houses run by the secret police exclusively for the interrogation of defectors who had been caught and brought back. He knew that such places existed; he had met men who had worked there; he had seen the bodies of some who had died there.

Would the door open soon and his accusers enter, Ackermann at their head, to ask about the man he and Issan had killed? And was it not true that he had read Western magazines, and had even criticized the ruling régime and said that life was better in America than Albania? Could he deny that this was his view?

Steinmann folded his arms and stood looking down at him as though he could guess his thoughts.

'We know something about you, Dr Krasna,' he said gravely, 'but before we are prepared to hand you over to other authorities, you will carry out the operation you and your son had perfected on a patient we will provide.

'According to how successful this operation is will largely depend your own chances of survival and freedom.

'It is no good you asking me where you are, or who we are, because our names and your location would mean nothing to you. The names are not our real names, and this location can be changed within hours, so you would learn nothing.

'Should you entertain any foolish ideas about escaping, let me disabuse you immediately of your chances. You are surrounded by desert. We will deliberately keep you short of water, so that under the heat of the sun, which can reach a hundred and ten degrees, you would speedily collapse. And should you attempt to escape by night there are wolves that hunt in packs. By day or by night, you would not run very far. Also, your son, who is in another part of this building, under an even stronger guard than you, would be our hostage. And I am sure you would not wish him to suffer.'

'I am not fit to operate,' protested Krasna.

He held out his hands towards the other man.

'Look. They're trembling. I can't operate like this.'

'You will eat and sleep and have a bath, and you will feel

better,' Steinmann assured him. 'You are in no danger so long as you cooperate. And if the operation is successful, you and your son may well go free, and unpunished. I cannot guarantee this, of course, for apart from deviationary thoughts and comparisons you have made between Albania and the West, you have also killed a man. But I promise you I will do my best to see that this is reduced to something like manslaughter in self-defence.'

'How is Issan?' asked Krasna. 'Is he injured?'

'He put up a tough fight, but then he is young and we expected that. He is not seriously hurt. As for the operation, you will be taken to an operating theatre, which is being prepared. Now, rest and eat. I will return in a few hours.'

Krasna did not know what time it was or even what day it was when Steinmann came back with two men in monks' robes, for he could not see the sky from his windowless cell. He was ushered out into a corridor lit by blue lamps, and there Issan was waiting for him, his face bruised, his lips split but otherwise apparently well.

Then they had both been blindfolded, their wrists tied behind their backs and they were taken outside. It must have been dark, because the air felt cool, and Krasna shivered as he was led into a car. There was a strong smell, a mixture of hair-oil and sweat, and they drove, it seemed, for hours. Then, still blindfolded, they were led across some flat surface – possibly a courtyard – up stairs, and along another flat surface that smelled of wax polish and disinfectant, so that both men guessed they were in a hospital.

They went through two sets of doors and their bandages were removed. They were standing in a small room, tiled in white, with a hand basin in the corner, mirrors on the walls and several surgical cupboards. It was the ante-room to an operating theatre. There were no notices on the walls, and the labels had been removed from all the bottles and phials in the cupboards.

Two attendants, already masked and in rubber boots, indicated that they should wash, and handed them surgeons' coats, gauze masks and sterile rubber gloves. Then they went through into the theatre. On the table, dressed for an operation, lay a girl. Krasna approached her, lifted up one eyelid. She was already under sedation.

'Here is your patient,' said Steinmann. 'Now, this is what you will do . . .'

How long ago had all that taken place? Was it days or hours? Time had telescoped, and Krasna had only a vague, confused recollection of scrubbing up afterwards, of being blindfolded once more and unable even to speak to Issan, because they both were driven back in separate cars.

Steinmann's voice cut into his thoughts.

'I have brought you here to tell you that your operation has been half-successful,' he told him.

'How do you mean, *half*-successful?' Krasna asked. 'It should be completely successful.'

'And so we all hope it will be. I will know one way or the other in an hour.'

'You talk in riddles,' said Krasna. 'What's happened to the girl? Has she had a relapse or something? Has her system rejected the electrode we introduced?'

'No,' said Steinmann. 'That part has been satisfactory. Indeed, she was ready to be moved from the Clinic when, under cover of some mock air-raid, an English doctor and a colleague – who I strongly suspect is involved with their Secret Service – kidnapped her.

'I don't know exactly where they intended to take her, but they ended up about thirty miles north of here. Possibly they could not leave the country. It can be difficult to leave if the police want you to stay.'

'Where are we?' asked Krasna wearily.

'I can tell you now, because you can make no use of the information. You are in Syria.'

'Syria?'

He repeated the word as though he had never heard it before. What were they doing there? Why had Ackermann not taken them back to Albania?

'Who is this English doctor?' he asked.

'It is immaterial. He and his friend are locked up not fifty feet from here. Your patient is also under this roof – in the next room, although last night she was with this doctor and his friend.

'She tells me that at four o'clock this morning she awoke. She says she had been dreaming of this monastery – she knew what it looked like although, of course, she did not know its name. And she had to come here, although she had never heard of it before. Interesting, eh?

'The only way here was by bus, so she caught the bus and walked in through our front gate. That's what I mean when I say your operation was half-successful.

'Now, Krasna, you and your son have still the most difficult part of the operation to perform. Then we will know whether it has been a complete success or not.

'On my instructions, you tuned the girl's mind to mine. Now, link up the electrode to the tape recorder, and then I'll know whether she has been able to assimilate my thoughts from a distance – as you claim is possible.

'Also, I will know whether the experiment has any elements of chicanery, because no one else can possibly know my thoughts. That is why I insisted you tuned our two minds. How long will this part of your experiment take?'

'About two to three hours. Largely because the tapes will need to run at least that long. The actual operation is not very difficult. In fact, she will only need a local anaesthetic, and under this we can fix the magnetic links to the electrode.

'Then the impulses of the brain will be transmuted into an electric current, and so into a memory bank and then on to the tapes. Then we remove the electrode. Of course, her thoughts will come out in English, because she is English.'

'Quite so, but then I speak that language. There is no difficulty on that score. Now, you had better see your patient.'

As he pushed back his chair, someone knocked on the door. Steinmann's hand automatically dropped to the right pocket of his jacket.

'Come in,' he called, keeping his hand in his pocket.

The monk inside slid back the bolt, opened the door. A man came through, dressed in monk's habit. His face was pale with the pallor of one who brings bad news and fears he may be blamed for it.

'They've got away, sir,' he announced hoarsely. 'The cell's empty. And Brother Brauer has disappeared. We had no signal from him, so I went in. They've all gone.'

Krasna looked bewilderedly from Steinmann to the monk. What was he talking about?

'It's impossible to get out of that door from inside,' said Steinmann slowly, his face a mask that concealed his feelings. 'Could they have bribed Brauer?'

'I don't think so, or he would have led them out through the door. Also, there seems to have been a struggle.'

'They must be hiding somewhere, in the building,' said Steinmann. 'Go back with Brother Saundra here and make a thorough search. Then report to me. We will be leaving in' – he glanced at his watch – 'in approximately four hours. But first we must establish where they are. Dead or alive.'

'And if they're alive, sir?'

'We cannot take them with us, and equally we cannot leave potential witnesses behind. If they are still alive – which I doubt – we'll have to kill them. But leave that to me. Your job is to find them – now.'

Love was the first to awake. The way he felt, as though he had been beaten all over with lead piping, he wished he could have stayed asleep. His clothes had stiffened with slime and water, and this throat was rough, as though it had been sandpapered.

He sat up slowly and painfully, for if he moved quickly he thought he might fall apart. Parkington stirred at the movement, opened his eyes, grimaced at Love's appearance, then sat up beside him.

'We look like something out of pond life,' he said hoarsely. 'God, my throat. Do you think this water is safe to drink?'

'I wouldn't,' said Love. 'We managed not to drink the stuff underground. This river looks like an open sewer to me.'

'Smells like one, too,' said Parkington. 'So do you, Doctor. Your worst friends wouldn't know you, let alone tell you. I suppose I'm much the same.'

He sniffed the sleeve of his jacket and wrinkled his nose in disgust. 'As I thought. I am.'

Love tried to dust his clothes and then gave up the attempt. At least he was alive, and the sun was shining, and he was warm, and for the moment this was enough. He picked up the plastic box, stuffed it into his pocket.

Then he glanced at his watch; half past eight, and judging from the sun, in the morning. But what morning, on what day? How long had they slept? How long had they been underground? The questions echoed emptily in his mind.

'We'd better get back to the car,' said Parkington, standing up and stretching himself.

'Where is the car? Where the hell are *we*?'

'Don't ask me,' Parkington replied. 'I've lost my compass button.'

'We could find where north is with the sun and my watch,' said Love. 'But that's no good, because we still wouldn't know what we are north of. As there's a river here, it's a fair chance there'll be a road alongside it. Let's take a gander.'

They climbed slowly and stiffly up the bank, through the sharp, speary-leaved bulrushes. A wind blew dust into their faces from the open, flat emptiness before them. To their right they saw a travelling cloud of dust, round and high like a peacock's tail, and in its centre, the glittering chromium snout of a lorry. It passed them a hundred yards away, and they watched the dust cloud until it was out of sight. Then they walked on until they reached the road.

Fifty yards to the right, a milestone stuck out of the landscape like a tooth. Love walked to it; Damascus, 72 km. Homs, 96.

'This is the main road,' he told Parkington. 'Our car should be about three miles along it, following that lorry. Can you make the distance?'

Parkington nodded without speaking. His face beneath the dirt and the bristles looked grey; sweat varnished his forehead. Love felt his pulse; it was a little fast. He was probably running a temperature, but there was nothing he could do about that now. There was nothing he could do about anything now except to keep on walking, fortified by the tag-end of his benzedrine pill.

'We'll take it easily,' he promised. 'We'll be all right when we reach the car.'

'You're joking,' said Parkington. 'Why the hell *should* we be all right? We daren't go back to Damascus, even if those bastards at the monastery haven't got a guard on the car or boobytrapped it, or something.

'I only hope there's a message on the recorder with some suggestions for getting us out, for I can think of nothing. Not only have we got the monks after us, we're also wanted by the police. They'll have had a description of the car from the car hire company by now, too, which won't help us any. And we're no nearer finding the girl, either. Thank God I'm a Civil Servant. In any other business, a balls-up like this would mean the sack.'

He began to shiver, and Love noticed, with rising gloom, that it needed a supreme effort for Parkington to keep up with him.

The sun burned down on them, and Love pulled out his pocket handkerchief, knotted the four corners, pulled it over his head to give him some protection.

Now and then a lorry or car thundered past, with a great blowing of horns, and they stood, heads down and backs to the road, until it was out of sight, partly in case they should be recognized, partly to avoid the choking cloud of dust that enveloped everything for hundreds of yards, until the next vehicle came along.

They had been walking for half an hour, when a Peugeot swung past them going north. The driver blew his horn angrily, and then braked suddenly. The car's two stop lights glowed like red eyes through the swirling dust. Someone opened the back door and held it open for them.

They ran forward eagerly. The action brought a sudden recollection of hitch-hiking years ago, in the Army. Love's mouth was as dry as a lime kiln. He peered into the cool, air-conditioned interior of the car, where pleated white curtains over the rear windows filtered the fierce harsh sun.

The driver smiled out at him. He was wearing a lot of gold in his teeth that year.

'Can I give you a lift, yes?' he asked.

'Yes,' said Love eagerly.

He glanced in the back of the car. A man was asleep, propped up in a corner, head back, a handkerchief over his face, under a panama hat. He snored slightly and moved one hand in his sleep to dislodge a fly that settled on his wrist.

Parkington jerked his head inquiringly towards this man. The driver smiled again.

'You will not wake him,' he said. 'And, anyhow, it would be his pleasure, as it is mine, to give a lift to two wayfarers.'

They climbed in, shut the door. As the car surged forward a welcome gout of cool air blew out from the air conditioner. Love sat back thankfully against the cord upholstery. The desert stretched ahead, faintly blue through the Sundym windscreen. 'Are you going far?' asked the driver.

'Only a couple of miles,' said Parkington.

They sat in silence. The two mosque domes of the monastery loomed in the distance to their left, stone breasts behind a protective wall.

'Here will do,' said Love, as the car drew level with the clump of trees where Parkington had left his Renault.

He turned to open the door, expecting the driver to slow.

'It's rather difficult to stop *exactly* here,' said a voice behind him.

He turned.

Khalif, the hospital administrator, was sitting in the seat behind him. He had pulled the handkerchief off his face, pushed up the panama. He smiled.

'I've an appointment at the Monastery of the Sacred Flame,' he said, 'and I'm already late. I think you will keep it with me.'

Love dredged for words and found none.

Khalif said: 'The last time we met, Doctor, you were digging up a grave. Remember? The next time – who knows – perhaps you will be *in* the grave.'

Love turned to the driver.

'Stop the car,' he shouted.

The driver paid no attention. Parkington ripped out the ignition key, but the engine did not falter.

'Dual ignition,' explained Khalif. 'You're too late, Doctor. Both of you, far too late.'

A Lüger had materialized in his right hand, covering first one of them and then the other.

'Sit right where you are,' he said, sucking his broken tooth, savouring the sudden, sharp spear of pain. 'Do you think it was by chance that I saw you in the road? I've been going up and down this stretch for hours searching for you.

'We knew you'd got away somehow, and we also knew that three rivers feed the underground lake, so if you were going to surface – which, frankly, we doubted – you would have to come out in one of these three places. We watched them all. Now I'll call off the hunt elsewhere.'

'We?' repeated Love, but Khalif ignored the question.

The driver handed a radio microphone over his shoulder. Khalif began to speak rapidly into it, in Arabic. The car swept through the monastery gateway, past the man selling melons and grapes, past the poor shabby people who waited hopefully for a miracle. Love knew now how they felt; now he could only hope for one himself.

Khalif tossed the microphone back on the front seat.

'Get out,' he said curtly.

The driver moved a lever that released the rear door. Wearily, Love and Parkington, prodded by Khalif's gun, climbed out to the same flagged courtyard they had last seen in daylight, only a day before. Or was it really a century ago? Or could the distance between then and now be measured by hours, or only by experience?

The great wooden gates of the monastery boomed shut behind them. Men in saffron robes dropped the familiar beams, big as railway sleepers, into the black wrought-iron hooks. A blue Mercedes waited in the shadow of the building. This could be the car that had crashed into Clarissa's Sprite, but what use was this knowledge now? What use was anything now?

'Well,' said Parkington bitterly. 'To coin a phrase – back to square one.'

One of the monks behind the door pulled a revolver from his clothes, broke it expertly to check it was loaded, snapped it shut again. He twirled it from the trigger guard as he walked towards them. He was smiling.

Steinmann came out from the main building. He wore a linen suit, dark glasses and a panama hat against the sun. He might have been any well-to-do Levantine merchant off for a Sunday by the sea. Love wished that he was.

'I got your signal,' Steinmann told Khalif. 'The others are on their way back. But why did you bring them here? We're leaving. My car's all ready.'

'My orders were to pick them up,' replied Khalif sulkily. 'What you do with them is up to you, sir.'

'Have you searched them?'

The monk with the revolver ran his hands expertly over their pockets. Then he stood back, covering them.

'Put your hands on your heads,' he told them in English.

They stood there dejectedly in the classic position of surrender and defeat. Through the door came Clarissa, still wearing khaki slacks and a bush shirt. For a moment she paused in amazement at seeing them there. The monk behind her pushed her on.

'Don't speak to them,' he cautioned her, and then turning to Love and Parkington, 'and don't you talk, either.'

Parkington reeled slightly on his feet, and his hands dropped to his side. A monk with puffed, goitrous eyes brought up his left knee into Parkington's stomach.

Parkington fell clumsily and heavily on the stones. Love, still keeping his hands on his head, knelt down by his side. Love lowered his hands and felt Parkington's pulse. It was slow and heavy. He moaned as pain pierced the mists of dizziness. The monk kicked Love in the chest, so that he rolled over.

'Get up,' said the monk.

Love pulled himself to his feet.

Steinmann turned to Khalif.

'Stand them both up on the edge of the well. Then shoot them, and let their bodies drop down the well. By the time they're found, it won't affect us. We'll be miles away. Only, hurry. We've a plane to catch.'

The scene seemed like a frame frozen from a film. Two men he did not know, unshaven, one old, the other young, with some similarity in their faces – father and son? – were standing by Clarissa. Horror, despair, bewilderment was on all their faces. Next to them stood two monks with revolvers, and then Steinmann in his light suit, his brown and white co-respondent's shoes, the blue car behind them coated with dust. A bird screamed hoarsely from the feathery leaves of a palm by the wall.

Well, this was the end of the run, thought Love, the last picture his mind would register. Questions sought answers it seemed he would never now learn. Where had he gone wrong? And what would happen to Clarissa?

He straightened painfully. His jacket was open. He glanced down at his torn trousers, his scuffed shoes, and remembered the plastic box. What transmitter could it control – and what message would the transmitter send? Was it possible someone might pick up the signal?

It was a chance, slim as a needle, faint as a mirage, but it was the only one he had. If he'd had another, he'd have used it.

He bent down to Parkington again.

'Can you walk at all?' he asked him loudly, so that Steinmann could hear.

Parkington nodded slightly and crawled to his feet.

'I must help my friend,' Love told Steinmann. 'I'm a doctor, and he cannot walk on his own. Even to his death.'

'Hurry, then,' said Steinmann irritably. 'And no tricks, or you won't even reach the well.'

Love helped Parkington to his feet, half standing behind him, so that his body concealed his own right-hand jacket pocket. He slipped in his hand; his fingers closed over the plastic box. He concealed it in his palm, holding his hand flat against Parkington's body as they began to walk towards the well.

Two monks walked with them, guns in their hands, amused at their slow and painful progress.

'Put them on the edge nearest me,' said Steinmann. His manicured right hand felt inside his jacket to a shoulder holster. The sun glittered on the snub blue muzzle of a handbag automatic.

'I'm a little out of practice,' he said and smiled.

Love saw his face grow suddenly hard and cold.

'I used to be quite good,' he went on. 'The rest of you stand back while I take the first shot.' His smile seemed as macabre as rouge on a chancre.

The monks manhandled Love and Parkington up on the small parapet round the well, then obediently moved away a few paces to each side of them. Love glanced behind him, saw a circle of water reflecting the sky and their faces a hundred feet down. He remembered how cold that water had been. If they couldn't escape, would they be dead before they hit it?

In front of him stretched dusty flagstones. Ten paces away, Steinmann and the others stood watching them. Clarissa held her hands before her face, and turned away slowly, huddled in misery over the bonnet of the car. The older man by her side appeared to be comforting her. The younger one, who looked so like him, was watching the scene as though mesmerized, his mouth half open in disbelief that this could be happening.

To their right was the brass ceremonial cannon, then the two heavy wooden doors of the main monastery building. Beyond this the two minarets, glittering with ceramics, soared to the sky.

In the nearest minaret, the door was slightly open; above the doorway, he could see narrow, vertical slits, like slots for bowmen in the round tower of an ancient English castle.

The two monks lowered their revolvers. After all, Steinmann had claimed the first shot. They could easily finish what their master might begin. Love turned to Parkington.

'If we get the chance,' he whispered, not moving his lips. 'That minaret.'

Parkington gave no sign that he had heard. What chance could they expect now? Love raised up both his hands keeping the fingers closed to conceal the box.

'Move closer together,' ordered Steinmann. He was enjoying the moment; it gave him the feeling of power he needed, as other men need strong drink and energizing drugs. Suddenly and obliquely, he was no longer middle-aged in a strange and shabby country; he was young again, in the courtyard of Count Eckdorf von Heifenstaub's castle. He was telling the Gestapo officer that Ingrid was responsible for hiding the paintings. His lips drew back over his grotesque china teeth as he remembered her screams when they led her away. He drew in his breath and his finger took first pressure on the trigger.

'Wait,' called Love desperately as he squeezed the plunger and held it down. 'Can I say something before you shoot?'

Steinmann lowered his automatic for an instant and let out his breath. His heart was beating fast, as though he had been running uphill, just as it used to beat when he had run all the way to the castle from his step-father's house in case he should be late.

'What is it?' he called back.

'This,' shouted Love, and let drop the plastic box. It splintered into pieces as it hit the flagstones. For a second they all stood, watching it. And in that second the whole courtyard filled with music – the wild, tremulous cacophony of Islamic chants, highly strung and nervous as an Arab stallion.

'The minaret!' yelled Love and jumped at the monk by his side.

As the monk's right hand came up with his revolver, Love brought down the edge of his hand just behind the man's wrist. The man screamed as the bone broke, dropped the gun. Love caught it, drove his left fist into the monk's face, and as he fell, brought down the butt on the back of his skull.

They were by the car, and firing wildly. Clarissa saw Parkington race for the minaret, and ran after him. Love dropped down behind the parapet of the well for cover, emptied the monk's revolver at Steinmann, missed him with every shot, threw away the empty gun, and ran for the door himself.

They slammed it shut, shot the ancient carved bolts into their sockets, and for a moment leaned back against the wall, sobbing for breath, sick with reaction.

'Up the stairs,' gasped Parkington. 'Hurry! We may find something we can use as a weapon.'

The tiny inner room was built in the shape of a circle, and out of it climbed a spiral staircase as in a lighthouse. The vertical windows, empty of any glass, cast golden slats of light on dusty steps and crumbling inner walls. A spider scuttled across its own web, seeking safety rather than food; this was altogether out of its league.

Hearts pounding, lungs almost bursting, they toiled up the stairs. About fifty feet above them was a small landing. On this stood a plain wooden table with a huge tape-recorder, and the grey metal cabinets of a transmitter. Parkington tore open the doors to reveal a mass of black dials etched with white. The big plastic reels of tape revolved slowly, and over the wail of music, a voice was speaking, slowly, quietly, with infinite persuasion.

'What the hell is this bloody thing?' Parkington asked, thinking aloud.

'Never mind that,' panted Love. 'What are those sods outside up to? Isn't there anything here we can use to defend ourselves with?'

He peered through one of the slit windows. Two monks were talking to Steinmann. Then they ran across the courtyard and returned wheeling the ceremonial cannon. Its iron wheels rumbled on the stones. Sunshine glittered on the heavily chased and scrolled characters, along its huge, blunt barrel; brazen serpents on the wheel bosses stuck out polished tongues.

'They've got that cannon,' said Love hoarsely. 'They'll blast the doors with it. It's only a matter of seconds now.'

'Can we stall them somehow?' asked Parkington desperately, flicking switches on the transmitting equipment. 'We may be able to get a message out on this thing.'

'That's what I hoped when I pressed the switch that started the music – but how, and to whom?'

As Khalif had told him in the car, it was all too late.

He peered once more through the window. In the courtyard, they were loading the cannon, and taking their time about it; after all, there was no hurry now. Love watched with horrified fascination, as a bird watches a snake prepare to annihilate it. The monks were ramming nuts, bolts, odd jagged ends of metal down the barrel, while Steinmann fixed the charge in the breech.

Love remembered the words of Sir Thomas Browne, in *Religio Medici*, 'There is nothing strictly immortal, but immortality . . . There is no antidote against the opium of time.'

It was quite true; there also seemed no antidote against recapture and defeat. He turned back into the room, conscious only of his own failure, his own weariness. He had done his best and his best had not been good enough. What was it his old Latin master used to say? *Jacta est alea*: the die is cast, and he could do no more. He leaned against the wall, eyes half closed, empty of all resolve.

Music still poured from the loudspeaker. The man was still talking against it. Even though Love could not understand a word, he could feel the immense persuasion in his voice. He should have a job reading commercials; maybe he had; maybe that was what he was doing.

'Listen!' cried Parkington excitedly. 'Just listen.'

'I am,' replied Love. 'I don't understand what he's saying. And I don't care.'

'I do,' said Parkington. 'My God, I do!'

He reached out and turned the volume up fully until the voice and the music deafened them, reverberating from the walls.

'Are you mad?' shouted Love above the thunder, but Parkington did not even hear him. Instead, he jabbed his finger at the window.

'Look out there!' he said. 'Look out there! You'll see what I mean!'

Love turned again to the window.

Down in the courtyard, Steinmann still crouched behind the cannon, his hand on the breech, but the other men had drawn apart from him, and stood in a little group watching him.

Their cowls were off their heads, and in the bright sunshine Love could see their dark faces contorted with hate, like the faces of ancient evil gargoyles. Their lips drew back from their teeth, their eyes narrowed, and, even as he looked, and as the tape-recorder blared away, the monks began to move stealthily towards Steinmann.

He saw them suddenly and stood up, and read the message of death in their faces, in their eyes.

He waved at them frantically with his hands, shouting something in Arabic that Love could not understand. But still they came on, slowly and in step, inexorably. It was like some strange ballet movement, the prelude to a kill: the saffron robes, the slippered feet, the cruel, implacable hatred in their faces; and behind them, the walls, red as blood dried by the sun, where palm trees shook their foliage like feather dusters, and the wild birds screamed dementedly at the noise of the music.

Steinmann dug into his jacket pocket, whipped out his automatic, and fired wildly. The monk on the far left clutched his arm, dropped his gun on the flagstones, and went down slowly on his hands and knees, his head bowed in pain.

The others still came on; not one of them even looked at their fallen comrade. Steinmann clicked the trigger of his toy gun, but the magazine was empty. He threw the useless automatic away, and leapt for the cannon, throwing his full weight against it.

He heaved it around on its solid wheels until the gaping muzzle faced the monks. He shouted to them once more, waving his arms in a frantic appeal to reason. They paid him no attention, but still walked towards him, not hurrying, their shoulders hunched, arms bent, their eyes fixed on his, as the eyes of hunters seek the eyes of the beast they mean to kill. Steinmann could wait no longer; he seized a hammer and smashed down the firing pin.

As the cannon fired, it recoiled on its wheels, knocking down Steinmann. For an instant, in the white cloud of powder, Love saw the monks' arms outstretched, transfixed in agony, like figures on an invisible cross, while the scrap iron charge tore through them. Behind them, the explosion blew open the two doors in the main monastery building. For a second, the darkness of the open doorway gaped at them emptily, and then, with a subterranean rumble, like a volcano in eruption, the whole building blew up.

Bricks, tiles, doors, window-frames, debris of every kind rained down on the courtyard, stripping branches from trees. A cloud of dust hung like a brown fog from the minarets to the far wall.

Parkington leaned over, switched off the tape-recorder. The music shrank to a whine and died. The room was suddenly silent; dust filtered the sunlight. Outside, someone was moaning, and then even that sound ceased.

'My God,' said Parkington shakily. 'What the hell did that hit?'

'Those oil fumes,' replied Love dully. 'The petrol gas that forced the water up through the foundations.'

He was already opening the door.

'Where are you going?' Clarissa asked him in a hushed whisper.

'There may be someone left alive out there,' said Love. 'I might be able to help them.'

He began to run shakily through the settling cloud of dust and the heaps of rubble to the crumpled bodies.

Epilogue

Miss Jenkins pressed the button on the desk in her outer office. The buzzer sounded on MacGillivray's desk, and the blue light flashed impatiently. He stood up, stubbed out his cheroot, pressed the switch to release the magnetic lock on his door. Parkington came in first, followed by Love and then Clarissa.

Parkington, shot full of antibiotics to avoid the incipient pneumonia he had suffered as a result of being submerged in the underground lake, looked pale and tired. Love, in a suit he had been given in Beirut, on the way back to London, looked rather better than he felt. Clarissa might have walked in from a hairdresser's appointment in Bond Street.

'Please sit down,' said MacGillivray.

He indicated the familiar shabby armchairs, offered around a box of cigarettes, and then sat back in his own swivel chair, elbows on the arms, fingers pressed together, jogging easily from side to side.

'So you found the car I sent to the airport all right?' he said, making conversation.

Love nodded.

'That's about the only thing that was all right,' he said dryly.

Had it all actually happened, or was it simply part of a dream, the legacy of some unwise mixture of lobster thermidor and double whiskies; some strange trauma of the mind, born of indigestion or imagination?

He glanced down at his hands covered with plaster patches that concealed the cuts he had received as he had torn away the rocks and rubble to see who was dead and who was dying in the courtyard of the monastery. It was no dream; it had all happened.

He remembered the dash out of the monastery gates to

their car, through a crowd of terrified locals – including the man who sold melons, the woman with the withered arm, who had sat so patiently hoping for a miracle, and had finally been rewarded with the destruction of the shrine she held most sacred. Love wondered whether she would class that as a miracle. He certainly did, but then he knew more about it now than she would ever imagine.

They had dragged Krasna, with a broken arm and severe concussion, and Issan, with two broken ribs, into the back of the Renault. Parkington played over the tape-recorder, picked up the message MacGillivray had sent. If they could reach the Lebanese border they would be met at the frontier with a full cover story; they were to travel there as a university team on an archaeological dig.

Back they drove to Maloula, where Parkington collected five blank passports from the stock he carried with him, took as many blurred photographs from a folder of dozens. He wrote in false names from a list concealed between two sides of a coloured postcard of Damascus, using the green ink essential for British passports. The visa stamps for all Middle East Arab countries had already been forged on the passports. They could take their pick.

Love set Krasna's arm, examined his son; he would need specialist attention when they reached the Lebanon; there was nothing he could do for him without drugs or instruments, except to wrap him in blankets from the hotel and hope he survived the journey.

The hard drive up through the mountain peaks fissured with snow, bleak and cruel, was something Love preferred to forget. At last they reached the frontier post with its barbed wire fence, the little police huts, the flags of two countries drooping at the poles.

On the other side, beyond the Customs shed, and the Lebanese soldiers with tommy guns, a Ford station wagon was parked under a cedar tree. Two men in anoraks and mountain boots stood leaning against it, enjoying the afternoon sunshine. As they saw Parkington they came forward slowly.

'My dear professor,' began the older of these men. 'How wonderful to see you again. I've brought Professor Blaikie to meet you.'

Parkington had described himself on his new passport as Head of the Department of Pan Arabic Studies, University of the Lebanon; Love was a Reader in Sanskrit, at the University of North Stafford.

There was commiseration with Krasna and his son (described on their passports as Readers in Arabic Archaeology at the University of Wales). They had fallen at a dig in Damascus, the man explained to the Customs officer. It was very important that they should get to hospital as soon as possible.

The Customs officer spoke to Krasna in English. Krasna's face puckered; he could not understand a word. The officer turned to Love.

'Why doesn't he speak English?' he asked suspiciously.

'He's a Welsh nationalist,' replied Love quickly.

'Ah, of course,' said the officer not understanding, but not wishing to appear ignorant. He stamped the entry visa, handed back the passport with a flourish. 'Welcome to the Lebanon,' he said.

One of the two men in anoraks drove Parkington's car while the rest of them travelled in the more comfortable station wagon with the man called Blaikie, so that Krasna could stretch out on the back seat with a shot of morphia to ease his pain. Blaikie opened a briefcase, took out a sheaf of leave passes of the type issued to British Servicemen in Cyprus, for seventy-two hour recreational visits to Beirut.

'There's a regular shuttle service of RAF transport between Beirut and Nicosia,' he explained. 'We've held seats for all of you. But I don't know if the two injured men are well enough to travel?'

'Who are we supposed to be this time?' asked Love.

'Three officers in the Royal Army Pay Corps. No one will ever query that. Miss Head here is a nursing sister.'

'Which I am,' Clarissa told him.

'Really?' said Blaikie, surprised. 'So we were right for once. Three cheers for us.'

In Beirut, they were hustled into an upstairs flat in a new block on the outskirts of the city. Here Krasna's arm was examined, and Issan was taken by private ambulance to hospital. Love, Parkington and Clarissa had hot baths, a meal and then chose, from a selection of clothes sent in on approval by a department store, the ones that fitted them best.

Parkington asked that the tapes he had collected from the monastery should be copied; the originals were put aboard a London-bound airliner addressed to Sensoby and Ransom, Covent Garden, marked 'Perishable: Lebanese figs. Sample. Treat as urgent.'

So urgently, indeed, were they treated, that a special messenger collected them at London Airport.

Within two hours, Love, Parkington, Clarissa and Krasna were at Beirut Airport. Here there was a short delay, because some visiting Arab dignitary was inspecting a guard of honour in their unpressed uniforms and unpolished belts, and they waited impatiently with some other British Servicemen and women in the departure lounge.

Then the flight to Cyprus, another change of planes, and, finally, the discreet Princess limousine waiting for them at a side entrance of the Europa Building at Heathrow.

It had all happened, right enough, but why? Who was the man in the light suit, whom Clarissa knew as Steinmann? Who was the man who spoke little English with the broken arm, who had written his name 'Krasna' shakily with his unaccustomed left hand when Parkington had asked him in French for his signature?

MacGillivray watched Love shrewdly, guessing at his thoughts.

'All told, a most successful venture, Parkington,' he said, swivelling in his chair.

'Successful?' echoed Love in amazement, before Parkington could reply. 'Successful? We've been shot at, imprisoned, nearly drowned and almost blown up. I've lost all my luggage and God knows what my reputation as a doctor is like now in Damascus – or here. If you call that successful, how do you rate failure?'

'There are degrees of success,' pointed out MacGillivray. 'And by our standards, this was all most successful.'

'In that case, I'm glad your standards aren't mine,' Love retorted. MacGillivray shrugged; there was no point in becoming involved in an argument.

'Maybe not, Doctor. I grant that you have suffered certain

– ah – discomforts. But consider what has been achieved. The man Steinmann, who was killed when the cannon set off the underground petrol vapour, had a unique plan for making an enormous fortune quickly.

'With his handful of men, he had captured a number of defectors or would-be defectors from the East and the West – before they could give themselves up to their new countries.

'He tried to kidnap Krasna with his son in Albania, but they escaped to Cairo. Krasna has explained in his report that he saw General Ackermann, the head of the Albanian Secret Police, in Cairo, and naturally assumed he was after them. In fact, he was. But not to arrest them – only to save them from being kidnapped.

'Dr Ronald wasn't defecting, of course. When his plane came down at Cairo to refuel, Steinmann approached him and asked him outside under the pretext of meeting someone. Then they simply kidnapped him and took him off to the Syrian monastery that figures so strongly in your report, Parkington.

'Ronald was working on applications of RNA acid, and other matters. I won't go into all the technicalities of this now, but, in brief, if you could inject minute quantities of this into someone else's body – or give it to them in a drink with another substance which we are still keeping secret – these people would assume the characteristics of someone with this quantity of RNA in their brain. For example, if you calculated the strength of RNA and this other substance in the brain of a coward, and then fed it to, say, a platoon of soldiers, and broadcast that they should desert, the soldiers would at once lay down their arms and do so.

'Now this is obviously a discovery of inestimable value, both politically and commercially. But Steinmann had to be *certain* it worked as well as he had been led to believe. He needed a place where he was unlikely to be disturbed, and where he could keep Ronald and Krasna prisoner until he had finished with them.

'He hit on the idea of using the Monastery of the Sacred Flame because, apart from two or three blind or infirm monks, all the brothers there were making a pilgrimage to Mecca, and would be away for two or three weeks, and this was all the time he needed. The locals wouldn't disturb them – they'd assume they were genuine monks. They'd have a base, a car – and a perfect cover.

'In addition, the monks there bottled water from the well and shipped it to various Muslim communities throughout Asia. This gave Steinmann the idea of testing Ronald's experiments with RNA himself. Ronald was made to take samples from one of the monks who loathed Europeans. Then the same concentrate of RNA was measured into the stone phials of holy water.

'He didn't doctor all the bottles, but only some, and made absolutely certain where these were to be delivered. Then, from his transmitter in the monastery, he broadcast music to blot out the usual Voice of Islam programme that so many cafés and coffee houses in the Middle East and Asia tune into, simply because they get good reception on it.

'Over this music he superimposed the voice of the man who hated whites. As soon as the listeners who had drunk the doped water heard this, they absorbed his hatred, too.

'The results were localized riots in which some Europeans were beaten up – but not general riots, which is what made me a little suspicious. I received routine reports of these, and checked that a local transmission *had* come in on the Voice of Cairo broadcast on one particular day – and what that transmitter said is on the tape you took from the monastery, Parkington.

'You only managed to get out, in any case, because Dr Love here tipped a flagon containing RNA into the well when you were both trying to escape. The monks drank that water, and so absorbed the acid. When the transmitter started again they had the same reaction of violence against white men. And, luckily for you, the only white man they could see was Steinmann.'

He paused, looking from one to the other.

'Why didn't Steinmann get infected with this violence?' asked Parkington. 'Didn't he drink any water?'

MacGillivray shook his head.

'He only drank bottled Poland water,' he explained. 'A phobia of his. What these fellows didn't know was that Ronald suffered from Addison's Disease. Cut off from cortisone, he would die. They were racing him to the Clinic for treatment when their car was in collision with yours, Miss Head, and Ronald died.

'This was both bad and good luck for them, because Krasna's experiment was in a different, if allied, field. His technique was to sink an electrode into the brain of some unsuspecting person and then tune their mind to someone else's so that they could pick up this other person's thoughts without either of them realizing what was going on. They could then be put into a hypnotic trance and would speak these thoughts to a tape-recorder.

'This condition would only last for as long as sufficient RNA remained in their body, probably a matter of twenty-four hours or so. Then they'd be back to normal.

'Steinmann had to be certain this technique also worked before he could offer it for sale anywhere, so when you, Miss Head, appeared so fortuitously, he got Krasna and his son to operate on you and tune you to *his* thoughts. This way, he would be sure there was no faking. There wasn't – which is how we know so much about Steinmann's plans.

'Both these secrets could fetch enormous sums if offered elsewhere, either politically or commercially, but now they won't be on the market. Others may catch up on these techniques, and probably they will. But right now we have them. I expect that the two Krasnas will be going to America when they are fit enough to travel. With the sort of research facilities they will be given in the States, there's no knowing what further break-throughs they will make.'

'I'm glad of that,' said Love, and then he realized that this remark could be taken two ways. Well, let it. He had had enough.

He suddenly remembered the shock of the searchlight as he opened the grave; the chilling darkness of the underground lake; the almost unbearable depression of driving through the monastery gates in Khalif's car.

'Khalif,' he said. 'The hospital administrator. What happened to him?'

MacGillivray shrugged.

'Maybe he was killed, maybe he wasn't. He was only useful because he could get them the use of a room and the operating theatre in the Clinic. He would probably have been expendable in any case after he had nothing more to offer.

The Syrians will no doubt deal with him if he has survived. He was only small fry, anyway.'

MacGillivray lit a cheroot.

Most people in the world go by that description, thought Love, and yet almost all were important to someone. Was he?

'Won't you have a cup of tea?' MacGillivray asked him. 'Miss Jenkins is brewing up.'

'No, thanks,' said Love.

He had had enough of explanations and mutual congratulations. He thought of the terrified pilgrims waiting outside the ruined shrine, of the genuine Brothers of the Sacred Flame returning to find their monastery a shambles. He thought of the whole involved network of hate and murder and torture and greed that he had inadvertently stirred, as a hand in a dark cave can disturb a spider's web. Then he thought of his Cord, still in London Airport garage, and glanced at his watch. If he left now, he could miss the rush-hour traffic, and be back in Bishop's Combe in time to take evening surgery.

That might surprise his locum, who wasn't expecting him for another two days, but then, if the man knew what had been happening to him, he wouldn't expect him at all. Also, the drive with the roof down would do him good. And he felt he needed to be back among ordinary people, to be doing the job for which he had trained.

MacGillivray might delude himself that all this had been successful, but so far as he was concerned, it had been a waste of time. He had missed the lectures for which he had paid; his luggage had been abandoned at the New Omayad. Why, he hadn't even been able to bring back the car badges he had bought in Damascus. And where could he find another Hispano-Suiza or Invicta badge in Somerset?

'Are you going, then?' asked Parkington in surprise as Love stood up. 'I thought we'd have a night out together.'

'Another time,' said Love, 'I'd love to.'

And he meant it; another time.

He turned to Clarissa.

'I can give you a lift back home,' he said. 'If you'd like to come now. But I should warn you, it'll be damn cold in that open Cord.'

204

'Like Maloula?' she said, and smiled.

Love smiled, too.

'Like Maloula,' he agreed. "All the way."

And then he'd open the door for her to follow him out into the sunshine.

Damascus and Maloula, Syria;
Stogumber, Somerset, England.

JAMES LEASOR

Meet DR. JASON LOVE . . . country doctor turned secret agent and 'Heir Apparent to the golden throne of Bond'.

PASSPORT TO OBLIVION
(Where the Spies Are)
(25p) 5/-

First adventure of Dr. Jason Love. 'A Secret Service thriller in the most expert manner . . . I can foresee a succession of thrills to please even jaded suspense addicts'—Oliver Warner, Tatler.

PASSPORT TO PERIL
(25p) 5/-

'Lots of casual killing and ditto sex, Technicolour backgrounds, considerable expertise about weapons . . . action driven along with terrific vigour'—Sunday Times.

PASSPORT IN SUSPENSE
(25p) 5/-

'This is how I like my thrillers . . . superb example of modern thriller writing at its best'—Sunday Express.

PASSPORT FOR A PILGRIM
(25p) 5/-

'No other aspirant for James Bond's crown has made a stronger claim than Dr. Jason Love . . . Here is the same swift action, the hints of brutality and undercurrents of sadism, all laced together in a fast-moving tale marked by an immense readability.'—Manchester Evening News.

GAVIN LYALL

'A complete master of
the suspense technique'
Liverpool Daily Post

SHOOTING SCRIPT
5/-
'The sky's the limit for this
fine suspense/adventure story'
Daily Mirror

MIDNIGHT PLUS ONE
5/-
'Grimly exciting ... original
in concept, expertly written
and absolutely hair-raising'
New York Times

THE WRONG SIDE OF THE SKY
5/-
'One of the year's best
thrillers'
Daily Herald

'Thrillers on this level
are rare enough'
The Daily Telegraph